Caramel and Magnolias

By Tess Thompson

To Sue
Happy reading!
Tess Thompson

Booktrope Editions
Seattle WA 2013

Copyright 2013 Tess Thompson

Cover Design by Greg Simanson
Edited by Jennifer D. Munro

This is a work of fiction. Names, characters, places, brands, media, and incidents are either the product of the author's imagination or are used fictitiously. Any resemblance to similarly named places or to persons living or deceased is unintentional.

PRINT ISBN 978-1-935961-82-6
EPUB ISBN 978-1-62015-086-3

For further information regarding permissions, please contact info@booktrope.com.

Library of Congress Control Number: 2013900889

For Katherine Sears
and Heather Ludviksson.
Beloved friends.
Trusted colleagues.

Acknowledgments

Thank you to the team at Booktrope, especially my superb editor, Jennifer Munro, for her careful and thoughtful contributions, cover designer Greg Simanson, and marketing expert Kara Mann. To my writer friends in The Lounge, thank you for your unshakable love and support. Teri Lazzara, for twenty years of friendship and allowing me to use Stewie as a character. Jacqui and Brent Farnsworth, Lynnette Bradbury, Maria Palmer, Natalie Sorensen, Jennifer Gracen, Tracey Hansen, Jesse James - thank you for always picking up the phone. And finally, to my friend who gently suggested it was time for me to get off the sidelines – thank you for inspiring this book and me.

Prologue

THE WIND OFF THE PACIFIC OCEAN brought the smell of seaweed and saltwater, everything encased in the constant damp and gray so that it seeped in through skin and flesh to bone, impervious to fleece or knit or rain gear. Alicia Johnson trudged across the Legley Bay High School campus on the way to gym class, the September drizzle on her cheeks and hands, her rain hood pulled over her head. She was coming from math class, thinking about the new teacher, Jack Ball, of the angry scars she'd spotted on his wrists. What had made him sad enough to attempt such a thing? Despite all her angst and disappointment, Alicia wanted to live. That above all. To stay alive and somehow make it through to a life outside of the small Oregon coastal town of Legley Bay that was nothing but the smell of fish and sea air that made houses, cars, and people gray before their time. Yes, this was the best she could hope for. And hoping kept her going despite failing grades and worry over her mother and the endless cycle of classes and her job at the minimart after school.

Alicia glanced up from beneath her hood. There was a woman just outside the metal gates, leaning against the fender of a white, four-door Mercedes, holding a bottle of water like a beer, as if she were at a tailgate party. The woman had blue eyes, so light they reminded Alicia of ice cubes, encircled by purple glasses. Unusual color, Alicia thought. And she was short, almost square, and wore a long, black coat and thick-soled shoes, the kind nurses might wear, only brown instead of white. Her hair was short and spiky, standing up despite the rain in a way that indicated wealth. Not from around here, Alicia thought. Anyone could see that.

The woman nodded and their eyes locked, as if they knew one another. Alicia felt the cold, more so than the moment before. Shivering, she pulled the zipper of her raincoat higher, averting her gaze to the muddy path between the main part of the high school campus and the gymnasium.

Later, in the locker room after gym class, Alicia pulled socks over damp feet. Lola was at the mirror, applying blue eyeliner.

"Hey," said Lola, catching her eye in the mirror's reflection.

"Hey," said Alicia, polite but not too friendly. Lola was the type of girl to attach herself to anyone who was kind to her. Like a puppy that followed you home, Alicia often thought. If she were too kind, she'd never be able to get rid of her. Lonely girls recognized one another. Regardless, she couldn't be seen with Lola. It might mean hazing and teasing, torturous taunts in the hallways and maybe even shoving or punching after school. No, it was better to live on the fringe, on the sidelines, skirting between classes, invisible and unknown, rather than caring whether you had friends or not.

"You wanna hit DQ after school?" Lola turned back to the mirror and put a thick coat of mascara on her lashes. "I'm supposed to be on a diet but life's short, right?" She laughed, her lips pulling up to show her gums, and snorted. Alicia turned away. She'd noticed Lola had gained a lot of weight this year. But so had a lot of girls. It happened. Alicia was skinny and never thought much about what she ate but her mother was always on a diet, living on cigarettes and diet soda.

"Can't. Have to work," said Alicia.

"You still at the minimart?"

"Yep." Alicia grabbed her sweatshirt and pulled it over her head.

"Well, tomorrow, maybe? I've got a new car. A Mustang." Alicia knew about the car. She'd heard Lola telling anyone who would listen about it.

"Where you working?" asked Alicia. It must be better than her minimum wage job if Lola could afford a Mustang, even if it was used.

"Nowhere. Nothing around."

"How'd you get the money for your car?" Alicia asked, working on a tangle in her hair with the brush she kept in her backpack. Lola's mother worked down at the Pig-n-Pancake near the entrance to Highway 101 and they lived in an apartment above some old man's house down a long, dirt road.

Lola turned to Alicia, her eyes darting back and forth. "Why? You need money?"

"Thinking about going to masseuse school."

Lola's eyes widened. There was a smear of mascara under her left eyebrow. "You mean drop out of school?"

"I hate it here," Alicia said, surprised by her sudden honesty and the lump at the back of her throat. "Just trying to stay under the radar until I can get out."

Lola joined her on the bench. "You have a plan?" She smelled of cherry lip-gloss.

"Not really. Costs ten grand," said Alicia. "I researched it on the Internet. It's probably just a dream for other people, not someone like me."

Lola glanced behind them. The locker room was nearly empty. "Meet me after school. I'll tell you about a way to get some money." She paused, lowering her voice. "But you have to swear to keep it a secret."

Later that night she was on the couch with her mother watching her mother's favorite show about rich women who were always fighting with one another. The rain was a steady drum on the tin roof of their mobile home. "You wanna diet pop, Mom?" she said.

"That'd be nice. Thanks, baby," said Jo, playing with a strand of her long, drab hair, her eyes fixed on the television. Jo wore sweats and a loose T-shirt, standard uniform for her one day off from the bar. Alicia recorded all her favorite shows during the week and Jo watched them on her day off, one after the other.

Alicia went to the kitchen and opened the refrigerator. There wasn't much in it, just a half case of diet cola, the generic kind they bought at Walmart, a carton of nonfat milk, and ketchup, mustard, and mayonnaise in the side door. Leftover cardboard boxes were stacked on the counter from dinner. On Tuesdays Alicia always brought them dinner from the minimart - a corndog for her sister Misty, a hamburger for her mother, and chicken strips for herself. They shared a dozen Jojo's between them, fried potatoes that only places like the minimart and deli counters at grocery stores sold. According to Misty, no matter where you bought them, they always tasted the same. "Some kind of secret molecular creation by scientists in plastic suits and face masks," Misty had said tonight, laughing, as she grabbed two more on her way out to her Math Club meeting at school.

Alicia laughed too. "You're such a show-off."

"These fabricated potatoes will probably kill us yet, but what a way to go," Misty added before the door closed behind her, causing the trailer to shudder.

Alicia grabbed two sodas and closed the refrigerator door. At the doorway, she paused. Something was dripping. Her eyes scanned the ceiling. There, to the right of where they kept the trashcan, was a leak – a brown stain the shape of a pineapple in the false-ceiling tile. She sighed and grabbed the bucket from under the sink and set it there, watching the water splash against the plastic. After a moment, she joined her mother back on the couch. "There's another leak."

Jo didn't take her eyes off the television. "Great. That's all we need. Did you put the bucket under it?"

"Yeah. I'll try and fix it tomorrow, Mom, don't worry."

"You're a good girl," said Jo.

"You're a good mommy," said Alicia, snuggling closer.

The women on television were at a spa. An attendant wrapped them in seaweed. "I'd like to work at a spa someday," said Alicia. "Maybe become a masseuse."

"You'd be good at that, baby. Such strong hands."

"Really, Mommy? You think so?"

"Sure. Once things pick up at the bar, maybe we'll send you to one of those schools."

"They cost ten thousand dollars."

"That much?"

Alicia shifted so she was sitting on the far end of the couch. "Give me your feet, Mommy. I'll rub 'em for you."

She held her mother's feet in her hands, listening to rain beat against the roof of the trailer. She thought about Lola's offer. If she did it, she could work in one of those swanky spas in the city and wrap women in seaweed. She could send money to her mother so she could fix the roof. And maybe Misty could go to college when she graduated in three years.

The next day Alicia sat slumped in her seat, watching Mr. Ball explain an equation by scrawling it in messy handwriting on the whiteboard. Jack Ball was a new teacher, young, without the wary defeat of the other teachers. He dropped his whiteboard pen and as he reached for it, his sweater sleeve inched up over his wrist. There was the angry red scar on the inside of his wrist again - this telltale sign of a sad man.

In the row next to her, Josh Wilson doodled a pattern like a checkerboard on his folder. His brown hair was on the long side, cut in the way all the boys wore it now, brushed over their foreheads. He shifted in his seat and glanced over at her, and seeing that she watched him, raised an eyebrow and smiled. He was an athlete and his arm muscles flexed as he tapped his pencil on the side of the desk and his thigh muscles pressed against the fabric of his jeans. He was considered good-looking but wasn't the most popular boy because he was on the sweeter side. Would he be interested enough in her to have sex?

What had Lola said to her? *All boys will do it with you if you let them know you want to.* So she smiled at him, hoping he would understand - *I am available.* It must have worked, she thought, since he grinned at her before he leaned back over his notebook, continuing his doodle.

After school, Alicia walked towards home with her hood pulled tight against the slanted rain, her gaze focused on the tips of her soaked tennis shoes. Large drops of water dripped from the edge of her hood like a mini-waterfall. A car pulled up beside her and stopped. She lifted her rain hood. Water splashed her face and ran down the back of her neck. It was Josh, in his blue Subaru. Leaning across the passenger seat, he rolled down the car window and grinned, his pale face flushed. "You wanna ride?"

She looked to the sky and let the rain fall upon her closed lids and her cheeks. When her gaze returned to Josh, he had one arm draped over the steering wheel, peering at her from under his fringe of hair. "Sure," she said, taking off her backpack and sliding into the bucket seat. Accelerating with a lurch, he pulled out to the highway and turned up the radio. It was playing some kind of hip-hop music she didn't like. Josh tapped his fingers against the steering wheel. She stared out the front window, holding her bag against her chest. "Don't you have cross country practice?" she asked.

"Had it this morning."

She nodded and licked her chapped lips, pulling lip-gloss from the side pocket of her bag and running it over her mouth. "You know where I live?"

"Sure."

"Yeah. I didn't have to work today." She let it dangle out there, knowing he would catch it if he were interested.

His eyes slid to her and back again to the road. "You wanna go down to The Landing, listen to some music in my car?"

She stared out the window. The Landing was the state park. A lot of kids went down there for parties and to hang out, both in the parking lot and on the stretch of flat, sandy beach. "I guess."

"Cool," he said, tapping his finger on the steering wheel.

She played with the zipper on her backpack. Her pants were wet from the rain where her coat hadn't covered them, and her legs were numb from the cold. "Could you turn up the heat?" she asked.

"No problem." They passed the Dairy Queen, heading south. The heater blew hot air onto her lap, and steam began to rise from her thighs.

When they pulled into the lot, Josh parked at the farthest spot from the entrance and turned off the car. She was instantly cold again. Rain pounded on the roof of the car. There was the sound of waves crashing below and the occasional seagull. Josh pulled the parking brake. "You wanna mess around?" She looked up at the firs surrounding the parking lot. They swayed from side to side.

"I guess." She made her mind numb, watching the drops of rain make their way down the passenger side window.

He gestured towards the back. "More room in the backseat."

They both climbed over the front seats to the back. Taking his wallet from his letterman jacket, he pulled out a condom.

"We don't need it," she said. "I'm on the pill." She looked at a rip in the car's ceiling upholstery. She hoped Misty remembered that the key was under the mat on the front porch if she decided to come home early from the library. She tugged at the wet jeans that stuck to her skin.

"Great," he said, grinning.

She kept her eyes fixed on the ripped ceiling. "I've got to get home soon, make sure my sister isn't locked out."

He ran his fingers through his shaggy hair and unzipped his pants. "That's cool."

"This is my first time," she said.

"Shit. Really?" His eyes searched her face. "You sure then?"

"Yeah. I don't want to be a virgin anymore. But you can't tell anyone."

"Totally uncool to kiss and tell, right? But why me?"

"I like the color of your skin," she said, staring at the vein in his neck that bulged near the muscle there.

He grinned and put his hand on her left breast and squeezed. "Good enough reason, I guess."

Afterwards, he drove her home. The rain had lessened and his windshield wipers were on intermittent. She counted two seconds between each swipe. "It only hurts like that the first time," he said, turning down the radio. "I hope it wasn't too bad."

"Don't worry about it. I figured." One-one thousand, two-one thousand, she counted in her head.

"Wanna try again?" He stopped in front of her house.

Her hand on the car door handle, she looked back at him. "Tomorrow?"

"You bet," he said.

Chapter One

DRESSED IN HER ONE COCKTAIL DRESS and knock-off Spanx undergarment, Cleo Tanner stood near the bar at the annual fundraiser for scholarships for underprivileged children. The smell of tiger lilies in vases on the dining tables set around the Seattle Art Museum made her eyes water. She dabbed at them with a cocktail napkin, wondering if her eyeliner was smeared. Her dress felt tight, like she was a mouse being ingested by a cobra. Why couldn't she stick with a diet? Really. Five pounds. Did it have to be so hard? It was the Sierra Nevada Pale Ales that did it. She should tell Nick to stop giving her so many free pints during her frequent visits to Cooper's. Who was she kidding? That would never happen.

It was the silent auction portion of the evening. Attendees perused the items displayed—gift baskets and a homemade quilt and weeks at vacation homes—on long tables covered in white cloths, all procured by well-intentioned but slightly frightening mothers of Cleo's little Montessori students. Late May, it was an unusually clear and warm night for Seattle, and the committee of mothers had decorated the room with blue and silver ribbons and sparkly things that hung from the ceiling.

She was about to head to the bathroom to adjust the torturous undergarment when suddenly there was a man standing in front of her, carrying two glasses of red wine. He was handsome, she supposed, if one liked the slick type, which she never had, even before Simon. He had an olive complexion and brown eyes and his hair was perfectly cut and blow-dried so that it gave the impression of being tousled instead of carefully groomed. He wore a well-draped, expensive suit, like Sylvia's husband often wore.

"I saw you were empty handed," he said, holding out the wine with a small bow, like an offering to the gods. "Can't have our best teacher without a drink."

She took the glass from his outstretched hand. His fingernails were manicured to a gleam. *Never trust a man with a manicure,* her father always said. But there was no reason to turn down free wine. "Thank you. Do I have your child this year?"

"No children," he said, sticking out his hand. "I'm Scott Moore."

"Ah," she said, keeping her voice light. "The big donor."

"Guilty," he said.

"Your scholarships are being well-used this year," said Cleo.

He smiled, sipping his wine without taking his eyes off her. "I'm pleased to do it."

"Am I right, remembering you're an attorney, Mr. Moore?"

"Trained as an attorney but I run an adoption agency."

She felt a pang, thinking of Sylvia. "Really? How interesting." Then a lie. "I have a friend contemplating adoption."

He raised his brows, took another sip of his wine. "I should mention the fees at my agency are a bit steep."

"My friend is a professor of music," she said, tugging on the skirt of her dress. "But she's from a wealthy Seattle family. Money is not a problem." She felt defensive. Did he only help rich people?

"Really? Would I know them?"

"You would," she said, keeping her voice cold.

"I see," he said. He was trying to hide his curiosity, she thought, watching his eyes glitter.

Everyone in Seattle was familiar with the Holm family and their business enterprises that ranged from oil to timber to technology during a span of 100 years. Sylvia's father was one of five sons, all of them successful in one venture or another, having inherited mass wealth from their oil tycoon grandfather, which they subsequently used to start ventures of their own. Her father was in biochemical engineering.

Scott Moore smiled and tapped his fingers on her bare wrist. "Come to my office sometime. I can explain how we do things. You can decide then if you want to pass the information on to your friend." This was the kind of man who made deals, who was skilled in the art of negotiating, Cleo thought. Someone who got what he wanted.

"I'll think about it," she said.

"Or I'd love to take you to lunch," he said. "Or drinks."

"I don't date," she said, keeping her voice light, without emotion, merely stating a fact. Just then a photographer came over to them, a "Press" I.D. around his neck.

"Pose for a photo, Mr. Moore?"

Scott Moore put his arm around Cleo's shoulder. "Sure."

The photographer snapped several photos of them before thanking them and moving across the room to a different couple.

She shrugged away from his embrace, trying not to shiver. There was something disturbing about this man. Despite her aversion to him, she paused, remembering Sylvia's puffy eyes two nights ago, after the fourth failed in-vitro procedure. "My friend would consider adoption. Her husband isn't so sure."

"What's his hesitancy?"

"I'm not sure."

"But you say she'll consider it. What's holding her back? Besides her husband?"

"She's afraid she'll be disappointed. Have a birth mother change her mind. It happened to other friends of ours."

"It never happens in my agency," said Moore.

"How is that possible?"

"We have ways of making sure a birth mother is certain before we commit to the adoptive parents."

"Is there a long waiting list?" asked Cleo.

He smiled. "You go out with me, I'll put your friend on the top of the list."

She felt her mouth fall open. She stared at him. Surely he was kidding? She laughed. "Very funny."

He smiled and shrugged his shoulders, his voice low. "I'm actually not kidding. I know it seems a bit unorthodox, but I want you to let me take you out. It won't hurt, I promise."

"I hardly know what to say."

He raised an eyebrow, his voice calm, like she was the crazy one for even questioning it. "I mean no harm. And I'm happy to help your friends, regardless. She just won't go to the top of the list."

"Thank you for the wine, but I should join my teacher friends at our table."

"I understand," he said. He handed her his card. "But call me if you change your mind."

She left the auction before dessert, slipping out the back after a quick goodbye to her table. Driving home, the pounding rain seemed to come out of nowhere just as she exited the West Seattle Bridge onto Admiral Way. Although she tried to dismiss it, the thought of Scott Moore would not leave her mind. What kind of man was he? Obviously, he was controlling and demanding, a man accustomed to getting his own way. But he had another thing coming if he thought he could manipulate her. And yet, she wanted nothing more than for her best friend to be a mother. It begged the question - how many times would she have to go out with him before he'd arrange an adoption? Would Sylvia and Malcolm even consider it? She didn't know. But it was worth asking. If it was something Sylvia wanted and would ease her pain, what were a few dates?

She set the wipers on high. But they had almost no effect against the Seattle downpour, and her shoulders tensed as she drove up the hill, winding up and around, past the main street of West Seattle before turning onto a side street where her apartment building was located.

She waited for the parking garage gate to open and then drove in slowly, her tires squealing on the wet cement. She parked in her designated spot and climbed out of the car, exhausted, anticipating her favorite jeans and a soft T-shirt. What kind of music was she in the mood for? A little Nanci Griffith, circa 1989?

As she exited the elevator, she saw Mrs. Lombardi from 3C going into her apartment, her white hair plastered against her pink scalp. She wore a flimsy raincoat dripping with water, which soaked the cheap carpeting that lined the hallway. "Mrs. Lombardi, why are you so wet?"

"Oh hello, Cleo," she said. "I couldn't find a parking space close to the front at the grocery store and I'm chilled to the bone."

"I wish you'd let me pick things up for you when you need them," said Cleo. "You know I'm happy to get whatever you want when I shop for my dad."

"You're a good girl, but I was out of cat food and you know how Stewie needs his food."

Stewie was the meanest cat ever born, and also one of the fattest. Going a day without food surely wouldn't cause him much harm, Cleo thought, stifling a smile. Sweet Mrs. Lombardi kept shrinking while her cat grew fatter with each passing day. It reminded Cleo of the Danish folktale she often read to her Montessori students, about the cat who ate all the people in the village and grew so fat he couldn't move.

Mrs. Lombardi wiped under her eyes, scrutinizing Cleo. "You look so nice. Did you go out with a man?" she asked in a hopeful tone.

"You know I don't date."

"Cleo, ten years without a man is too long. And thirty years old is so young. You know what I would give to go back and do it all over again? You should be out living it up."

Cleo didn't say anything. She heard this quite often from Mrs. Lombardi. And Sylvia. And, of course, there was Nick. He probably lectured her the most, which was ironic, given that he'd pined for Sylvia in secret for four years, never having the courage to tell her his true feelings. And now it was too late. Four years ago Sylvia had married arrogant and distant Malcolm, whom both Cleo and Nick hated, without ever knowing Nick's feelings. *I'm not good enough for her*, he always said to Cleo. Which, in Cleo's opinion, was absolutely not true. But he saw only that he was a poor bartender trying to make a living as a glass blower. *It wouldn't be enough for her*, he said, time and time again. *She wouldn't respect me.*

"And you're so pretty," Mrs. Lombardi said now. "Men should be lined up around the block for you."

"I'm not interested. You know that."

"Maybe you should get a cat."

"Very funny," said Cleo.

"You want to turn out like me? Alone at sixty living with a cat that only loves me when I feed him?"

Cleo ignored her. "I'm making chicken cacciatore for Dad tomorrow. I'll drop some off for you before I go over there. But only if you promise not to give any to Stewie."

Mrs. Lombardi opened her door wider and stepped inside. "You know I can't promise that." They both laughed. Just then, Stewie came running to the door, leaping into the hallway and sitting back on his hind legs, hissing at Cleo while holding his front paws like a boxer.

"Stewie, nice to see you," said Cleo. He hissed again, this time with even more venom. "I'll check on you tomorrow," said Cleo, backing away. The cat scared her. No question.

"Goodnight, dear."

Cleo crossed the hall to her apartment, 3D. Living alone, she kept it tidy, her familiar objects pleasing during long, rainy afternoons and evenings. It was only 900 square feet - just one bedroom and a front room divided by a counter into a sitting area and kitchen. She'd decorated it in white and blues, replicating photos she found in a beach house magazine she'd purchased standing in the grocery store line. There was an attractive off-white couch, which she kept spotless by almost never sitting on it, and two soft reading chairs in light blue. She'd hung white, filmy curtains over the front windows along with various Impressionist prints and Ansel Adams photos on the walls. Between the two front windows was her one prized possession: her mother's old turntable, set inside a white cabinet and surrounded by books and several photos.

She paused, gazing at the photo of her mother and father on their wedding day, the other of she and Sylvia, arms linked in front of their dormitory room at USC the second week of freshman year. They'd already been best friends by then. She picked up the frame, peering into their eighteen-year-old faces. *So young.* Their cheeks were rounded with youth, eyes sparkling with the possibility of everything. It was before Simon then, before she even knew him and loved him, before the empty space left when he was gone. And the years since for Sylvia? She felt trapped in a loveless marriage, Cleo suspected, although her friend never confessed to it. And maybe she didn't even know herself because all Sylvia wanted was a baby. So much so that all other dreams had faded.

If someone took their photo today, what would they see? Cleo knew the lens would not lie. It would capture two women living on the edges of life, waiting and yearning for that which they could not have.

In her bedroom, she kicked off her dress and slipped into her favorite jeans and T-shirt, which were draped over the reading chair near the window. Then she padded to the kitchen and poured a glass of red wine from an open bottle on the counter.

She took one sip before going to the hall closet and pulling a purple hatbox from the top shelf, next to an umbrella and a Mariners baseball cap. She carried the box and her wine to the bedroom, placed the glass on the bedside table near her mother's high school portrait, and settled cross-legged on the bed. Then she emptied the contents of the hatbox: two photos, a slip of paper with one sentence scribbled on it, a DVD labeled *The Soup Kitchen*, and a typed manuscript entitled *Cleo*, held together with a large, black clasp.

The first of the photos was of her and Simon lounging on the fountain outside of Bing Theater on the USC campus. Each morning before their ten o'clock classes they would spend fifteen minutes together, either chatting or dozing or practicing Cleo's lines for scene class, before Cleo headed into the theater and Simon went to the film school for his graduate level screenwriting class. How they had gloried in the symmetry of that one small thing: class at the same time. It indicated to them that they were meant to be, that the future they envisioned would come to fruition because of that small aligning of the universe: a writer and his muse - an actress and her filmmaker.

The second photo she'd taken of Simon was on the set of *The Soup Kitchen*. He was behind the camera, setting a shot, his shoulders slightly curved, his face focused. She allowed herself to stare at this one for several minutes. But tonight the tears didn't come. She hadn't had enough wine. Instead the cavern in her chest opened wider until all that was left was the terrible emptiness that had once been him.

Next, she held the manuscript to her chest, knowing the story of the Seattle girl and her young mother dying of cancer not only because she'd read it so many times but because she'd lived it once. It was her story before Simon captured it so beautifully in his manuscript. And now it was nothing but these sheets of fading pages in her hands.

Lastly, she picked up the slip of paper. The last words he'd ever written to her. *Gone for donuts.* Gone. Never to return.

She put everything carefully back into the box and returned it to the closet, next to her ordinary things - this Pandora's box of another time and place.

Then she went to her stereo, kneeling on the floor as she rifled through her old LP's for music to suit her mood. There was every type of music, much of it from her mother's collection but some added in the last several years because of the resurgent interest in old LP's as collectors' items. She was embarrassed to say how many hours she spent on the Internet finding and ordering from vinyl sellers all over the world.

She chose Pink Floyd. As the lyrics to *Wish You Were Here* engulfed her as only music could, she grabbed her wine and curled up in the blue chair closest to the stereo. The rain continued outside, cascading down the window in sheets.

From her purse by the door, her cell phone rang. She uncurled from the chair and reached into the bottom of her bag. What was this number? Should she answer?

Against her better judgment, she answered.

"Hi, Cleo. Scott Moore here."

"Hi, Scott. How did you get my number?"

"One of your teacher friends gave it to me. Hope you don't mind? I promise I'm not calling to ask you out."

"All right." What was wrong with this man?

"That's a lie. Actually I am." He sounded amused, which annoyed her further. "No, I'm calling because I just talked with someone from my office and it turns out we have several birth mothers who specifically put in their profiles that they wanted musical adoptive parents. I couldn't help but remember you said your friend is a music professor."

She shivered. The hair on the back of her neck stood up. What did this mean? Was it a sign? Just then her phone buzzed in her hand, indicating another call. She held it away from her ear and looked at the small screen. It was Sylvia. Was it another sign? She looked out the window. The rain still pounded against the pane. "I'll let her know," Cleo said. "I'll have her contact you if she's interested."

"Does this mean you'll agree to go out with me?"

She hesitated. "Let's not get ahead of ourselves. Let's see what she says first." She said goodbye and clicked over to Sylvia.

"Can you meet me at Cooper's?" asked Sylvia.

"I'll be there in thirty minutes," she said, already heading towards the bedroom to find her favorite sweater.

Chapter Two

THE STREETS OF DOWNTOWN SEATTLE were slippery from a recent rain and deserted. Peter Ball yawned, weary from the insomnia that plagued him. His car clock said 2:16 a.m. Maybe he could fall asleep when he returned to his own bed. Insomniacs were always hopeful, staring at the ceiling thinking sleep would come at any moment, he thought. He was on his way home from his woman friend Melissa's apartment. Melissa called him whenever she was on the outs with her married lover, knowing he would always come and hold her and make love to her so that she might forget the pain of loving a man who was unavailable, at least for a time. Last night the call had come at ten. She'd broken it off, once and for all. Could he come over? Of course, he was happy to oblige, although as they lay intertwined in her bed, he was unable to resist a gentle lecture about giving herself to someone who didn't deserve her, thinking, as always, about his mother and all those nights she'd spent waiting and watching for his father to come home, crying into her needlepoint.

After his lecture she shifted in bed to look into his eyes. "Peter, are you ever lonely?" Women always smelled of two things. Melissa smelled of vanilla and freshly mowed grass.

"Every day of my life, sweetheart. But you know how I am."

Her question had jolted him, had made him think about things he didn't want to think about. It was just his work, he knew, that sustained him in a life purposely lived on the outside of things, like a house perched on the outskirts of town, almost part of a community but not quite. It was his childhood that had molded and shaped him; there was no need for a shrink to explain that to anyone. He knew all those nights of listening to his mother cry had made up his character: jittery, driven, suspicious, questioning - a perfect detective. He could piece together false mutterings and shards of gossip. He could smell the truth of a thing before anyone else.

He often said to his brother Jack, when they were still speaking: *cops beget cops and all that.*

Jack. As it so often did when he thought of Jack now, the clasp in Peter's chest tightened from missing him and worrying about him. Eighteen months with no contact. And the feeling of betrayal, too, was there at the center of the pain. What was he doing right now, Peter wondered? It was early June and Jack would be done with his school year of teaching high school math back in their old hometown.

At home, Peter tossed about restlessly for hours, still unable to sleep. Eventually he must have drifted off, because he wakened with a start to the sound of his cell phone ringing. Rubbing his eyes, he reached for it, figuring it was the precinct or his partner, Brent.

"Peter, it's Jack."

He sat up, plucking at the covers with his free hand. "Jack?" He glanced at the clock – it was a few minutes before seven.

"Yeah, hey, I'm downstairs. Can you buzz me up?"

Peter put his bare feet to the floor. The carpet was soft between his toes. He crouched over so that his chest was on his knees, his stomach sucked to his ribcage. "Jack?" he repeated.

"Can you let me in?"

"Yeah, okay."

Peter walked blindly to his front door and pushed the buzzer. Through the intercom, he heard the downstairs entrance into the condominium building open and click shut. Then he leaned against the wall, pulling absently on the waistband string around his sweat pants. After a moment, there was a soft knock on his front door.

And there, standing in the hallway, was his brother. He wore a button-down cotton shirt and khaki pants with creases above the thighs. His hair was longer than he used to wear it, curling on his forehead, and disheveled. But his blue eyes were the same: clear-sighted, intelligent behind wire-rimmed glasses.

Next to him was a teenaged girl. She was thin, with a fitted T-shirt over protruding hipbones and leggings.

Peter gripped the side of the door, unable to think of anything to say. Jack spoke first. "May we come in?" *May we* instead of *can we?* Like their mother: unflappable, proper. But that was the old Jack – just eighteen months ago – before the razor blade and the blood that spilled over white tiles.

Then they were in his living room. Jack had his hands shoved deep into the pockets of his khakis. The girl pulled on a strand of mousy brown hair, her eyes red-rimmed and glazed. She smelled of black licorice and peaches. Peter looked around the condo, hoping there were no stray pairs of underwear or packages of condoms or Victoria's Secret catalogs. But the cleaners had come yesterday and everything was dusted and vacuumed and put away in its proper place. The standard off-white walls were bare of paintings or photos and the only furniture was a black leather couch, a tan easy chair, and a glass coffee table with a yellow decorative bowl his mother had given him for Christmas a couple of years back. The year Miriam came to visit. His eyes darted to Jack. Would he remember that Miriam had helped their mother choose it from Legley Bay's one kitchen store? But Jack's gaze roamed the room. "Hired a decorator, I see," Jack said with the banter so familiar between them.

"Sure, a guy with purple fingernails named Fifi," said Peter, the clasp in his chest tightening. *Oh, little brother, I've missed you.*

The girl standing next to Jack cocked her head to the side, her eyes flickering in the way people's do when they're trying to understand something.

"Peter, this is Misty Johnson," said Jack. He sounded almost fatherly. "She's my best math student at Legley Bay High School. We came to ask for your help."

Again, he could think of nothing to say. His once-promising brother was now a small-town teacher. It was hard to fathom, given that eighteen months ago Jack had been a semester away from finishing his doctorate in physics, that he now taught high school math and science instead of working at some research institute or other prestigious organization.

"Because you're a cop, right?" said Misty.

"He's detective status," said Jack. "Promoted at thirty."

"Cops beget cops, and all that," Peter said to Misty with a grimace, almost apologetically.

"Yeah, I know your dad," said Misty. "He busted up a kegger couple weeks ago down by the creek."

"He's still doing that, huh?" said Peter, glancing at Jack. "Some things never change."

"My sister Alicia's disappeared," Misty said without emotion, like a person in shock.

"In Legley Bay?" asked Peter.

"Yeah," said Misty. "In the middle of the night."

Peter's gaze darted to Jack. "Why didn't you take it to Dad?"

Jack's face flushed. "I did. He thinks she's a runaway."

Peter looked over at Misty. "And why don't you think the same thing?"

Misty squared her shoulders, speaking with a defensive edge to her voice, as if she were accustomed to people not believing her. "For one, because Alicia's been acting weird all nine months of the school year - crying all the time, and sick a lot. I tried to get her to tell me what was wrong but she always just clammed up, which is not like her. We're close. Best friends." Her voice wavered; she put her hand up to her mouth, staring at the floor.

"And what's the second thing?" asked Peter.

"Because I followed her and saw her meet a woman. A woman I'd never seen before."

He motioned them into the sitting area, pointing to the couch. "Here, sit. I want you to tell me every detail you remember." He grabbed his notepad from the table next to the door and sat across from them.

"I remember my sister wore a trench coat she'd found at the Goodwill a couple of months ago, buttoned but not belted, and no hat," said Misty. "And her red rain boots."

They always began with, *I remember*, like a poet's writing prompt, thought Peter. Most tried their best to be precise, to tell their recounting of a particular moment as accurately as possible, but whether in interrogation or simple conversation, they had only memory to inform their stories. And Peter knew memory was an unreliable mistress. All cops knew this. As did storytellers. For tales are only fragments, snatches of time, drawn from perceptions, from our noticing of something we may or may not be asked to recount later. But he urged her to continue. "How many days ago was this?"

"Two," she said, her eyes filling.

"Go on. It's okay. Take your time," said Peter.

"It was foggy," she continued. "We call it pea soup."

Peter nodded. "I remember. I grew up there too."

"Oh, right," she said, her brows knitted over eyes that searched his face for some kind of recognition of a similar life, but she could see that he felt far away from her reality. "It was a little after midnight. She walked straight towards town, resting every so often like she was out of breath." Misty pulled on the neck of her T-shirt. "We live just blocks from the high school."

"They live in the Wilson's old place," said Jack.

"Yeah, I know where that is," said Peter. It was a green mobile home, set back from the street, decaying even twenty years ago. He could only imagine what it looked like now.

"And I saw her meet a woman outside the motel. The one next to Dairy Queen," said Misty.

"The Dew Drop Inn?" asked Peter.

"They renamed it," said Jack. "It's just Legley Bay Inn now."

"What did she look like?" asked Peter.

"I couldn't see that well in the dark but she had short, brown hair and a dark coat. She wore glasses." Misty closed her eyes, as if to conjure the image in her mind. "They were purple." She opened her eyes. "And she kind of looked like a man. Like a fat, square man."

"Did they go into the bar or the restaurant at the Dew Drop Inn?" asked Peter.

"Neither, they went into a room. Room 12. The one on the end. I went down there and knocked, loud, again and again." She held up her hand, revealing bruised and scraped knuckles. "But no one came. I put my ear against the doorframe but heard nothing." She paused, her lips trembling and her eyes filling with tears once again.

"Tell him what happened next," said Jack, gently. "Go ahead."

"I went across the street to Sissy's Tavern. My mom works there. She got the motel night manager, Patti Robertson, to open the room. My mom went to high school with her brother so she did it as a favor."

"You remember Jim Robertson," said Jack. "He was in the class two years ahead of me."

Peter nodded, an image coming to him of Jim at a party on the beach - kids sitting around a bonfire passing a bong. "Sure, I remember him."

"But when we opened the door, there was no one there," said Misty.

"Was there any indication anyone had been there?" asked Peter.

"The bed looked like someone had sat on it – the top cover wrinkled," said Misty. "The woman must've seen me cross the street and they slipped out then – well, I don't know." She hesitated, waving her hands in the air like she was trying to dry them over an open fire. "That's just it. Where did they go?"

"And this woman, you have no idea who she is?" asked Peter.

"Never seen her before," she said, shaking her head. "But there is one thing." She reached into her pocket and pulled out a glossy piece of paper, folded in three. "This was on the floor near the bed."

It was a brochure for a Montessori preschool in Seattle's Queen Anne neighborhood. A woman's name was scrawled across the top: "Cleo Tanner – 206-555-1425."

"You think it means anything?" asked Jack.

"No idea," said Peter. "But it's something, at least."

Misty, looking paler than the moment before, sank into the back of the couch. "So, you'll help us?"

"I'll do my best," said Peter. "In the meantime, I think you two should stay here until we figure out if this woman is dangerous or not, since she can identify you."

Misty's eyes reddened. "I'll have to call my mother and let her know."

Jack looked uncomfortable. "I don't know, Peter, if that's such a good idea."

"Why not?" asked Peter. "School's out, right?"

"Please, Mr. Ball," Misty said to Jack. "I'll be safe here."

Jack's eyes flickered and turned towards the ceiling before turning back to Peter. "Yeah. Okay."

❉

After they settled Misty into the guest room, Peter and Jack met in the kitchen. "I only have tea," Peter said, setting a package of green tea on the table.

"It's fine," said Jack.

"I know you like coffee."

"Don't worry about it." Jack's eyes were soft, making it seem that he was still his same, small brother, whose arrival had found the dormant clasp in the middle of Peter's chest, which tightened and loosened according to Jack's safety and happiness.

Peter put a steaming cup of tea in front of Jack. "How you been?" He felt the sting of betrayal creep in, tightening the clasp in his chest, approaching the surface of everything.

Jack ran his hands through his hair. "Better."

"How's Legley Bay?"

Jack's mouth twitched and he crossed his leg, adjusting the bottom of his pants over his ankle. "The weather's terrible. I forgot that."

"Mom says you rented a little house near the high school. How's that working out?" asked Peter.

"It's fine. Small. Affordable. And I don't have to eat Aggie's cooking."

"You regret it?" asked Peter, in spite of his best efforts to remain on neutral territory.

"Which part?" Jack kept his eyes on the cuff of his pants, rubbing the cloth between his fingers.

"Leaving the doctorate program."

"I don't know."

Peter bristled. How could he not know? Either you knew something or you didn't.

"After Miriam died," Jack said, and then paused, clearing his throat. "After Miriam was murdered, and I got out of the hospital, going back to finish seemed ridiculous suddenly. None of it mattered anymore."

Peter leaned against the doorway between the living room and kitchen. And there it was: an image of Jack slumped over the bathtub, wrists gushing blood onto the white tiles. That was eighteen months ago. Eighteen months without any contact. "Did you get any of my messages?" It came out strangled, the hurt and anger so near the surface.

Jack nodded, still examining the cuff of his pants. "Peter, I'm sorry if I hurt you. It was something I needed."

"What's that?" He tried to keep his voice even, nonchalant, as if the clasp wasn't tightening in his chest.

"Time. Away from you. To figure some things out. Without you acting like my father." Jack's eyes glistened and he took off his glasses, blew on one of the lenses, before hooking them back over his ears. He played with the fringe of his sock and then shivered. "It's freezing in here. Don't you turn on the heat?"

"Sorry. It's June. Can't use the heat in June. I know, I'm cheap. Just one of the many ways I'm like Dad."

"You're nothing like Dad." Jack rubbed the scar that ran over his wrist, and Peter wondered if he realized he did it? Was the movement subconscious, the reality of what he'd done such a part of who he was now?

Peter went to the window over the sink. The dark clouds from earlier had parted so the sun looked like it had arms, extending from the heavens.

"I've been seeing him," said Jack. "On and off since I got back."

Peter turned and stared at him, unable to think of what to say, this new betrayal hot in his chest. Jack saw their father and yet refused to answer Peter's phone calls? "You're kidding, right?"

Jack blinked behind his glasses and ran his hand through his hair. "He's lost some of the old arrogance. Sort of humbled or beaten down or something."

"Well, if you're such pals now why didn't you take this case to him?"

"I told you. I did. He's convinced she's a runaway," said Jack.

Peter took a sip of his tea. It was hot and burned the tip of his tongue. He set it on the counter, too hard, so that it splashed over the tan tiles. "Look, I want to help you, but this is out of my jurisdiction. And this girl needs to be with her mother, not us. I mean, shit, we don't know anything about teenagers."

"Peter, I know exactly what she's going through."

"You're still dealing with your own stuff and to take this on, well, I don't think it's a good idea."

"Because I'm too emotionally fragile? Is that what you mean?"

Peter felt the anger bubble to the surface now. His voice came out a low roar. "Yeah, that's exactly what I mean."

Jack's voice was angry too. "My wife was killed for the fourteen dollars in her purse. One minute she was squeezing my hand, wiping away tears over Colin Firth's performance as an English King and the next minute she's bleeding out on a sidewalk. I know about night terrors, irrational fear, bargaining with God, and finally, just wanting the pain to stop."

"No," Peter said, holding up his hands. "Don't."

"Peter," Jack said, his voice soft. "This is why I can't talk to you."

The anger Peter felt only moments ago was replaced with a sense of helplessness. Another image of Jack came sweeping in: of him almost drowning in the public swimming pool when he was only five years old, his fragile arms flailing about in the water and Peter all the way down at the other end of the pool. He swam fast, his athletic body unfailing despite his panic, and reached him in time, pulling him to the edge of the pool and holding him as he choked up water. But nothing, not Peter's physical or mental gifts, could save Jack from despair when Miriam was murdered. Nothing, even all the years of being a cop, had terrified him as much as his kid brother bleeding out on the bathroom floor. Nothing had sickened Peter more than admitting him to the psychiatric ward.

Peter tossed his teabag into the trash and turned his gaze to the light playing on a tree's branch outside the window. He spoke quietly. "We all loved Miriam, Jack." He faced his brother, looking him in the eyes, despite the pain he saw there, the pain he felt too. "I've grieved for her too. I never had the chance to tell you how much."

"I know. But not like I did." Jack paused, his thumb rubbing the ring left on the table from his teacup. "No one loved her like I did."

No one loves you like I do, Peter thought as he dumped his tea into the sink. He turned to Jack. "The Captain's been after me to use some of my vacation days. After I take a run and shower, I'll go into work and ask for some time off. I won't have jurisdiction on this but if I find anything I can send it to Dad. First thing is, I'll try and get a lead on this Cleo Tanner."

Jack sighed, the tension around his eyes disappearing. "Thank you. That's a good start."

Chapter Three

SITTING AT THEIR USUAL PLACE at the bar, Sylvia waited for Cleo. She doodled flowers on a napkin in an attempt to keep from staring at Nick, who worked steadily behind the bar making drinks or filling the dishwasher with dirty glasses. Cooper's was located in lower Queen Anne, not far from the Space Needle, and was a remnant of the old days of Seattle, before Microsoft money and its offspring brought so much wealth to the city that it changed from gritty and grungy to gleaming and new. Serving only bar food, chicken wings, and nachos and burgers, it was dimly lit and rugged like neighborhood bars should be, Sylvia always thought. The bar was made of dark wood and the seats were round stools covered in red vinyl. Small, square tables sat upon scuffed wood floors the owner never bothered to refinish. It smelled of fried food and spilled beer and numerous women's perfumes.

For a Friday night it was quiet, with only half the tables occupied. When she and Cleo first started coming to Cooper's four years ago, it was packed on a Friday night. But that was before the recession brought so many entertainment establishments to a grinding halt. Then again, she and Cleo didn't get out as much as they used to since Sylvia married Malcolm four years ago.

Just then Cleo came in through the front door, her long honey-colored hair slightly damp. She was breathing hard. "Sorry I'm late. I took the bus and had to run in the rain like four blocks to get here." She smiled, fluffing her hair. "I've already had some wine. Auction tonight," she added, as if Sylvia didn't remember. They talked several times a day. There wasn't a thing they didn't know about one another. Except for one thing - Sylvia's one secret - too big for even Cleo to know.

Slipping out of her coat, Cleo climbed up on the barstool. "And it's still pouring. Of course. I mean, what do we expect in June, right?"

Sylvia smiled. This was a favorite pastime of Seattleites - always talking about the rain and complaining about the weather as if it weren't the same every year, and as if their talking about it could change it. Summer didn't begin until after July Fourth.

Cleo waved hello to Nick. He nodded and smiled as he poured several shots for the older gentlemen in the seats closest to the door.

"I'm so glad you agreed to come out," said Sylvia, resting her head on Cleo's shoulder for a moment. "I know it's late already and short notice but I just had to see you."

"I'm glad you called, actually," said Cleo. "I have something to ask you."

Cleo's cheeks were flushed like they did when she was agitated over something. Before Sylvia could ask what was wrong, Nick came over to them. "Usual?" he asked.

"Sounds good," said Cleo, grinning. "Does it bother you we're so predictable?"

"Not one bit," he said, matching her grin with one of his own, glancing at Sylvia. "It's good to see you, Sylvia. Feels like a million years since you've been here."

"I know," she said. "How's your work going?" Nick was a glass blower. To her, his work was exquisite. She owned at least a dozen of his pieces, bowls and vases mostly, displaying them in all the best locations around her home. If only Malcolm knew what they represented, she often thought, as she gazed at them or held them in her hands like she might hold a lover on a long languid night.

"Same. Still struggling to make it," he said, his face clouding.

"You know the offer stands to talk to my dad about you," said Sylvia, trying to keep her voice light in order to disguise how much she wanted it for him. Her father, as a donor and an art aficionado, had deep connections in the art community. For years she'd offered to talk to her father about getting Nick featured in different galleries or helping him come up with a business plan to sell his work in shops. But he wouldn't do it.

His eyes went flat. "You know I can't let you do that."

"But why?" asked Sylvia, for what felt like the hundredth time. *Because you're too proud*, she thought, wishing she had the nerve to say it.

"Because I can't let my best girl ask for favors from her father. I have to do this on merit, not because someone helped me," he said, smiling in a way that didn't reach his eyes.

My best girl. Every time he called her that, it made her heart swell. But it wasn't really true. She wasn't his best girl and she never would be. She was married to Malcolm. And she was certain Nick loved Cleo.

If only I'd known you before I agreed to marry Malcolm, she thought, for what felt like the thousandth time.

"Well, that's ridiculous," said Cleo. "That's how the world works. It's nothing but who you know." She threw her hands in the air. "But I'm a broken record on this point. He doesn't listen," she said to Sylvia.

Nick shook his head. "Art's different. It has to sell because it's good, not because somebody hooked me up. I just need to keep working at it until I'm good enough." Nick reached for a pint beer glass and tipped it, filling it with Sierra Nevada Pale Ale from the tap before setting it in front of Cleo, his biceps pushing against the sleeves of his T-shirt like camel humps. He became better looking as he aged. She'd known him for four years now and every year he grew more handsome. His father was Italian and Nick inherited his dark complexion, but his mother's Swedish genes gave him height. He was over six feet, tall and broad. Despite Sylvia's own height of five-eleven, he made her feel petite when she stood next to him. He had thick brown hair, and his face, once round with youth, had thinned out and become chiseled over the years. But it was his eyes she loved the most. They were the color of dark coffee and glittered or twinkled or turned liquid like the glass he formed over hot flames, depending on his mood or the conversation. The first night she'd met him, she'd taken one look into those eyes and thought: *I'll never be the same.* And she was right.

"I have to run to the ladies room," said Cleo, scooting from the stool and heading towards the back where the restrooms were.

Nick reached under the bar and pulled out a bottle of red wine not on the menu. "Have a new one for you to try. Found it last weekend at their tasting room up in Woodinville. I've been saving it, hoping you would come in." He poured a taste for her in a wine glass. She swirled it and breathed in - it smelled of tobacco and mold.

"Has a little funk on the nose," Sylvia said.

"Yeah, I know how you love that."

Her shoulders loosened, for what felt like the first time in months. Nick always made her feel lighter. She took a first sip. It tasted like blackberry pie with a little pepper on the finish. "Oh, Nick, it's good."

He poured a full glass for her from the bottle. "You all right?" His voice was gentle. "I've been worried about you."

"Not really. In-vitro didn't work. Again." She tried to fight it, but the tears came anyway, hot on her face.

Nick handed her a stack of napkins. "I'm sorry, Sylvia." He shook his head, squeezing her wrist for a brief moment. "I know it hurts."

She wiped under her eyes, covering her wrist where he'd touched her. How good his fingers felt on her skin. "It does. Really bad."

Cleo slid into the stool beside her. "What happened?"

"Talking about the in-vitro," said Nick.

Cleo put her arm around Sylvia's shoulders. "I wish I could help."

"Malcolm's angry with me all the time lately," said Sylvia. "And I don't blame him. I'm a mess all the time."

"Well, he has no right to be angry," said Nick. "He should understand."

She felt Cleo stiffen next to her. "That's right, Sylvia. He doesn't know what you're going through. Not to mention the hormones from the in-vitro procedure."

Two days ago, shortly before dinner, she'd felt dampness in her panties and sure enough, it was her period: yet another in-vitro procedure that didn't take. The last one, she and Malcolm decided afterwards. Enough was enough. Malcolm had been particularly adamant on this point.

And then, the next morning she was in her office at the university, keeping busy with mindless paperwork, crying into her wine glass, her eyes raw and puffy from the night before. There was a tentative knock on her office door. It was one of her graduate students. "I've some news," she said in a shaky voice. "But it won't affect my studies. I just wanted you to know before I started showing."

No, Sylvia screamed inside her head. *No, no, no, not this girl too.*

A strange hum started between her ears like an electric fence she could not silence.

There were pregnant women everywhere, on the street, in the grocery store, at family holiday dinners. Her sister, Margaret, married to a man who seemed to Sylvia to care nothing for his own children, given the way he looked at his wife whenever one of them needed something, had three children and another on the way. "An oops," Margaret whispered to her during a family dinner at their parents'. And Sylvia was so angry she'd had to go home, making an excuse about a migraine, Malcolm following her helplessly to the car. They were silent until they reached their garage, when he turned off the car and without looking at her, spoke through gritted teeth. "You've got to get over this. You're letting it ruin your life."

"Over it? How do you suggest I do that?"

"I don't know," said Malcolm. "But you have to move forward somehow."

"What about adoption?"

He rested his forehead against the steering wheel of their Mercedes sports utility vehicle – a car made for a family, purchased so happily and hopefully. "You know how I feel about that," said Malcolm.

She cried into her hands, not bothering any longer to hold it in, feeling hopeless and angry and sad. And bitter. Terribly bitter towards this man who would deny her the one thing she wanted.

She heard his car door open and watched as he disappeared into the house. After that, for a week, after work, she'd locked herself in the spare bedroom, unable to face him. She watched old movies for hours, trying in vain to escape her thoughts. Their housekeeper, Minnie, sent in meals that remained untouched; Sylvia felt her body mass shrinking and could see the bones right underneath the skin and yet she didn't care, couldn't care.

Year after year, she'd yearned so for a child that it felt almost like another entity in her body, this longing, and it was in everything she did, making her feel like she might explode with rage from her own desperation and obsession to have a child. For the first time in

CARAMEL AND MAGNOLIAS   35

her life playing her beloved piano did not help. Even music could not save her.

Now, Cleo was peering at her, with those eyes that knew almost everything about her. Nick put a glass of water in front of her. He didn't shrink away like most men would, she thought, when a woman cried. It was because he had so many sisters. Men with sisters were never afraid of tears.

Cleo leaned closer. "Listen to me. I met a man at the auction," she said. "His name is Scott Moore. He runs a private adoption agency."

Sylvia didn't say anything, flicking her gaze between her glass of wine and the glass of water. "You know what Malcolm says about that."

Nick's fingers thumped on the top of the bar but he didn't say anything. She wondered what he thought. He never said a thing about her husband but she had the feeling he didn't like him.

"He said he would put you on the top of the list. If you wanted," said Cleo.

"Why would he do that?" said Sylvia.

Cleo's eyes flickered to the ceiling. "I think he likes me."

Nick wiped an imaginary spill with a white towel that smelled of bleach, his eyes fierce. "What do you mean?"

She stared at Cleo, trying to grasp what she meant. "Did you agree to go out with him?"

"No. But I will, if it means he would help you."

"Cleo, really?" asked Nick.

"It wouldn't be a real date if I just did it for Sylvia," said Cleo. "It's different."

"What are you talking about?" said Sylvia. "You are not doing that." She emphasized each word.

"He told me he'd put you and Malcolm at the top of the list if I'd go out with him." Cleo shifted on the barstool. "What could it hurt? A few dates?"

"Absolutely not. You're not going out with some creep just so I can get to the top of the list. Anyway, it doesn't matter. Malcolm says no adoptions." She felt the tears come again. "But I love you for wanting this for me so much that you'd even consider it. Especially, you know, given your..." She trailed off, not wanting to say what they all knew. *Given your decision to live like a dead person.*

Cleo reached out for her hand. "You have to ask Malcolm to reconsider. Just think about it. Please. This is a chance. Scott called me just before I came here because he said he has several birth mothers delivering in the next couple of weeks. They want musical parents."

A shiver went down the back of her spine. "Really?"

"Really."

"How many times would you have to go out with him?" asked Nick, concern in his voice, his eyes still glittering.

"As many times as it takes to get Sylvia a baby," said Cleo.

"It's absolutely out of the question," said Sylvia. But even to her own ears, she didn't sound convinced.

Sylvia arrived home after midnight to an empty house. Malcolm was working late, preparing for trial, sitting third chair on a case against a large pharmaceutical company. She went upstairs and ran a bath, as hot as she could stand it, and put her headphones on. Adele was what she needed, she thought. She closed her eyes, wishing the hot water and music would make everything better. But it didn't. All she could see was Nick's face, like a movie playing on her closed eyelids. It was always the same after she spent time with him. This is why she tried to stay away from the bar. She was married. She'd made her choice and she must remain committed. There was no going back. Not that Nick wanted her anyway. That was perfectly clear.

She'd met Malcolm at one of her mother's garden parties on a warm August afternoon. They chatted for an hour near the pool about their work mostly. He was an ambitious attorney, trying to make partner in one of the long-standing firms downtown. He was handsome, in a bland sort of way, hair the color of sandpaper and placid blue eyes, dressed in a Tommy Bahama linen button-down shirt and khaki shorts. After that afternoon, he pursued her with a relentlessness that made him a good attorney.

After several months of dating Malcolm, she and Cleo discovered
Cooper's. And with Cooper's, came Nick. She'd felt an immediate,
visceral reaction to him that she tried to set aside, to place into a
container that had nothing to do with her real life. *This is Nick. He's
wrong for you. And he's probably not even interested. He's a friend. And he
most likely wants Cleo.*

Malcolm asked her to marry him on a cool April evening at a
window seat at the Flying Fish in downtown Seattle. Nothing came
out of her mouth at first. She thought only, wildly, heart beating fast:
Is this the one? And then, *Nick.* "Yes," she said. Malcolm was steady
and successful, a perfect match for her. *He will make a great father.*

"Excellent." He nodded and waved for the check, almost like
he'd finished a business transaction.

The next night, she called Cleo. "Meet me at Cooper's?"

They both drank multiple cosmopolitans made by a shake of
Nick's sexy arm. Cooper's was empty, just the two of them at the bar
and Nick. After Sylvia's third pink drink, she got up the courage to
tell them about the proposal. "Malcolm asked me to marry him
last night."

Nick, wiping wine glasses, stared at her. "What? Is it that serious
between you?"

"He seems to think so," said Sylvia, emboldened by drink.
"Because he asked the big proverbial question. And I said yes."

The wine glass in Nick's hand suddenly shattered. Blood
squirted from his thumb. "Crap," he muttered. He took a towel from
under the bar and wrapped it around his thumb. "Good thing you
guys are the only ones in here."

"Are you all right?" asked Sylvia.

"Sure," he said, wincing. "No big deal. Just a minor cut." He
pulled a first aid kit out from under the bar.

"Put your hand on the counter here," said Sylvia. "I'll put the
bandage on for you." She took his hand between her own. The cut
wasn't bad, just a few centimeters. His hands had so many scars
from burns. *The hands of a glass blower,* he always said.

"Put some of that antiseptic stuff on it," said Cleo. "Nicky,
you've got to be more careful." She always called him Nicky when
she was drunk.

After he was bandaged, Cleo grabbed her arm, turning to stare into her eyes. "Now back to this big announcement. Are you sure?"

"He's perfect for me," she mumbled.

"If you say so," said Cleo.

"I say so," she said, feeling defensive.

After closing that night, Nick drove them both home. They dropped Cleo off first and then headed across the West Seattle Bridge back to Seattle.

Resting her head on the back of the car seat, she watched him as the headlights from oncoming cars flickered across his handsome features. And there it was, again. This feeling of wanting him that was always there, like an unrelenting disease. She wanted his mouth on her own, his hands on her skin, to crawl inside him or wrap herself around him. But it wasn't to be. He didn't feel that way about her. He'd never confessed but she was sure he loved Cleo. Nick and Cleo had an ease with one another that was so familiar, so comfortable. Cleo said it was like brother and sister but she knew Nick felt differently. "How come you don't have a girlfriend?" She played with the tennis bracelet she always wore, a gift from her parents on her twenty-first birthday, turning it round and round on her wrist, her eyes on his profile.

"Want the truth?"

"Always."

"I'm in love with someone who can't love me back," he said, glancing over at her.

Her stomach felt like she'd been dropped from a tall building. She was right all along. He loved Cleo. Of course he did. She'd known it for years. "I wish you didn't," she said. "It's useless, you know."

"I know," he said, flinching. "But you don't choose who you love."

"I guess not," she said, softly. "I wish you could."

"Me too."

She put her feelings aside after that night, determined to try and make a life despite this cavern in her chest that made it hard to breathe. She walked down the aisle towards Malcolm on a warm July day, vowing to never look back.

Every day since she prayed the same prayer. *Please God, let me love my husband like I should and please send me a baby.*

And she carried this secret love around, never allowing herself to utter the words to a single soul. She loved Nick. And he loved Cleo. And Cleo loved Simon, gone for over ten years now.

But Cleo was her best friend, no matter all the rest of it. Who understood the magic of friendship? It was not possible to explain how some people made their way into your life as if they'd always been there, their soul lurking with yours until bodies met in the physical world. Their friendship was the unraveling of fate, the two of them destined by a random computer selection when they were put together as roommates their freshman year at USC.

So many years had passed since then, so much loss for both of them, robbing them of the girls they'd once been. She was assigned to a dormitory suite; eight girls were to share a common living room and kitchen but were grouped in pairs for bedrooms. Cleo and Sylvia arrived, coincidently, at almost the exact same moment, smiling shyly at one another while riding up in the elevator, suitcases in hand, only to discover that they were roommates.

As they unpacked, they discussed their backgrounds, discovering to their mutual delight that they were both from Seattle. "Two Northwest girls in the city of angels," Cleo said. "What are the odds of that?"

Sylvia grew up in the wealthy community of Medina, whereas Cleo grew up in a modest part of Seattle called Ballard, the daughter of a plumber and a housewife. But there was one important commonality between them: they were both artists. Cleo had auditioned and been accepted into the drama program. Sylvia was studying concert piano at the music school.

That night, they shared their first pizza together, sitting on their twin beds in their small dormitory room. Cleo was a girl you might not notice at first glance, Sylvia observed. She was of average height and build and had a quiet presence, moving in a way that made Sylvia think of a breeze on a summer day – there but not there – unnoticeable except for providing a cooling presence. But when you looked closely, you saw Cleo's natural beauty. Her features were even and her honey-colored hair hung long, highlighting her fair skin and beautiful light green eyes. She reminded Sylvia of the paintings of the Swedes who populated the Midwest in the later part of the nineteenth century – like a heroine in a Willa Cather novel.

"You don't seem like an actress," Sylvia said.

"Why do you say that?" Cleo asked.

"I don't know. You seem genuine. Without any vanity. Not like the girls from my high school that were in the drama club."

Cleo shrugged and tucked her hair behind her ears. "A lot of actors are introverts," she said. "Sensitive."

"I never knew that." Sylvia leaned back against the wall, stretching out her long legs and sipping on her diet soda. She rubbed her manicured feet together in a rhythm, one hand placed idly in her lap, like she did when she was comfortable.

"You're so pretty," Cleo said. "And tall and thin. You could be a movie star."

Sylvia blushed. People told her she was pretty but she didn't see it. She was almost six feet tall, with long brown hair and almost translucent white skin. Her eyes were too wide apart in her small face and were a nondescript color, somewhere between green and hazel, depending on the light. "Gosh, no. I hate to have people look at me. I can imagine nothing worse, as a matter of fact. Plus, there's never a boy tall enough for me."

Cleo smiled. "With a campus of thirty thousand students, there's gotta be at least one boy tall enough for you."

Now, the water in the tub was growing cool. She shivered, thinking perhaps Cleo was right that she should ask Malcolm to reconsider adoption. There was no reason why she couldn't ask. This might be a chance for them. Maybe Malcolm would see it her way if she presented it to him that it was practically just a phone call away.

The next night Sylvia dressed, did her make-up, and blew out her long brown hair until it was shiny about her shoulders. She had Minnie make Malcolm's favorite dinner: meatloaf and mashed potatoes. And she asked again, telling him of Cleo's connection to Scott Moore, of his agency that would put them on the top of the list. Despite her best intentions, her eyes filled with tears as she watched Malcolm push his meatloaf around on his plate, knowing he would say no. Finally, he looked up. "If it's what you really want. Let's do it."

Chapter Four

PETER RAPPED HIS KNUCKLES on the doorway of Captain Wilson's office. Wilson sat at his desk, looking through a report, his right hand on a cup of the gut destroying precinct black coffee. "What's up, Pretty?" He glanced at Peter's empty hands. "Coffee shop out of green tea this morning?"

"Already had it at home. Cheaper that way."

"What's a guy like you need with frugality? No wife, no kids, nothing on the horizon but relaxing nights in front of football, no one harassing you for conversation or a night out during the slow march towards death."

Peter chuckled, resting his hands on the back of the visitor's chair next to Wilson's desk. "You always make marriage sound so appealing, boss." He paused, debating on whether to sit or not, but remained standing, his right foot tapping the floor under the chair. "So, Jack showed up at my house yesterday."

Wilson blinked a couple of times in rapid succession. "That right?"

"Brought one of his students with him. Says something's fishy with her sister's disappearance." He told Wilson the rest of what he knew, including Cleo Tanner's name and number on the scrap of paper.

"What's your gut?" asked Wilson.

"The kid seems pretty sure something's not right. I think it's worth sniffing around. I know it's out of my jurisdiction and all, but I have all that vacation time saved up and thought I might use it to look around a bit. Figure out the Cleo Tanner lead. Get a read on her first. Then head down to Legley Bay. See if I can find anything." He paused, flicking at a piece dust off the back of the chair. "It gives me a chance to get back in Jack's life."

Captain Wilson nodded. "Yep. Nothing better to do with your vacation than that. I know it's weighed heavy on you."

"Yeah," he said, avoiding the Captain's eyes. He'd worked for Wilson so long now and although he knew they'd never admit it, they were fond of one another in a way that went beyond just work. Peter's mother and grandmother came every year for a visit and Wilson always insisted they come to his home for dinner. Two years ago at their annual visit, they'd all enjoyed one another so much that his mother insisted Wilson and his wife Joan come to Jack's wedding. Such a great night that had been, too, Peter thought, with a pang.

"Jack took it to your pop already?" asked Wilson.

"Yeah, the genius thinks she's a runaway."

"You'll have to hand it off to him if you dig anything up. You know that, right?"

Peter edged towards the door. "If I find anything."

"You check in with him when you get down there. I don't want any crap from Legley Bay that we're stepping on toes. Regardless of your personal feelings, it's professional courtesy."

"I got it," said Peter. "And Brent wants to take a few days off too. Wants to go with me if I head to Legley Bay."

"You two lovebirds can't be separated for a few days?"

"Longest relationship of my life," said Peter. It was true. He and Brent had been partners for six years now. No one had his back like Brent, despite the fact that they bickered like an old married couple.

"Fine. Go. Have fun. Say hi to your mom and Aggie for me." Wilson's face softened. "How *is* Jack?"

Peter hesitated, hovering in the doorway. "Better. I think."

"How was it to see him?"

"Hard," said Peter.

"Give him my best."

"I will. I'll call you if I find anything."

❉

Brent was at his desk, finishing paperwork from their last case. He was a large man, once a decent basketball player but now with a few extra inches around his waist and his face fuller than it should be. "He give the go ahead?" he asked.

"Said I have to check in first with my dad, but, yes," said Peter.

"Can we stop at Top Hat donuts on the way out of town?"

Peter grimaced, adjusting his tie and moving towards the exit. "How can you be this much of a stereotype?"

Brent shrugged, looking blank. "Are you trying to hurt me?"

"Anyway, I've got some trail mix in the car if you're hungry."

"I wish I didn't have a woman as a partner."

Sitting in the passenger seat, Brent shoved a large piece of blueberry muffin into his mouth.

"That's full of fat." Peter waved at the muffin.

"Your point?"

"I thought you were on a diet?"

"You sound like my wife," said Brent.

"You shouldn't eat so fast."

"Shut up."

They drove up Queen Anne Avenue to the older upper-class neighborhood of Queen Anne. Once a working-class neighborhood with Craftsman-style bungalows built in the thirties and forties, it was now sought-after real estate, with almost every home remodeled and the entire top section of Queen Anne Avenue bustling with trendy, upscale restaurants, bars, and businesses. Peter understood this was all part of the new economy of Seattle, the Microsoft era, but there was a part of him that missed the old, gray Seattle, with grungy neighborhood bars and diners, places regular people could patronize instead of the rich people who worked at Microsoft and its offspring, the smaller tech companies started by rich ex-Microsoft executives.

Peter glanced at the address on the brochure and turned left on a skinny residential street with cars parked on both sides. After several blocks they saw a large yellow house and a patch of grass behind a tall steel gate displaying the name Queen Anne Montessori. Peeking out from behind the house was a bright blue playground. There was a gravel paved loop around the school and on the left side a sign that said, "Drop-Off Time 8:45-9:10" and "Pick-up Time 2:45-3:10."

They parked several blocks from the school, near a neighborhood park, lonely seeming, empty of children, warm June rain falling into mud puddles near a set of swings. They entered the lobby of the school, where a plump older woman wearing a sweater embroidered with spring flowers stood behind a chest-height counter. Hanging on the wall behind her were photos and a sign that read, "Our Staff."

The woman stood. "May I help you? I'm Martha Clemmons, Head of School." She enunciated every consonant and spoke at a slow pace, all the while looking Peter directly in the eyes.

"We're looking for a preschool for our daughter. Your school was highly recommended."

"That's very nice to hear." She looked at Peter and then at Brent. "And we're certainly open to alternative families. We believe love makes a family."

Brent laughed and waved a hand. "Oh, we're not—."

Peter interrupted, trying not to smile. "Thank you. We appreciate your openness to our situation."

Martha's wide face wrinkled into a smile but her brown eyes were disapproving. "That said, surely you realize it's way too late to enroll a child for this coming fall. We have open enrollment in February." She played with her necklace, which spelled out "Children First" in primary colored beads. "And, it is June." She emphasized every word.

"February? For daycare?" said Peter, genuinely taken aback.

Martha coughed and widened her eyes, as if it were difficult to be polite. "We consider ourselves a school, not a daycare. Maria Montessori developed this method of teaching over one hundred years ago. Did you know that children's personalities are fully developed by age five? This, amongst other data, is more than enough reason to get your child off to the right start for a fully realized life."

"Fine, sure," said Peter, feeling almost guilty over his imaginary child and her now partially diminished life.

Martha, Head of School, picked up a clipboard, lips pursed, and in a patronizing voice asked, as if they were on the slow side, "Is this your first child?"

"Yes," said Brent. "We tried for years." He waved his hand in front of his eyes, as if he were about to cry.

Peter hid a smile behind his hand.

"What's her name?"

"Matilda," Peter said.

"Matilda Rose," said Brent. "For our mothers."

"Yes, well, let me write down the name of several other preschools you might try," said Martha.

"So, you don't conduct interviews?" said Brent. His face was concerned, brows wrinkled and his hand at his heart.

"No, it's first come, first served," said Martha. "We had mothers who slept on our steps the night before open enrollment."

"It's too bad," said Peter, using an apologetic tone. "We're new to this." He turned, as if to go. "Just so you know, in particular, one of your teachers came highly recommended. Cleo Tanner?"

Martha pointed to the last photo in the line, of a pretty young woman with long blond hair, squinting into the sunlight. "Oh, yes, Cleo's been with us for five years now. We're very lucky to have her. She was educated in the theater before she came to us." She picked up a pen, holding it against her mouth, looking pensive. "You're the second person to ask about Cleo in the last two weeks. Strange."

"Really? Another parent, like us?" asked Peter, keeping his voice casual.

"I don't think so. This woman wanted her cell phone, which I hesitated to give out but she flustered me. She had these intense eyes – almost the color of ice - that made me so nervous I ended up giving it to her. Matter of fact, I got the feeling she was an employee of another school, trying to poach Cleo from us. She wrote her number down on one of our brochures. Then, I felt guilty about giving Cleo's number away without her permission and had to confess the next day. She's such a doll, though. Said she couldn't care less who had her number. 'Nobody ever calls me anyway,' she said to me. But I'm not giving it out again, I can tell you that."

Peter put up his hand, as if in protest. "Oh, we have no interest in getting her number. We just heard she was a fantastic teacher."

"Oh, well, that's true. Best I've ever had. Don't know why I told you all that. Still feeling guilty about it, I suppose." She now spoke with a conciliatory tone. "Shall I add you to our waiting list for the fall?"

Brent sniffed, like he was offended. "No, I think we'll find a school that has a more vigorous selection process. You know, interviews and such."

"Well, f-fine," said Martha, raising her eyebrows. "But you won't find a better school than this."

On the sidewalk, Peter reached in his pocket for his car keys. "You realize you're going to Hell, right?"

Brent laughed. "Yep."

They slid into the car. As Peter reached for his seatbelt, he thought about what they knew of Cleo Tanner thus far. *Best teacher I've ever had.* "You know, if this Cleo Tanner is involved in anything illegal, I'm going to be very surprised."

"Why's that?" said Brent.

"Gut. And the fact that teachers are special people."

Brent chuckled. "Well, that's true. Although you're somewhat biased there, given your mother and brother are both teachers."

Back at his desk Peter typed "Cleo Tanner" into Google while Brent searched the police system. Nothing came up on the personal or criminal searches, not even a Facebook page. The only reference they could find to her was a link to a week-old article from the *Seattle Times*. In it was a photo of Cleo Tanner standing next to a man, his arm tightly squeezed around her shoulders. Under the photo was a caption. "Local adoption agency CEO, Scott Moore, at *Kids First* fundraiser, and date, Cleo Tanner." In the article Scott Moore was profiled, citing his recent donation of a million dollars to a local children's fund and his scholarship sponsorship at several local schools, including Queen Anne Montessori. It went on to say that Moore was an attorney who had started a small adoption agency fifteen years ago and was responsible for over 100 adoptions a year. There was no mention of Cleo Tanner.

Later that afternoon, Peter drove back to the Montessori. At three o'clock the children filed into the yard and stood in an orderly line, small backpacks slung over their shoulders, raincoats covering their heads, until one by one Cleo Tanner and an older woman wearing a pink knit hat escorted them into a myriad of minivans and SUV's. Cleo leaned into each of the vehicles, fastening child seats. After the last car left the driveway, she disappeared inside the building, appearing moments later in the window of a classroom, stacking chairs on tables. Then the light clicked off and a few minutes later Cleo walked out of the building and slid into the driver's side of an old Honda Civic.

Peter followed her to the freeway, where she headed across the bridge towards West Seattle. He continued to tail her as she exited at California Street and turned right onto a side street. She pulled into the underground garage of a modern apartment building. He parked across the street and waited. Fifteen minutes later, she drove back out of the garage and headed towards Alki beach. He followed her down the curvy, steep hill until she reached the shore area where there was a walking and bicycle path. Dressed in running tights and a fleece coat, she put earphones in her ears, adjusted what looked like a small iPod, and began speed walking down the path, in the opposite direction of his car.

Peter walked across the street to a coffee shop and ordered a green tea. He stared out the window at the gray sky reflected in the waters of Puget Sound. Forty-five minutes later, Cleo Tanner was back at her car. Peter sprinted across the street to his car and followed her back up the hill to Ballard, north of downtown Seattle, driving south for ten or so blocks before she turned right and pulled into the driveway of a brick house, similar to many in this formerly working-class part of town. She went around to the passenger side of the car, pulled out a casserole dish covered in foil, and opened the house's front door with a key. After a few minutes she came back outside, walked to the mailbox, and took the mail out. She stood there, sorting through the mail, and then walked to the side of the house and put part of the mail in the big blue recycle bin. Then she sat on the steps and opened the remaining envelopes, piece by piece, frowning and biting her lip before stuffing it all into the pocket of her fleece jacket and disappearing inside the house again.

In a few minutes, she came out with an older man. He was slightly overweight and frail, and he hung on to the metal railing of the steps as she walked back to her car. He waved to her as she drove down the street.

Peter followed her back to West Seattle and parked across the street from her apartment. He checked emails on his phone, glancing occasionally at the front door to her building. After thirty minutes or so she drove out of her building's lot and headed towards the freeway. He pulled out and followed, over the West Seattle Bridge and through downtown. She exited at a stop on lower Queen Anne and disappeared into a bar with a red awning named Cooper's.

By the time Peter parked and made his way in, she was already sitting at the bar sipping a pint of amber-colored beer. There was a young couple near the back, talking quietly and sharing a pitcher of beer, and a man in a suit typing on a laptop in the corner booth.

Peter took a seat at the end of the bar. Behind the counter was a large mirror and shelves stacked with various liquors and bottles of wine and beer. A bartender was cutting a lemon into small slices on a white plastic board. He was nice-looking, with olive skin, brown eyes, and well-developed muscles stretching the fabric of his T-shirt. When he came over, Peter ordered a scotch, up.

"Any special brand?" asked the bartender.

"Glenlivet, please."

"Anything to eat?"

"Maybe later," said Peter. "You have a newspaper?"

The bartender reached under the counter. "From this morning," he said. "Slightly used." He handed it to Peter. There were several coffee rings on the front page. "I'm Nick. Haven't seen you in here before, have I?"

"No, I just happened to be in the neighborhood," said Peter.

Nick excused himself and went through the kitchen doors. Behind the newspaper, Peter watched Cleo Tanner in the mirror. She appeared to take no notice, simply sipping her beer and folding and unfolding a paper napkin, occasionally glancing at her watch. After a time she pulled a paperback with a library tag on the cover out of her purse. It was a novel with a serious looking title that Peter didn't recognize. She opened to the middle of the book and appeared to read, turning the pages in the usual amount of time, every minute or so, allowing Peter to observe her closely.

Her clothes were of the cheap variety. Peter had been with enough rich women to know how designer clothes drape over a body. And there wasn't an ounce of drape anywhere near this Cleo Tanner. Her sweater set was baggy in the wrong places and the bottom button hung by a thread. Her shoes were black loafers made of a shiny plastic meant to imitate patent leather, sold at one of the discount places.

But then, something remarkable – as Cleo read, her expression changed - he presumed in reaction to the book. At one point she actually flushed, as if something had made her angry. A few moments later she brushed a tear from the corner of her eye.

After a few moments there was the sound of a cell phone ringing, and she pulled out a mobile phone out of her bag. It was one of the old flip phones, the free one from Motorola. Peter hadn't seen one in years.

"I'll be right there," she said into the phone. She grabbed her bag and put some money on the counter. Then she looked over at Peter. "Excuse me," she said. "But will you tell the bartender, Nick, I had to run and that I'll call him later?"

Peter nodded. "Sure."

Then she was gone.

Nick came through the swinging doors of the kitchen, carrying a plate of chicken wings.

"The woman, there," said Peter, pointing to the seat where Cleo Tanner had sat only moments before. "She had to leave. Said she'd call you later."

Nick put the chicken wings on the counter. "That's odd," he said.

"Got a phone call and then took off," said Peter.

"You want these wings?"

"No offense but I don't eat stuff like that," said Peter.
Nick smiled. "I shouldn't either, but I do."
"You and the woman there an item?" asked Peter.
"Cleo? Oh no, just a friend. She doesn't date."
"Really? Why's that?"
"Broken heart."

Chapter Five

CLEO, RESISTING THE URGE TO SPEED, drove around Queen Anne hill towards Ballard. Her father had called. He was sick with a cold and felt worse this evening than he had this afternoon, he'd told her. Could she come by and bring him some cough medicine? Without hesitation, although sad to leave the chicken wings she'd ordered, set out for his house in Ballard. On the way she stopped at the neighborhood drug store and purchased both nighttime and daytime cold medication and some cough drops.

Her father's home was on a street of 1940's houses, mostly remodeled and expanded during the boom in the late nineties, when so many young professionals had taken over the neighborhood. His house was the standalone from another era, a small brick house, untouched from its original design, looking faded and shrunken next to the remodeled and rebuilt Craftsman style homes so popular with the Seattle demographic.

She let herself in through the front door. Her father, Chester, was in his usual place in front of the television, a box of tissues on his lap.

"Cleo girl, thanks for coming," he said, sounding congested. His eyes were red and weepy looking.

"Dad, you don't look so good. Sure you don't want to get into bed?"

"Maybe after dinner. Right now I'm watching a really good *Law and Order*."

"Found one you hadn't seen before?" she asked.

"I've probably seen it but don't remember." He tried to chuckle but it turned into a cough.

"Here," she said, measuring a dose of the nighttime cold medicine into the small plastic cup. "Take this and I'll go warm up your dinner."

"Thanks, honey." He made a face as he swallowed the medicine. "This is terrible."

She went into the kitchen. While she stood at the old stove, the same one her mother used to cook on, she could hear her mother's soft voice instructing her. It still comforted her, even after all these years.

Cleo was just shy of her thirteenth birthday when she sat by her mother's bed and held her dry hand, watching the life seep out of her with each ticking of the second hand on the grandfather.

After she was gone, the night was the hardest. Cleo would awaken, the house quiet, and remember that her mother was no longer asleep in the room down the hall. And in that silence was fear – the opposite of love.

Her mother's most verbal worry when she heard the news of her terminal cancer: who would cook for Chester? So she taught Cleo how to make his favorite dishes, one for every night of the week. He was a creature of habit, she told Cleo. "He'll be happiest if you stick to the same schedule." As if Cleo didn't know that already, but she played along, pretending for her mother's benefit that this was new information because it seemed to soothe her to go through the details.

Sunday was pot roast and he liked it with little red potatoes and carrots, slow cooked on the stove in the big black Dutch oven, so she should start it at two in the afternoon so that it was ready for his dinner at six.

"You know, Cleo, how he must eat right at six."

"Yes, Mommy, I know."

Monday must be tacos and he liked the crispy little shells that came all stacked together and ground beef with Lawry's taco seasoning. Tuesday he expected chicken cacciatore. "Don't forget to ask the butcher to cut the chicken up for you, so you won't cut yourself with the knives your dad only sharpens once a year." On Wednesday it was meatloaf made with tiny pieces of onions and breadcrumbs and topped with ketchup. "The ketchup is his favorite part." Thursday he liked sloppy joes. "Use the kind from the package but make sure to get the buns with sesame seeds on the top." On Friday it must be fried cod because it reminded him of his childhood in Wisconsin, where they had a fish fry every Friday. On Saturday he liked spaghetti. "Don't forget to stir the noodles or they stick together."

The chicken cacciatore was the most complex of the dishes and they practiced together just several weeks before her mother died. Cleo remembered every detail of that afternoon.

The dish required browning the pieces of chicken before tossing them all in a big pot with tomato sauce and oregano and basil. "Now you've got to be careful of bits of grease popping out of the pan when you first drop the chicken in, so move away quickly." She held up her arm to show Cleo a tiny scar from the time a bit of grease had burned her.

Suddenly, her mother's face crumpled and she began to cry. She reached for Cleo, hugging her tightly against her body, so frail by then. "I'm so sorry you have to do this, but it can't be helped."

Cleo cried against her mother's cotton dress while her mother stroked her hair and rocked her. "Just try to hold on to this feeling right now," her mother said. "Remember the feel of my arms around you and when you're sad or lonely for me, call on the power of my love—it it will come to you from wherever I am. I will always be with you, as long as you can remember this moment."

Now, using the microwave – she'd finally convinced him to get one – Cleo warmed several pieces of chicken and some white rice and then set it on a tray with silverware and a napkin.

He looked up when she came in and sat up a little straighter in his chair. She put the tray on his lap.

"Looks good Cleo girl."

"Thanks, Dad. Same as it is every week."

"I do enjoy this chicken. Never gets old."

"Apparently not." She smiled, her heart soft, and watched him for a moment, standing slightly behind him so he would think she watched the television. He looked old tonight, she thought. He worked too hard for a man almost sixty years old.

"Dad, can you take tomorrow off?"

"Oh, I don't think so now. Got two big jobs."

She sighed. There was no way she'd be able to talk him out of working even though he was sick. He was stubborn and proud. Just like her. They were similar in so many ways. Neither of them knew how to move forward after grief. It was like something was broken in them, the way they stubbornly clung to the past. And they knocked around this life, spouseless, an unspoken agreement between them that certain things were not discussed, her father being uncomfortable with emotion of any kind, most especially any tinged with dusty grief. He chose instead to go to work and fix pipes and unplug drains without complaint but without any joy, seemingly as stuck in the past as she.

She leaned over and gave him a quick kiss on his cheek. "Dad, I'm going now. Please go to bed after dinner."

"I will. Right after this show's over."

"Love you."

"Love you back."

Chapter Six

SYLVIA'S HANDS SHOOK as she handed the stack of paperwork to Scott Moore, who sat behind a large mahogany desk. "I hope the photos are all right," she said. "I hardly ever have my picture taken these days and I'm afraid I look stiff." I wish my mother were here, she thought. Everything would be easier if her mother were with her. But her parents were in Italy, celebrating their thirty-fifth wedding anniversary. They would be gone another six weeks but surely they would return before the adoption was complete. Of course they would, she told herself. It could take months and months to be chosen by a birth mother.

"Were you a model at one time, Mrs. Green?" asked Scott Moore, pulling her from her thoughts.

Malcolm laughed, as if that were a preposterous idea. She felt herself blush. "Oh no. I just meant, y'know, as a child you have your photo taken all the time," she said. "My mother must have a dozen albums of just me and my sister."

Malcolm shifted in his seat. "I'm an only child. My mother took a photo of me every day for the first five years of my life."

Sylvia held back from saying anything, especially in front of Scott Moore, but it did say a lot about Malcolm and his family. No wonder he thought the world revolved around him. Malcolm's cell phone buzzed from his suit coat pocket. He jumped, as if the sound had bitten him. "I'm sorry," he said. "Probably work calling." He reached in his pocket and glanced at the screen before putting it away.

Sylvia's eyes shifted to her hands. "Anyway, we made a recording of ourselves, like you asked. It should be in your email."

"Yes, I got it this morning," said Scott.

"Do you think anyone will pick us?" she asked.

He nodded, his voice smooth and reassuring. "I'm sure we can find the perfect match for you."

"This reminds me of dating," said Sylvia, pulling on a strand of her hair. "Always waiting for the phone to ring."

Scott chuckled. "I've heard that before." He paused. "How's Cleo?"

Sylvia played with her earring. "Fine."

"Tell her I said hello."

"Certainly," she said, avoiding his eyes. Was he trying to give her a message that they'd be on the top of the list if Cleo called him?

"I'm putting you two on the top of the list," he said, as if reading her thoughts. "Please tell Cleo I'm doing that for her." He smiled in a way Sylvia suspected was supposed to be charming. "I'm hoping this might convince her to give me a chance?"

She could think of nothing to say, but it didn't matter because just then Malcolm's cell phone buzzed again from his pocket. He stood, like something was on fire, and reached inside his jacket for the phone. His eyes darted to the screen. "Sorry, I thought I turned this off. But I really have to take this." He looked at Sylvia. "I'll see you at home tonight."

After Malcolm left, Sylvia turned back to Scott. "I'm sorry about that. He's working on the biggest case of his career. But he's not always married to his work. I mean, no more than most men are about their jobs. He'll be a wonderful father." She stopped. Why was she talking so much? *Just be quiet*, she told herself.

"No worries, I understand perfectly," he said. His intercom buzzed. "I have Alva on line two," said a female voice.

"Please have her hold," said Moore. "I'll be right with her." He looked back at Sylvia as he stood. "Let me walk you out." At the doorway, he put his hand on her back. "I'll hope to see you very soon with good news. Again, tell Cleo I said hello."

Chapter Seven

MONDAY MORNING PETER AND BRENT LEFT at six a.m. to make the five-hour drive to Legley Bay from Seattle. Peter had driven this stretch of highway so many times, every pine and fir and clump of ferns familiar, rising from wet soil under a low, gray sky. Brent, in the passenger seat, played on his phone and ate cheddar popcorn from a bag between his thighs. The radio was tuned to a pop station, but Peter didn't hear the music. His mind ambled and turned, twisting between what he knew of the missing girl's disappearance and his brother's sudden appearance. He'd left Jack and Misty at his condo with a list of the best places to order take-out, advising them to stay inside if they could. No reason to put Misty at risk if they didn't need to.

He thought of his father, too, and the anger habitually pushed down for all these many years bubbled and churned as if no time had passed, as if he hadn't untangled himself from his father's life in every way except for this one tie. Cops beget cops and all that. He passed a camper on a long, straight stretch of highway. It was so typical, he thought, that something so clearly in the Legley Bay police department, indeed in Tim Ball's jurisdiction, was now in Peter's own consciousness, born of his long-ingrained inability to refuse his baby brother anything and his deep desire to be that which their father was not. He never wanted to let Jack down. Ever.

After two and a half hours, they stopped for gas and to use the restroom in Kurt Cobain's hometown of Aberdeen, as gray and depressing as Peter's own Legley Bay. For the last hour of the trip, along the coastal highway, Brent dozed, his head bent towards the window, a smear of cheese powder on his chin.

They passed Cannon Beach and Manzanita and then another fifteen miles later exited right into Legley Bay. He drove slowly along the main street. It gave him a start to realize fifteen years had passed since he left for college. He looked at it with hungry eyes, as he did each time he came to visit his mother and grandmother. Regardless of the fact that he no longer wanted to live there, it was still his home. Although the main street had the same buildings, there were different businesses occupying most of them, some of them having received a facelift sometime in the last ten years. But it was the underbelly of the town that was different, according to his mother. Meth had arrived, creating an atmosphere of danger and violence never seen in Peter's childhood. The towns farther north, like Cannon Beach and Manzanita and Seaside, thrived on wealthy Seattle and Portland residents investing in second homes built on the beach or nestled in firs overlooking the water. Those towns had shops and restaurants that catered to a sophisticated clientele able to afford fine dining and retail shops filled with beautiful beachwear and kitchen accessories. But the tourist trend hadn't reached Legley Bay. His grandmother, Aggie, claimed it was the lack of sandy beaches; the shore was mostly craggy and dangerous, with cliffs above a tumultuous raging ocean that even during low tide revealed only a rocky surface unsuitable for walking or kite flying or reading. The only suitable section of beach for walking or running was the State Park at the very end of town, which the locals called The Landing.

Peter drove through the middle of town and turned left onto Seagull Drive and then right into the parking lot of the police station. He turned off the car and sat for a moment, mustering the energy he needed. Brent stirred. "We here already?" He wiped his mouth with the back of his hand.

"Yep."

"How long since you've seen him?" Brent's tone was soft and careful.

"Since Jack was in the hospital."

"Right," said Brent. He tapped him on the shoulder. "C'mon, I've got you covered."

A few moments later, they stepped into the station. The woman at the front desk was middle-aged, with an inch of dark roots anchoring bleach blond hair. She was wearing a red-and-white-striped satin shirt, its buttons straining against her generous stomach. "Tim Ball available?" asked Peter.

"You're his son, aren't you?" said the woman. "You look just like him."

"That's what I hear," said Peter, glancing sideways. He saw his father sitting with his feet up at a desk, talking on the phone behind a glass window.

"I'll let him know you're here," she said.

Peter and Brent took seats in the small lobby. There were two orange plastic chairs and tattered copies of *Field and Stream* and *Us Weekly* piled on the table. Brent picked up a *Field and Stream* with a photo of a fly fisherman casting on some river in Idaho. Feeling nervous but vowing to remain calm, Peter fidgeted in his chair, crossing and uncrossing his legs. After a few minutes, Tim Ball hung up the phone and came out to greet them.

"Peter," he said, putting out his hand.

Peter shook it in one quick motion. He introduced him to Brent. "Been my partner for six years now," said Peter.

"Good to meet you," said Tim, motioning them into his office. He shut the door as they took the two green vinyl guest chairs opposite his desk. "Everything all right with Jack?"

"Jack's fine. He came to see me," said Peter.

Tim raised his eyebrows. "That right?"

"Yeah," said Peter.

"That the first you've heard from him?" asked Tim.

Peter kept his voice even. "Yep."

Tim leaned back in his chair, crossing his hands behind his head like he was getting ready to do a sit-up. He'd gained weight since Peter last saw him eighteen months ago. His belly was hanging over his large silver belt buckle with the engravings of cactus flowers on it. The new wife was from Arizona. "This about the missing girl?"

"That's right," said Peter. "Jack said he couldn't get you to look into it, so he came to me."

Tim didn't say anything but simply looked at Peter. Peter stared right back.

Brent shifted in the seat and cleared his throat. "We're down here, hoping to dig up something."

"Right," Peter said, feeling suddenly like a child. He wanted to say, *yeah, because your lazy, fat ass wouldn't do anything, he had to come to me, just like always.*

"Jack's better," said Tim. "Don't you think?"

Peter shrugged. "I guess."

"How's your mother?" he asked. "Heard she's retiring this year."

"She's well," Peter said. He'd be damned if he was going to discuss his mother. The usual rage surfaced. He could feel it hot in his chest. "Anyway, we just stopped by as a professional courtesy, to let you know we think something's not right."

Tim Ball made a small movement with his mouth, almost like a nervous twitch. "Suit yourself." His eyes moved to the window. "But you've been gone a long time, Peter. You don't know what it's like here. Nothing but meth-heads and low-lifes. This girl is just another one, probably mixed up in drugs and ran off with some boy."

Peter rose too fast and the back of his chair slammed into the wall. "We'll let you know what we find."

Brent rose to his feet as well.

"You boys aren't gonna find anything," said Tim. "Waste of time."

Peter was at the doorway by then and turned back to look at him. "Thanks for the advice, Dad." In the lobby, he said under his breath, "Asshole."

Peter pulled out of the station's parking lot and headed back to the main street. They drove in silence, the windows fogging. Peter pushed the button for the air conditioner with more force than was needed.

"You all right?" asked Brent.

"After the hospital, I vowed not to ever see him again if I could help it," said Peter. The rain turned to mist and the windshield wipers made a squeaking noise. "Can't stand him."

"Dude, I get it. But listen, we did as Wilson asked. No reason we need to see him again." Brent paused, as if he wanted to say something further. "Know what I mean?"

"Yep. I hear you."

"Hey, I have an idea," said Brent. He was pointing at the Dairy Queen. "Let's get an ice cream."

"You can't be serious?"

"Ice cream will make you feel better. Maybe with that chocolate sauce stuff that turns into a hard shell. That's the best."

"There's no helping you," said Peter.

Chapter Eight

THE CALL FROM SCOTT MOORE came just as Sylvia was getting out of the shower.

"You sitting down?" Moore asked.

"No, yes, it doesn't matter," she said.

"We have a baby girl available for adoption. This is a somewhat unusual circumstance in that the birth mother gave her blessing to our agency to choose adoptive parents and then disappeared. She was very young and wanted nothing to do with the child. Wouldn't even hold her. This will be a closed adoption, meaning she'll never be able to learn the identity of her birth mother. You'll have to explain this to your daughter after she's older. It's my experience that most adopted children, or those who never knew one of their birth parents, become very curious about their origins, usually during their teens."

A closed adoption? It was too good to be true. She sank onto the side of the bed and looked out the window to Lake Washington. "Really?" Several speedboats carrying water-skiers dressed in wetsuits sped around in circles on the gray water.

"The baby's on her way to Seattle. She'll be here by tomorrow morning," said Scott.

"I can't believe it."

"Believe it." He paused. "Do keep in mind that nothing's legal until after the six-month waiting period."

"Yes, I understand," she said. But if it was a closed adoption, it was unlikely that anything could come up between now and then, she told herself.

"I don't suppose you'd put in a good word for me with Cleo?"

"Of course," she said. *When Hell freezes over.* This guy was unbelievable. She must keep him far away from Cleo.

She hung up, reeling, and dropped to her knees, thanking God, grateful tears dripping down her cheeks onto the cross she always wore at her neck. Then, realizing her teeth were chattering from both excitement and cold, she wrapped her wet hair in a towel before pulling on her terry cloth robe that the housekeeper had draped over the end of the bed.

She went down the spacious hallway, habitually running her fingertips over the lip of the white wainscoting, imagining the tea-colored walls one day lined with family photos. She stood at the top of the stairwell, looking for Malcolm. His keys were on the hall table and his briefcase was sitting near the front door but the spacious den off the main foyer, where he often had a drink after work, was empty.

She found him in the kitchen, still wearing his suit from the office. He stood at the counter, typing something into his phone. On the counter was a glass of red wine. Red wine? That was odd. Maybe he'd poured it for her.

"Malcolm," she said, moving towards him. "Scott Moore called. We've been chosen. They have our daughter." Tears started at the back of her throat.

He blinked as if trying to figure out who she was, like she was an American acquaintance in a train station in Paris. She almost expected him to say, "How do I know you?" Instead, he sighed, running his fingers through his hair. His eyes looked guilty, evasive. She shivered. Rain fell in slants onto the patio furniture in the courtyard beyond the French doors. She tugged on the end of the towel still wrapped around her hair. "What is it?" she asked.

"I thought I'd have more time," he said, almost like he was speaking to himself.

She felt relief, tightening her robe. He was only shocked, that was all. "Well, they say you're never prepared. We'll just have to dive in."

He faced her, shoving his hand into his pants pockets. "No, I've come to a decision. An important decision."

She watched him. He seemed jittery but also resigned. What had he done? Quit his job? Bought a vacation home without telling her? "What is it?" she asked again, this time with impatience.

He cleared his throat and looked out the window. "I've met someone else. I want a divorce."

She felt her legs go weak. She leaned against the counter for support, trying to understand what he was saying. "But we're about to have a baby."

"All four years of this marriage, Sylvia, it's just been you and your obsession with having a child. There's been no room for me in this house." His cell phone buzzed. He set it on the counter but she saw his eyes moving. He was reading a text from her. She expected to go into a rage. She could almost see herself lunging towards him and snatching the phone, perhaps even calling the number and accusing the woman on the other end of wrecking her life. But somehow she was stuck, rooted to her place in the doorway, with the rain now sliding off the gutter and dripping on the black metal table in the courtyard where they liked to have coffee on a summer morning.

Malcolm's eyes and voice were expressionless. "She actually notices I'm in the room. I'm in love with her."

For a long moment, she stared at him, untangling his words like a knot on a package she urgently wanted to open. "But what about the baby?"

He took a step back. "This is what you say when I announce our marriage is over?"

"Well what do expect me to say? We're supposed to go pick up our baby. You told me you wanted this too."

"I never said that. I agreed to it because I knew it was what you wanted. But I don't. Realizing this is actually happening makes me know more than ever that this marriage was a mistake. You've never loved me."

"That isn't true."

"At this point, wouldn't it be better to stop lying, Sylvia?"

She gaped at him, rage coming now, roaring and crashing like waves between her ears so that she heard nothing but that hum like an angry electric fence. "You're the liar. I've been loyal to you every minute of this marriage, which is more than I can say for you. Who is she?"

He turned away, his eyes darting to his phone. "You don't know her. Someone from work."

"How long has it been going on?"

He looked back at her. "A year."

"Oh my God. I think I'm going to be sick," she said, rushing to the sink, where she vomited up her breakfast.

"Sylvia, I'm sorry."

"Get out," was the surprising thing she uttered, wiping her mouth with a paper towel. And then she pointed at the door, as if he didn't know where it was. "My father will be delighted he pushed me on the pre-nup."

In her bedroom, she sat on the king sized bed she'd shared with Malcolm for the last four years. Everything so carefully put together: the flower pattern on the comforter chosen for a certain shade of blue, the color of a robin's egg she'd said to the designer, and the walls eggshell white and the furniture dark walnut. This house was 5000 square feet and looked out on the lake, where there was a boat waiting with life jackets made for children and a picnic basket filled with settings for four. And there was a pool with a slide, and a barbeque and fire pit and pizza oven, and the perfect nursery ready for a baby that never came. Every ounce of the house carefully pondered and planned, with so many meetings with the designer that she and her mother lost count. And for what? The family she yearned for but would never have.

She went down the hallway to the nursery and stood at the window, holding the filmy curtain between her fingers. She remembered picking out the fabric with her mother. *Mom, I wish you were here,* she thought. *I need you.*

In a lifetime of wonderful memories with her mother, one of the best was decorating the nursery. It was yellow, the crib and changing table and bookshelf in a dark mahogany with cushions in a pure white. There were bears and bunnies, childhood books her mother had saved for her, and prints of favorite book covers. But the months and years had passed with no baby. *I just want the chance to be the kind of mother my mother was,* she'd thought, hundreds of times.

And now, here was her baby and Malcolm had walked out the door.

What had he said? *She notices I'm in the room.*

She'd suspected Malcolm had someone on the side but she'd denied it to herself for months now. There was no use denying it any longer. After his Christmas party last year, they'd had a terrible argument. The next morning, she'd had the courage to ask the question that needed to be asked, but had she listened to the answer?

"Malcolm, are you happy? I mean, with me?" she asked him, standing in the kitchen, as he made a sandwich.

His features softened. "Of course. Why do you ask that?"

"I wonder sometimes. And last night you were so angry."

He set aside his sandwich and came to stand next to her, taking her hand. "I'm sorry about that. I don't know what gets into me sometimes. I'm just tense because of work. And I don't know how to help you work through this baby stuff."

"I'm sorry too. These hormones have me wacked out."

He embraced her, holding her for a moment. "I just wonder if maybe we should let this baby stuff go for a while. Try and find us again."

"What do you mean? We're halfway through in-vitro."

He sighed and let her go, walking back to his sandwich. "Right. Of course."

She ignored the defeated look in his eyes and left the room, going to her piano, all the while thinking of the soft cheeks of a baby and convincing herself that everything was fine between them.

Now, sitting in their bedroom, she remembered the look in his eyes that day. She had ignored how lonely he was. And lonely men sought company elsewhere. Everyone knew that. She was just too selfish to notice.

She cried, uncontrollable tears of shame leaking out of her eyes. This marriage had fallen apart because of her obsession with having a baby. And, it was true - she didn't love Malcolm as she should have. He was right to leave, to seek love from someone who noticed he was in the room.

They have my baby.

How could she do this alone? Was it selfish to still so desperately want the baby, regardless of the fact that now the baby was twice fatherless when she was less than a day old, abandoned by two men before she had the chance to utter her first cries of protest? The baby that, in the instant it took to get the phone call, she'd already begun to think of as her own. If only her mother were here. But she couldn't call them and ruin their time in Italy with all this. Knowing them, they would cut their trip short and come home. And she couldn't allow that to happen. They'd planned this trip to Italy for three years. Her mother was so happy to have her father all to herself, without the distractions of work. She must remain strong.

Cleo. Cleo would know what to do.

She wiped tears from her face with the back of her hand and blew her nose. Then she picked up the phone and dialed Cleo's number.

"Scott Moore called. They have my baby."

"What? Already? Oh my God. I'm so happy for you." Cleo paused for a moment, laughing. "And I didn't have to go out with him after all."

"He told me to put in a good word for him."

"What a creep," said Cleo. "But who cares? You're going to be a mother."

"Malcolm's left me," she said next. How was it that she didn't say this first, she wondered? *Because I care more about a baby than my husband. He was right.*

Cleo was silent. There was the sound of glasses in the background - Nick behind the bar at Cooper's. *Nick.* Her heart ached, as it always did when she thought of him. "What do you mean, left?" said Cleo.

"He wants a divorce. He's in love with someone else." The words strangled in her throat.

"I'll be right there," said Cleo.

Chapter Nine

RIGHT AFTER THEY LEFT Tim Ball's police station, Peter and Brent went first to the bar where Misty's mother, Jo Johnson, worked. It was on the other end of Legley Bay from the Dew Drop Inn, but equally depressing, a square building made of concrete blocks painted a hideous blue. There were two small cars plus an old Ford pickup truck in the parking lot. Jo Johnson was behind the bar, filling a pitcher with Budweiser for the two drunks slumped on the end of the bar.

Jo Johnson couldn't have been much older than Peter but he didn't remember her from school. She was skinny, wearing tight jeans, a sleeveless top, and a gold cross around her neck. Her hands were red and chapped, her fingernails short. When they sat at her bar, she greeted them right away, with a hint of suspicion in her voice. Strangers in a small town: not to be trusted. Peter introduced himself, showing her his badge.

"You're the teacher's brother?" she asked.

"That's right," Peter said. "Jack and I grew up here. Did you know that?"

"I heard that," she said, pulling on a strand of hair. It was a drab brown with streaks of gray at the temples.

"You from here?" Peter asked.

"No. California. Came here after I had Alicia." She pulled a pack of cigarettes from under the bar. "You mind if we go outside for a minute? I'm dying for a smoke."

Brent indicated the men at the end of the bar. "What about your customers?"

She called out to them. "You boys be all right if I go out for a smoke?"

"Sure thing, Jo," one of them said.

Brent said on the way out the door, "Aren't you worried they'll help themselves to the till?"

She made a scoffing noise. "No way. Those two been coming here longer than you've been alive. Might top off their beers but they're not gonna take from the till."

In the light of the afternoon, Peter looked at her face, searching for a hint of her daughter. But whatever youthful blush she once had was gone now, replaced with a shell, cracked and discolored like an old bomber coat. Her hands shook when she lit her cigarette and after a deep drag, she coughed and then apologized, saying she'd had a cold for weeks she couldn't shake. "And since this thing with Alicia, I can't sleep."

"Mrs. Johnson," Peter began, keeping his voice soft. "Do you think Misty is right that something's happened to Alicia?"

She looked confused for a moment and then her faced turned hostile. "Of course something's happened to her. Where else would she be?"

Brent put his hand up, as if he were going to pat her shoulder but just kept it hovering there, a little trick he often used to give witnesses a sense of his trustworthiness: his wholesome cop act. "You have no reason to believe she simply ran away?"

She shook her head, tapping the end of her cigarette with the tip of her finger. "I know what you people think of us." She waved her hand in the air. The ash from her cigarette drifted to the ground near her ratty sneakers. "I'm poor. I work in a bar. But I'm not a drinker. And we're close. The three of us. I'm a good mother." The cigarette was down to the butt by now and she tossed it into the gravel at their feet and stomped it out with her shoe. She looked Peter in the face. Her eyes were puffy and Peter knew she'd been crying on and off for days because that's how his mother had looked so many times. Then she began to cry in front of them, little heaves that made the rattle in her chest start again. "I know Misty's holding out hope she's alive, but I know she's dead. I feel it in my bones. That woman killed her. When Misty came tearing into the bar like her hair was on fire I filled with a coldness and I just knew something terrible had happened. I hoped to God I was wrong but soon as we opened the door to that motel room and saw it empty, I fell down on my knees, screaming. I knew it then. She was dead. I can't explain why I know. But I feel her watching me from up there." She pointed towards the sky. She inched closer to Peter. "I just don't know why they killed her."

"We're going to find out," Peter said, taking her dry hand in his. "You can trust me on that."

❋

From the car, Brent pointed to the Dew Drop Inn restaurant. "I'm starved," he said. "Let's eat."

Peter grimaced. "Not there," he said. He suggested a new sandwich shop he'd spotted several blocks down on the main street. But Brent was having none of it.

"No way I'm eating kale or some other weird green shit you come up with for lunch," he said. "Town like this, we need to get some fish and chips."

"There's no helping you," said Peter. He turned left, past the bank and grocery store to a fish and chips hole that had been there since the eighties, called Myrnas, with no apostrophe. Apparently Myrna didn't know about possessive nouns. But she knew everything that went on in Legley Bay.

"C'mon, no time like the present to encourage your heart attack," said Peter, opening the car door. "Plus, Myrna might know something."

"You take the fun out of everything," Brent said.

Myrna was there when they came in, standing behind the counter wearing the same hairnet she'd had when she opened the place in 1982 with her fisherman husband. Peter supposed this, actually, having no evidence that she hadn't replaced it once or twice, but if so, she was able to find the exact same shade of purple each time. She was short and plump around the middle and had rounded shoulders. Her white frizzy hair stood straight up under the hairnet like a troll in a children's story. However, that was where the resemblance ended, for she was always laughing and teasing her customers, giving the impression a party was just about to erupt.

She didn't recognize Peter. He could tell by her generic smile when she called out for them to sit anywhere they liked. The place was empty; it was late in the afternoon for lunch. They took two seats at the counter and she gave them menus and poured glasses of ice water into maple-colored plastic glasses. "Hi Myrna," Peter said, feeling suddenly like no time had passed since the days when he'd sat there as a high school student. "You remember me?"

She stared at him for a moment, narrowing her eyes and then breaking into a grin. "Well, if it isn't Peter Ball." She came around the counter and pulled him into her arms so that he was squished against her soft body. He hugged her back, smiling too; she smelled of grease and Dial soap. "What're you doing here?" she asked. "Come to see your mother?"

"No, I'm actually in town on police business." He introduced her to Brent, who was busy looking at the menu, deciding which deep fried food he was going to stuff himself with; then he'd complain of gas all afternoon.

She went back around the counter and crossed her arms over her ample chest. Her ruddy complexion had aged since he'd last seen her. There were deep lines that ran across her face and her eyelids had a slight droop to them he didn't remember. "This about the Johnson girl?"

"How'd you know?" he asked, feeling a surge of energy. Myrna was the type of woman who knew everything in town, not only because her customers told her everything but also because she was interested in all gossip and town happenings.

"One of the regulars from Jo's bar was in here the other day, telling anyone who'd listen that Jo thought Alicia been murdered."

"What do you think?" Peter said.

"Well, I told your father this already so you probably already know."

"Don't count on it," he said.

She smiled, like an indulgent grandmother of a troubled boy. Which Peter supposed was how she thought of herself: grandmother of Legley Bay. "Well, he's probably busy with other cases. After all, a lot of kids do run off for short periods. Y'know, when they get a wild hair or whatnot. Anyway, what I told him is that we have this regular customer the last year or so. A large woman, most awful haircut you ever did see, makes her look almost like a man, and she wears purple glasses, which I find an odd choice."

Peter stifled a smile, thinking of both Myrna's hairnet and purple scarf. "Yeah, what about her."

"Well, you know my best friend Sue works at the hardware store. We've been friends forever and a day. Anyway, she said that this man-type woman came in one day and purchased a large supply of rubber gloves, rubbing alcohol, and those big blue tarps some of the men use on their boats. Charlie doesn't, you see, because he favors the clear plastic, says they're easier to move around. Let's see now, where was I going with this?"

"The man-type woman," Peter prompted.

"Right. When Sue described her to me I knew at once who she was because she comes in here every Tuesday for our all-you-can-eat cod and oyster special we run at lunch, and I always get a downright creepy feeling about her. We discussed at length how odd it was that a woman, who obviously doesn't live here, would be buying all that. Well, then we found out she has a storage unit she rents from Al Peele. You remember Al, don't you? You were in the same class."

"Sure," Peter said, marveling that she could remember they were in the same class. Peter only vaguely recalled him: red hair and glasses.

"He took that old warehouse his father had and turned it into storage units, which we all thought was crazy. Who would spend money to store their old things? But beat it all if they aren't full all the time."

"She rents a storage unit?" he prompted, once again.

"Yes," she said, slapping the counter. "And Al says it's full of all kinds of doctor-type things."

"Like what?" Brent pulled out his notebook.

"Medicines, surgical-type instruments, like you see on the boob tube, and some kind of thing that looks like an I.V. dispenser."

This had to be the same woman Misty described. "Why do you think this has something to do with Alicia disappearing?" said Peter.

She leaned closer, lowering her voice. "Because ever since she arrived in town, there have been girls running around here pregnant that have no business having a baby." She tugged at her hairnet.

"Listen, no one but me and Sue suspect anything, but we've been on this earth long enough to know those girls are hiding big stomachs under sweatshirts and big jackets so their mamas don't know what's going on, but it's obvious to me. And after awhile these girls have no babies but a lot of new clothes that no longer cover their midsections. One even bought herself a car. I know these folks, Peter, and none of their parents can afford any extras."

When Myrna left to take their orders back to the kitchen, Peter looked over at Brent. "These girls are having babies for money?" Peter swallowed hard. Could this be the truth? "And what happens if one of them changed her mind?"

"Murdered?"

"So the article in the newspaper with Cleo Tanner's photo? She was with a big shot that runs an adoption agency?"

"Right," said Brent. "You think that's the connection?"

"Gotta be."

Peter took out his phone and did a search on Cleo Tanner and pulled up the article once again. "Scott Moore is his name. Tanner must be his girlfriend."

Chapter Ten

SYLVIA'S LEGS SHOOK as she walked into Scott Moore's office. He sat at the desk signing something when she came in. He stood, smiling and gesturing towards the guest chairs. *Two chairs. And I'm only one.*

"Where's your husband?" he asked.

She tried to control her voice but it wobbled. "He left me."

A muscle on the side of his face twitched but other than that remained unreadable. "I'm sorry to hear that."

"I remain committed to the adoption."

"Have you thought this through?" he asked, not unkindly.

"I have. I have the resources. I can hire a full-time nanny if I have to. As I'm sure you know, money is not an issue for me."

"You might be surprised to learn – this isn't the first time this has happened in my experience running this agency. Sometimes the finality of it is too much for men. It can be the deciding factor." He sat forward in his chair, reaching for a stack of papers, his eyes steady.

"So you won't change your mind over this?" She felt her throat tighten, waiting for his answer.

His expression didn't change. "Because the birth mother isn't in the picture at all, Sylvia, it's really just up to me. And I see nothing wrong with adopting for a woman of your resources." He shuffled through her file. "I'll just make a few changes to your paperwork. Delete your husband, so to speak. Don't worry, we'll take care of the required forms later."

"You can do that?"

"Of course."

She took a deep breath, ignoring the feeling of alarm down in the pit of her stomach. "So the baby can still come home with me today?"

"As long as you're sure?"

"More than I've ever been about anything," she said.

"And did you bring your cashier's check?" he asked.

"Oh, yes." She opened her purse and took out the check for $150,000. "Here."

His eyes flickered. "Wonderful." He looked up at her. "I don't know if Cleo told you or not but we've been talking on the phone for a week or so. I think she's almost ready to agree to a date. So, thank you for putting in a good word for me."

Cleo. What did you do?

"How did you get her number?" asked Sylvia.

"Had my right-hand person go to the school where she works. Alva is hard to say no to."

The door opened and a young woman came into the room. "I see it's time," Moore said, getting up from the desk. "Your daughter's arrived."

As they stood, the young woman disappeared for a moment, returning with a bundle wrapped in a pink blanket. "Sylvia, meet your daughter," she said.

Sylvia, over the years, had heard from other adoptive parents that when they held their daughter or son for the first time there was a feeling of distinct inevitability, or destiny, a rightness, that this child was meant for them and they for her. During the years of infertility and subsequent treatments she'd questioned the truth of it. How could a stranger's baby really feel like your own? But the moment the baby, her daughter, was placed into her arms, she knew. *This is the baby God made for me. This is my child.* And, just as her own mother had described the experience of giving birth to her own biological children, Sylvia was filled completely with a love so deep and profoundly shattering that all other matters ceased to have impact or value.

"I'm going to name her Madison," she said, to no one in particular.

Later, she would remember the moment as a spiritual experience, a time in her life when she felt the presence of God on her flesh, and inside too, where the mysterious soul lurked unseen. Madison was already known to her there: soul to soul.

There was nothing but this warm, helpless bundle in her arms. She examined the baby, taking in every detail: the tiny hands and fingers, dark fuzz on her head, dimple on her chin, glassy blue eyes that stared up into her own. And there, in Scott Moore's pretentious office with the oversized mahogany desk and leather chairs, she was transformed. She became a mother.

Chapter Eleven

IT WAS LATE AFTERNOON when Peter and Brent arrived at Legley Bay's high school. Despite the fact that school had been out for three days, the lingering scent of overcooked vegetables and sloppy joes remained. They went into the main office. Behind the counter was a woman, typing into a computer. Peter showed his badge and asked for the principal.

"He's not here this afternoon," the woman said. She had the voice of a smoker. "He's at a district meeting." She rolled her eyes.

"Hard to believe we're still wearing sweaters in June, huh?" said Peter, leaning on the counter. "But I must say, the blue of your sweater matches your eyes perfectly."

She flushed. "Oh, thanks, my daughter-in-law got this for me. She's the fancy type, works in Portland for one of the big department stores and gets everything with a discount."

"Well, she has good taste."

She smiled. "Maybe I could help you?"

Peter nodded toward Brent. "My partner and I are investigating the disappearance of one of your students. Alicia Johnson. You know her?"

"Sure, I know all the kids. Better than the principal does, matter of fact." She lowered her voice. "He's the fly by night type, just building his career, and then he'll move on soon as he gets the chance for a bigger high school in a city somewhere. That's what they all do. We had a graduation ceremony last week and he pronounced half the kids' names wrong when he gave them their diplomas."

"Well, then, it's our lucky day that he's not here and you are," said Peter.

She smiled and smoothed her hair with the tips of her fingers. "I'd be happy to help." She paused, glancing up at the ceiling as if a roster was written there. "I heard through the grapevine that Alicia disappeared – what is it now, almost a week?"

"Five days ago," said Peter.

"And, of course, we knew she missed the last two days of finals."

"Do you think there's a chance Alicia Johnson was pregnant?"

She looked shocked for a moment and then shook her head. "I'd be surprised. I wouldn't have thought her the type. She was a nice girl." She glanced at the hallway, as if the kids were still in school. "Now that you mention it, there've been quite a few pregnant girls this year. But I didn't think Alicia was one of them." The woman stared at the counter for a moment, obviously thinking. "I haven't mentioned this to anyone because I'm not one for idle gossip, but one day I was in one of the science classroom storage closets, taking inventory of some supplies. It was a good fifteen minutes before the bell rang for first period and a group of girls came in. They didn't know I was in there and I heard them talking about getting pregnant together. Kinda, 'I'll do it if you do it' type thing. One of them said, 'Just pick any boy, it doesn't matter because they'll all do it if you tell them you want to,' which I have to admit, no offense, is pretty much true about men, unless they play for the other team or something." She paused, as if collecting her thoughts. "The other one said, 'As long as he's white it doesn't matter who he is.' Then the teacher walked in and they went quiet."

"Was Alicia Johnson one of the girls you heard that day?"

"No. Alicia Johnson was more the loner type. She didn't hang in that crowd."

Brent cocked his head to one side. "You think it was a pregnancy pact, like those girls on the east coast a few years back?"

"I never heard about that," she said, shrugging her shoulders.

"Can you tell us their names?" Peter took out his pad.

"Britney Maguire and Connie Waggoner. The girl they were trying to convince was a sophomore named Sherrie Olson."

"Are they all pregnant now?" said Brent.

"Britney and Connie were pregnant. They must've had their babies by now, because that was back in September. They didn't come back to school, but I heard through the grapevine that they run around town here with no babies. So, I guess they put 'em up for adoption. Which, if you ask me, is the right thing to do."

"What about Sherrie?"

"I saw her in the grocery store just last week with a big belly. I'm guessing she'll have that baby anytime now."

"You know where these girls live?"

She hesitated. "I could get their addresses from their folders, but I'm not supposed to give that kind of thing out."

"We just want to get someone to talk to us, see if we can figure out what happened to Alicia."

"Fine, but just don't tell anyone I did it, okay?"

"You got it, blue eyes," said Peter.

She flushed and waved her hand dismissively. "Oh, you're a charmer, I can see that. Wait here, I'll be right back." She came back with the names and addresses scrawled on a piece of scratch paper.

"We can't thank you enough for your help," said Peter. "Can we have your number in case we have any other questions?"

"You bet. Let me know how I can help your investigation." He could see the idea excited her and Peter worried suddenly about whether she could keep quiet.

"I should mention," he said, "this is a highly confidential investigation."

"Understood." Her eyes gleamed as she smiled. "You can count on me."

The address for Britney Maguire was a rundown house outside of town, sorely in need of a paint job and with several old cars parked in the dirt driveway. A dog started barking as they walked up to the house and knocked on the door. An overweight girl of about sixteen, dressed in leggings and a big T-shirt, answered. When they flashed their badges, she stared at them with wide eyes. "You here alone?" Peter asked, glancing around the yard.

"Yeah. My mother's at work."

"You mind if we ask you some questions?" asked Brent.

"About what?"

"About a missing girl," said Peter.

"Alicia?"

"That's right," said Peter. "You think there's any chance she might've been pregnant?"

The girl shrugged, shaking her head. "Didn't know her that well."

"You were pregnant as well? Is that right?" asked Brent.

She nodded, her eyes darting to Peter and then to the driveway. "I gave the baby up for adoption. Far as I know that's not a crime."

"Didn't say it was," said Peter.

"Then I got nothing more to say." She slammed the door.

Peter and Brent looked at each other and silently headed for the car. The next address was in town at one of the rundown apartment buildings, behind a Laundromat. A small boy answered the door and told them his sister was working, pointing to the Laundromat.

"Where's your mother?" asked Brent, looking around the kid into the apartment.

"She's gone. We live here with my dad. He's Connie's step-dad, my dad. He drives a truck, between here and Portland. He's gone right now."

They found Connie folding laundry on a big table in the back of the building, near the industrial-sized washers.

"All Laundromats smell the same, soap and dryer lint," said Brent. "Reminds me of every Saturday morning of my childhood."

Connie looked up as they approached. She was a tall, thin girl with reddish-blond hair. "You guys dropping off laundry? I've got kind of a backup here so I won't have it done until tomorrow. That okay?"

"You Connie Waggoner?" Peter showed his badge. "We'd like to talk to you about Alicia Johnson, if we could."

She put down the shirt she'd been folding and stared at them. "Yeah, what about her?"

"You know she's missing?"

Connie looked around the empty Laundromat. "I heard that." She picked up the discarded shirt, folding it into a neat square.

"We heard she might've been pregnant."

"I guess," she said.

Something about the girl's demeanor, the way her hands trembled, made Peter suspect that they might actually get something out of her. Brent put his hand on the folded shirt. "You scared of something?"

The girl looked first at Peter and then Brent. "Yeah," she said, barely audible.

"You're safe with us," Brent said.

"These are bad people," she said, her face turning pink. "They killed Alicia for her baby. She didn't run away like our idiot cops think."

Peter rested his hands on the table. "What makes you think that?"

"Because when I tried to change my mind about my baby, she threatened me."

"Threatened you how?" Peter said.

The girl started crying. Black mascara ran down her face and she wiped at it with the back of her hand. "I was already pregnant when the girls told me about the people who would pay you for your baby. My stepfather." Her face twisted and she started to cry harder. "He comes sometimes at night and does things to me. I got pregnant and some girls at school told me about this woman who'd come and take your baby and give you money. I thought it was a chance, you know, to get away from him. But, when I had the baby, I sorta changed my mind. Started thinking, what else do I have? What's ten grand compared to this baby that might love me no matter what and I told the lady, this midwife lady, that I changed my mind. But she told me no way, that it was already done. They already had a home for him and what would everyone think, if they found out my stepfather was the baby's father. She told me my stepfather would go to jail and my brother and me would have to go to foster care. I wouldn't be able to keep the baby if I was in foster care. Someone would take him whether it was now or then so I didn't have any other choice but to let her take him. And then another friend of mine, she tried to run away with her baby and this midwife found her in the parking lot and threatened her with a gun, told her to give her the baby or she'd shoot her. So, what could she do? Anyway, what I think is Alicia wouldn't back down. And they killed her to send us all a message, including Misty. The woman, she's been looking for Misty. Came in here two days ago to ask me if I'd seen her. I don't know what happened to her but I hope she's far away. There's a bunch of us, you know. Most of them got pregnant on purpose, after they heard what was happening. We were all happy at first because of the money and some of the girls figured why not get pregnant, what's nine months if you get ten grand? Plus, if we convinced some of our friends to do it we got an extra thousand each time." Connie's face was smeared with mascara and eyeliner. She hiccupped.

Peter looked around the room for a box of tissue, but Brent handed her a handkerchief from his pocket. She took it, wiping her cheeks and staring at them with big eyes. "I can't believe I just told you all that."

"It's good you did," said Brent.

"How many others are there?" Peter said, softly.

"At least a dozen. Maybe fifteen," she said.

"What did you do with the money?" said Brent.

"My stepfather found out. And he took it. So, I couldn't get away after all and here I am." She looked around the Laundromat. "Still folding shirts. Will I have to go to jail now?"

"Why would you think you should go to jail?" Peter said.

"For taking money for my baby? Isn't that illegal? That's what she told me too, when I said I wanted to keep him. She said I would go to jail."

Peter and Brent exchanged a look. Peter went around the table and put his arm around Connie. "Listen, we want to help you. You're not going to jail. You're not the criminal here. You've done nothing wrong. But, there are some adults, your stepfather included, who've done some heinous things and we need your help to make things right."

"What about my brother? I don't want him to go to foster care. I'll be eighteen in two years so it won't be so bad for me, but what about him?"

"We know some people in social services. We could make sure he gets a good family. You, too."

"Can you keep us together?" she asked.

"We can try," said Peter.

"What do I have to do?" She sniffed.

"Tell the truth," said Peter. "That's all."

They dropped Connie at the station, in the capable hands of Tim Ball's deputy. After filling him in on the details of the investigation, they left Connie with him so she could give a detailed account of her story and answer questions. Brent stayed behind while Peter went to Sherrie Olson's address. This time a plump, middle-aged woman wearing a brown waitress uniform answered the door. No, Sherrie wasn't there. She'd run off, just three days ago, after that Johnson kid went missing, she told Peter. "She was pregnant you know, due any day. I've been worried sick but she'll be back when she needs money. They always do." The woman led Peter into her small trailer and sank onto a stained green couch. It smelled of mildew and stale cigarettes. There was an orange rug covering the floor, and photos of kittens hung on the fake wood walls.

"Do you know why she'd run away, Mrs. Olson?" asked Peter.

"I want her to keep the baby and she wants to give it up. I'll be damned if I'm going to let my flesh and blood get out of this family. So, she run off, I guess, to punish me. That's the kind of kid she is. Rotten from the minute she was born." She pulled a cigarette from a pack on the coffee table. "Mind if I smoke?"

"Actually, I do," Peter said.

She sniffed, put the cigarette deliberately back in the pack. "She went out and got pregnant on purpose, you know, after all her friends came around knocked up. She won't tell me who the boy is, but I have a feeling she might not even know. I work nights and can't always be around to see who she opens her legs to. I've got to put food on the table, but do you think she pays that any mind?"

"If you hear from her, give me a call." Peter handed her his card.

"What's this about?" she asked, heaving herself from the couch.

"The missing girl. And the fact that a lot of girls in this town seem to get pregnant."

"It's always been that way here. Happened to me, will happen again. Before we're old enough to know how a kid can wreck your life, right?" She laughed and tugged at her uniform.

"Right. Thanks for your time," said Peter.

They went to see Peter's mother and grandmother on the way out of town. "Should we have called first?" Brent asked as Peter drove up the steep driveway and parked behind his mother's old Toyota.

"I really don't need a wife," Peter said, "when I've got you."

"Well, did you?"

"Yes, I called this morning before we left. They're expecting us."

His grandmother Aggie lived in the family home: a large Victorian perched on the hill above the main street of town. On a sunny day, one could see the ocean from both the large bay windows in the sitting room and the sweeping porch that wrapped around the front of the house. In its prime the house was the crown jewel of Legley Bay, but it was in decline now, the years of salt air and harsh rains taking their toll. Any hint of a family fortune was long since gone; the needed repairs piled up on a list Aggie kept in a wire notebook near her telephone, waiting for a better day. All that was left of an earlier, better time was the house and Aggie's memories of a nursery filled with opulent toys and December parties alight with a Christmas tree adorned with candles and apples stuffed with cloves.

Aggie always made soup on Sundays, which she ate every night for the rest of the week, except for Saturday, when she drove fifteen minutes up the coast to a buffet dinner at Harry's Chuck Wagon. She had an old-fashioned stove, the same one put in by her mother in the 1940's. All day the soup would simmer while Aggie read the *Portland Oregonian* from front to back.

The sun was sneaking a few rays between the clouds as they shuffled up the mossy walkway. The house looked like it was sagging, reminding Peter of the last days of autumn when the leaves cling to their branches for dear life until a gust of wind tosses them and they fall, tumbling to the ground. "The place needs some work," Peter said, using the old-fashioned metal knocker on the door.

"You and I should come down one weekend. Do a little yard work. Paint the house," said Brent.

"Isn't Jennifer always complaining because you never get anything done around your house?"

Brent shot Peter a scathing look just as the door opened. Aggie stood, dishcloth in one hand, opening her scrawny arms to embrace them both at once. "Boys, so good to see you. I have soup."

Peter avoided eye contact with Brent, afraid they'd laugh if they looked at one another, as Brent knew all his stories about Aggie's notorious cooking. "We ate, Aggie," said Peter. "Down at Myrnas. I wanted to see if she knew anything about the missing girl."

Aggie chuckled. "That old hen would go out of business if it weren't for her clientele's insatiable craving for gossip."

Aggie, even at eighty years old, was an unusually tall woman, especially for her generation. She wore her faded blond hair cropped short and dressed in jeans, T-shirts, and tennis shoes almost every day of the year. Peter didn't think anyone would have described her as pretty, even when she was young, as his mother was; she was more the handsome, sturdy, no-nonsense type, with wide, square shoulders and narrow hips over long, skinny legs. When he was a kid, he imagined her coming out west in a covered wagon. For as long as he could remember, she had insisted they call her by her first name, Aggie. "I'm too young to be anyone's grandmother," she always said, which was both odd and funny to Jack and Peter when they were children. She was in her sixties then. That was practically ancient.

Now, Brent laughed at something Aggie had said, loud and hearty with his head thrown back. He was such a suck up, thought Peter. But Aggie beamed. "Not to worry, in honor of the occasion, I stopped at the bakery and bought one of Rita's pies," she said, glancing at Peter and raising her eyebrows.

"Rita?" said Peter.

Aggie put her hands on her hips. "You took her to senior prom."

"Oh, *that* Rita," said Peter.

Aggie turned to Brent. "She's married now with six children. Can you imagine? Six. Had a couple already when she got married, not sure who the father or fathers were," Aggie said, pulling her face in a horrified expression, as if she actually cared. "And he had a couple and now they have two together."

Peter's mother, Louise, came into the foyer just then and pulled Peter and then Brent into an embrace. "Yes, poor Rita got around a bit after high school."

"Your mother says she was easy," said Aggie. "But she just looks like a middle-aged housewife now."

Peter did remember Rita and her easy ways. She was quite a prom date. Brent laughed and patted Peter's shoulder. "Sounds perfect for you."

Peter smothered a smile behind his hand, avoiding his mother's eyes. "I bet Brent would like some of that pie," he said.

Brent patted his ample tummy. "Sure. Got some room in there for sure."

Aggie took his arm. "I think you've lost weight since I saw you last."

"I've been working out," Brent said, grinning. "Can you really tell?"

"I most surely can," said Aggie. "Sit here." She pointed to the chair nearest the back door. "The others are getting a little rickety."

The pie was cherry, with that god-awful thick filling that reminded Peter of the glop they used to make sweet and sour sauce at every greasy Chinese restaurant in America. "None for me," Peter said.

Brent shook his head in mock disdain. "Peter never lets me have any dessert."

Peter rolled his eyes as Aggie patted Brent's hand. "Peter's no fun."

"Yes I am," Peter said, chuckling. "I just worry about your health."

"No wonder Peter isn't married," said Louise. "You two sound like an old married couple."

"No offense, Lou, but if I was married to your son, I'd quickly end up in the loony bin," said Brent.

Louise's face went pale. Brent, realizing what he said, turned ashen. "I'm sorry," he mumbled. "I shouldn't have said that."

Aggie set a large piece of pie in front of him. "Now, let's not make a fuss. It's just a saying anyway. We know you didn't mean it."

"Of course we do," said Louise, patting his shoulder. "Don't worry one second about it."

After Aggie cut herself a piece of pie, Peter asked his mother if she wanted to take a walk on the beach before they had to leave. She quickly agreed and pulled on her sneakers and a sweater before they headed out and down the hill towards the beach. It was cloudy again but with no rain or wind, and the ocean was at low tide so they were able to walk along the sandy shore.

They talked first of her retirement, what it felt like to not be returning to the classroom she'd occupied for twenty years. "I'm sure there will be things I'll miss, Peter. But right now it feels pretty good. I feel so free." She threw her hands up in the air, almost like a child.

They walked a ways farther and she took his arm. "Peter, I have something I need to tell you."

He stopped, fearing the worst. Was she sick?

"I've met someone."

Peter stared at her. "Met someone?" He couldn't fathom what she meant.

"A man someone," she said.

"Like a boyfriend?"

"Right. A boyfriend," she said.

He felt odd, almost sick.

"We're going on a trip. To France," she said.

He didn't say anything. There was only the sound of the waves crashing. Finally, she spoke. "What do you think?"

"Where did you meet this man? This someone." Even to his own ears, he sounded like a cop. Suspicious. Skeptical.

"Online," she said.

"What?" Every alarm, every siren in the universe shrieked through his head.

"That's how everyone does it nowadays. There's not the stigma there used to be."

His head began to pound.

"Matter of fact. You might try it," she said, playfully nudging him in the ribs with her elbow.

"Mom, I don't need help getting dates."

"I know, but quality people. Not the kind you meet in bars."

He stared at her. "Mom, how long has this been going on? How well do you actually know him?"

"One year."

"And this is the first I've heard of it?"

"I wanted to see if it was something important or not first."

"And it is?"

"We're getting married." She wiped under her eye with a fingertip and turned towards the water. "Actually, France will be our honeymoon."

Peter couldn't decide if he needed to walk or sink onto the wet sand. He chose walking. His mother followed, practically running to keep up with his new pace.

"He's a spiritual man," she said, panting. "I put it in my profile that I wanted a church-going man and poof, there he was."

"What denomination?" Surely his mother wouldn't consider anyone outside of the Methodist church.

"Well, actually, he's Jewish."

He jerked to a stop. "He's Jewish?" He said it louder than he'd intended.

Her eyes looked almost frightened. "Well, even Aggie's all right with it." She put her hands on her hips. "I wouldn't expect this from you. When was the last time you worshipped at any Christian church?"

"How does this keep turning to me? We're talking about you." He put his hand in the air. "And for the record, I do not have any problem with him being Jewish. I'm just surprised that you don't."

"Well, I'm more open-minded than I used to be."

"I guess so," he said. "Does he work? I mean, who's paying for this trip to France? And please don't tell me he's moving in with you and Aggie?"

She grinned. Actually grinned. She was enjoying this, Peter realized. His concern amused her. He felt huffy then – like he wanted to pout and run off to his room. "He's a doctor," she said. "A surgeon."

"Here? In Legley Bay?"

"No, he lives in Portland. I'll be moving there." She paused and then said, sounding slightly embarrassed, "He's quite wealthy."

Now he started to lose it. He sputtered. He looked up at the sky and used his best parent voice. "Mom, what about Aggie?"

"Aggie? Oh, she's staying here."

"You're just leaving her here? Alone?"

His mother turned pink. "Aggie's fine. She's happy for me. Said she's thinking about going online herself." She laughed and clapped her hands together. "Can you imagine Aggie's profile online? Opinionated eighty-something seeks same. Good cooking skills a plus." Despite his shock, the idea of Aggie on an online dating site did make him smile.

He stepped back a foot or so from his mother. He really looked at her, as he'd maybe never done in his life, and saw her. She was making a joke. She was happy. For the first time ever, he thought, she was happy, just for herself, not for her children, or Aggie, or even his asshole father back when they were married. He felt tears come to his eyes. "Mom," he said.

Her eyes filled then too and she came towards him, taking his hands and squeezing them. "Peter, I'm just crazy in love."

Then he really did think he might vomit.

On the way home, he told Brent about the conversation he'd had with his mother.

"Your mother found a rich Jewish doctor. Every girl's dream," Brent joked, slapping the dashboard.

"My mother's hardly a girl," Peter said, but he'd lost his ferocity. "I just don't want her to get hurt."

Brent looked over at him. "Peter, you're the one that doesn't want to get hurt."

"What're you talking about? I'm not going to get hurt if he doesn't follow through. I'll just string him up by his balls."

Brent shook his head. "Not by him, you idiot. That's why you don't get involved in anything serious. You're afraid to get hurt."

Peter turned on the car stereo. "You know that's not it. I just know I'm not made for marriage. If my father realized that a long time ago, my mother would've been happy all her adult life instead of waiting until she was almost sixty."

Brent shrugged. "If you say so, man."

"I do say so." Peter turned up the car stereo. He had his iPod connected and turned on some old Waylon Jennings, just to annoy Brent. Brent hated his hillbilly music.

But Brent started singing along, most likely in an attempt to annoy Peter out of his funk. They *were* like a married couple, he thought. Peter knew his role was to make a crack about Brent's terrible voice but he suddenly felt exhausted and depressed.

Brent stopped singing and turned to look at him. "You all right?"

"I don't know. This thing with Jack."

"I know. But he reached out. That's a good sign."

It was approaching two a.m. by the time they reached Seattle. Peter dropped Brent off at his house and headed home, ready for a hot shower and bed. The front room of his condo was dim, with just a lamp on in the corner where Misty was curled up in a big chair, asleep, the latest copy of his *National Geographic* on her chest, the light throwing shadows across her face. Peter watched her for a moment, wondering of what she dreamed, thinking too of the town they had in common, how place had shaped and formed so much of who they were.

His thoughts went to Jo Johnson. She was certain her oldest daughter was dead, which was highly unusual in police work. For the most part, in his experience, families held onto hope until the very last moment, which usually came when and if a body was discovered. But in this case, there was no body, no physical evidence of anything other than an empty space where Alicia once dwelled.

He went to the child sleeping in the chair, touching her shoulder with the tips of his fingers. Her eyes flew open as he knelt beside her. "Time for bed," he said.

She sat upright, wiping her eyes. "Did you find anything?"

"I've got some solid leads. But I'll tell you about it in the morning."

He expected her to protest, but she merely nodded her head. "Goodnight," she said, hunched over like an old woman as she trudged towards the bedroom.

Chapter Twelve

IT WAS MONDAY, LATER AFTERNOON; Cleo sat at the nearly empty bar, celebrating the last day of school by munching on the only salad on the menu, a surprisingly good Caesar with grilled chicken, and sipping on a pint of Sierra Nevada Pale Ale. Nick was taking drink orders at a table near the back from a group of young men dressed in button-down shirts and khakis – a group from the same office, she guessed. She glanced at the man at the end of the bar. He was here the other night, she remembered. He'd been reading a newspaper. This afternoon he sipped green tea, occasionally twisting the cup in a circle.

She stole glances at him in the mirror. He was handsome in a rakish kind of way. Did anyone use the word rakish anymore, she wondered? If not, they should.

Then, in a habit leftover from drama school, moving her salad around the plate, she began to concoct a story about him. He was the type who could have any woman in the bar if he wanted, with just a smile and a compliment, especially given the way his dark blond curls fell over his forehead. His lips were too full for a man. Indeed, they were the lips of a player, of a man aiming to get a woman into bed and leave before the sun rose in the sky. He was a charmer who lured innocent women into his bed only to play the *I don't want a commitment* song in the morning. Or, perhaps he was a grifter, looking to bamboozle lonely, innocent women into a Ponzi scheme.

"Cleo Tanner?"

She jumped, startled. Had he just said her name? She shifted on her barstool to look over at him, somewhat frightened. "How did you know my name?"

He reached into his jacket pocket and pulled out a badge. "I'm a cop. You have a minute to answer some questions about Scott Moore?"

"What do you want to know?" She tried to sound more sure of herself than she was. "I don't know him that well."

"You dating him?"

"No. He's a friend. Sort of. His agency helped my best friend adopt a baby. Just two days ago, in fact." She took a deep breath. Why was she rambling, like she was guilty of something?

"I'm investigating Moore for some possible illegal activity related to his adoption agency."

Her stomach lurched. "I don't understand." What did he mean? It felt like she was turning pages of a book, trying to find the place where she'd left off. She took a deep breath, thinking only one thing. *Sylvia.* From the corner of her eye, she saw Nick moving towards them.

The cop indicated a booth towards the back. "You mind if we talk there?"

She nodded, following him, suddenly cold enough to shiver.

"How did you know I knew Scott Moore?" she asked, sliding into the booth.

"Your school brochure with your name scrawled at the top was found at a crime scene. And there was the photo of you and Moore in the paper that linked you as well."

"I didn't know my photo was in the paper."

"Yeah, society section, with Moore, at some function."

She nodded, remembering the photographer now. "My school's auction. The one and only time I've ever met him, actually."

"Most women would know if their photo was in the paper."

She shrugged, pulling her sweater closed. Why was he looking at her as if she were guilty of something? "I guess."

He pulled out the school brochure, pointing at the spot with her name and number on it. "Is this your handwriting?"

Cleo looked at it carefully. "No, and it doesn't look like either the administrator's or the Head of School's." She looked up from the brochure. "I know their handwriting very well." She paused, wrinkling her forehead. "Did you come to the school, looking for me?"

"Yes. I met the headmistress and saw your photo hanging on the wall."

"That's kind of creepy," she said. *Shut up now*, she ordered herself. *He's a cop. This is serious.*

But then he chuckled. His face relaxed somewhat. "It's the job, what can I say?"

He proceeded to describe the woman at the crime scene as a short, chubby woman with spiky hair and purple glasses. "Does that sound like anyone you know?"

"I can't think of anyone," she said. "I know every parent and staff member at our school and she doesn't sound like any of them." She took a sip of her beer, her brow wrinkled. "Wait a minute. The headmistress at my school told me someone came in a week or so ago asking for my number. She wrote it on a brochure. The headmistress said she had ice blue eyes. Does that sound like the same woman?"

"It does," said Peter. "Any idea who she is?"

"I think she works for Scott Moore, because not long after that, he started calling me. When I asked him how he got my number he said he asked at school and they gave it to him. But he must have sent his employee over to get it."

Bingo. This Cleo Tanner was on the level, he thought. She had nothing to do with this or she wouldn't be so forthright. For some reason, this made him feel good. He hadn't wanted this sweet-seeming teacher to be mixed up with something illegal. She hadn't even been out with Moore. Her name on the brochure was just a coincidence.

He pulled a photo out of his jacket pocket and handed it to her. "This is the missing girl."

She held it in both hands, peering at it closely. The girl was pretty, smiling into the camera. She had a round face with a dimple in the middle of her chin and blue eyes. "She's so young. Do you think she's dead?" she said, feeling another chill.

"I don't know."

She squirmed a little in her chair, sliding her drink in a circular motion. "Listen, I'll do whatever you need to help. But I don't know anything. Like I said, I barely know Scott. It's really been all about setting up this relationship for Sylvia." *Sylvia and Madison.* Her heart raced. What would happen to Madison if it turned out the adoption wasn't legal? "If there's something illegal going on, does it mean my friend's adoption could be in jeopardy?"

"I don't know," he said. His mouth was set in a grim line.

"What do you think he's doing?"

"I believe he's running some kind of ring where he convinces teenage girls to have babies and give them to him for adoption in exchange for money. One of the girls described the woman exactly as the missing girl's sister did. As did your headmistress. She's a midwife, according to the girls. This girl thought there were at least a dozen of them, all sort of connected as part of a social group."

"But why would they do it? They have their whole lives ahead of them."

"They're either desperate for money or starved for love. In either case that makes them prime targets for scumbags like Moore."

Cleo stared at him, trying to make sense of what he was saying. "So, that's how he gets the babies? By coercing teenage girls?" She put her head in her hands, her stomach sick. "I can't believe this."

"You all right?" he said.

She nodded, her face still in her hands. "This is a lot to take in."

"I know, but listen, we got one of the girls to talk. She gave an official statement."

"Is she safe?"

"Yeah, we got her to protective services. And away from her stepfather."

"Wait. Her stepfather raped her?"

He scratched the back of his head, grimacing. "I'm afraid so."

"My God," she said. "I don't get involved with men. With people really. Sylvia and Nick are my only friends. Ever. And now, the one time I do, it turns out he's a criminal."

"Possible criminal."

"Right. Possible criminal."

"Why don't you date?" he asked. "I'm sorry. That's none of my business."

She gazed at him, shocked by the question. "No, it's a legitimate question. But someone like you wouldn't understand."

He chuckled. "Very discerning of you." He put the photo back in his pocket, scooting to the end of the booth's bench. "Anyway, Miss Tanner, if you think of anything that might help, just give me a call." He slid his card over to her. "This is my precinct address. My cell phone number is on there too. Call me night or day. Even if it seems small or like nothing."

�֍

After she left Peter Ball, she drove to her father's house. She let herself in, bringing the damp newspaper in from the lawn. Her father was asleep in his easy chair, snoring loudly. The television was blaring CNN, running the day's headlines. She turned the television down and went into the kitchen, putting the newspaper on the table. He'd read it before bed, sipping a cup of warm milk, a habit left over from the days right after her mother's death. A friend had told them after her mother's funeral to drink warm milk before bed so they might trick their grief-stricken minds into sleepiness. It had never worked for Cleo, but her father, always a creature of routine, had integrated it into his daily schedule.

She glanced at the clock. Six p.m. Monday – taco night. She would put a couple of tacos together for him before she woke him from his nap. She found the shells in the small pantry next to the back door and heated the already-cooked taco meat on the stove, then scooped it into shells along with some tomatoes, cheese, and lettuce. All the while her mind replayed the conversation with the cop, a rising sense of panic in her chest. If it turned out something illegal had happened with the adoption, Sylvia could lose Madison. She set the thought aside. *It can't happen. Please God don't let that happen.*

When her father's plate was ready, she put it on the kitchen table, pouring chips and salsa into small bowls and setting a fork on a paper napkin.

In the living room, she put her hand on her father's shoulder. "Daddy. Time for dinner."

He started awake, rubbing his eyes. "Cleo? When did you get here?"

"A few minutes ago. Tacos are ready. And I put out some chips and salsa for a treat."

He rubbed his round belly. "Terrific. I'm starved. Had six jobs back to back today."

"You feeling better?"

"Tip top," he said.

Cleo washed dishes while her father ate. He told her about a particularly tricky plumbing job involving popcorn and cat hair, which made her think briefly of her neighbor Mrs. Lombardi. She should bring her some of the chips and salsa, she thought, absently. There was no way she could feed salsa to Stewie.

Her father brought his plate to the sink. "Cleo girl, you're distracted tonight. What's on your mind?"

She told him about the conversation with the detective.

"Oh, now, this isn't good," he said. "What're you gonna do about it?"

"I don't know. Pray?"

"I suppose that's all we can do," he said, tossing his napkin into the trash.

"Dad, that goes in the recycle," she said, reaching in and grabbing it.

"Never can get that straight."

After she left her father's, she drove over to visit Sylvia, ringing the doorbell and waiting under the front door awning as a dark cloud moved across the sky. Sylvia answered right away, dressed in her pajamas and holding the baby.

"Oh, Cleo, I'm so glad to see you." She looked at Madison. "Auntie Cleo's here, baby girl."

Cleo held her arms out for the baby. "Had to get a little snuggle time before I go home." She sniffed the top of Madison's head. "Oh, she smells so good. My dad says hi. He wants you to bring the baby by when you're ready."

"I wish he'd come over here," said Sylvia.

"You know he doesn't venture to this part of town unless it's a job," said Cleo, laughing.

Sylvia laughed too. "You'd think he'd make an exception for my baby."

Cleo sat in Sylvia's living room in the big chair by the window, holding the baby, alternately kissing the top of her head and rocking her. *Auntie Cleo*. She liked the sound of that. She'd never really thought of it before, but to be an auntie in her otherwise stark world was good. So good.

She stroked the baby's cheek, watching her sleep. Madison wriggled and stretched and made a face almost like a smile. And that's when she saw it. A dimple. Right in the middle of her chin.

Chapter Thirteen

MADISON WAS JUST FINISHING a bottle when Sylvia heard the doorbell ring. Holding the baby against her chest, she went downstairs, walking carefully in her socks on the hardwood floors. *Must be careful not to slip*, she thought. *Everything is different now. Even how I walk around the house. I am responsible for this helpless baby.*

The days were a blur. She had no idea what time it was. Madison didn't sleep more than two hours at a time. She'd never been this tired in her life, she thought as she looked through the peephole, expecting it to be Cleo. But it was Nick, his head enlarged in the skewed image through the peephole. She opened the door. "Nick, what're you doing here?"

"Hey," he said and smiled. In his arms was a white basket with a pink blanket and an adorable white teddy bear. "I brought a gift."

"This is Madison," she said, pulling the blanket off the baby's face.

"She's perfect," he said, his eyes shining.

Sylvia smiled, her heart swelling. He saw what she saw. "I agree."

"I won't stay." He paused. "But I wanted to check on you." Another pause. "I heard about Malcolm."

She opened her mouth to speak but nothing came out. What could she say? *Yes. He left. He loves someone else. And I love you.* She leaned against the doorframe, fighting back tears, holding the baby tight against her chest.

Nick. He looked so good standing there. What would it feel like to have him open his arms and let her fall into them?

"How are you? I mean, here alone, with the baby?"

"She doesn't sleep," Sylvia said. "And I'm so afraid I can't do this." She hadn't expected this to come out of her mouth. It wasn't right to admit how scared and tired she was. She was the one who had wanted this. She was the one who had thought she could do it on her own. *No right to complain,* she chastised herself. But now the tears came, rolling down her cheeks and into the folds of Madison's blanket. "And I'm so tired."

Nick stepped closer. "Oh, hey, now don't cry. Let me help. I have seven sisters. You know I'm the oldest. Practically raised the last bunch. C'mon, let me in. You can take a nap."

She put up her hand. "No. This is my job. I can't ask for help. If I can't do this I don't deserve to have her."

"Ridiculous," he said. "The first couple months are hell. Almost impossible to do it by yourself."

She looked down at Madison. Was it true? Would it get easier if she could just get through these first months?

"Show me around the nursery and kitchen and then go upstairs and crawl into bed. I'll handle everything."

She wanted to protest but was too tired not to accept the favor. She left him in the nursery, rocking the baby, and went across to her room and fell into a deep sleep almost immediately.

Sylvia slept for four hours, waking in a cold sweat, frightened when she saw the time and heard nothing. It was quiet. Was Nick still here? Where was the baby? *This is it,* she thought. This is what her mommy friends had talked about for years. Motherhood made you feel constantly guilty and perpetually tired. She glanced out the window. It was still light out, so it must not be too late. Had Nick gotten the baby to sleep? She stumbled, still groggy, down the stairs and into the living room. The sun shone through the sliding glass doors, having appeared suddenly in the evening as it sometimes did during June after a cloudy day. Nick was on the couch, sketching with a pencil and tablet. He seemed taller than he did behind the expanse of the bar at Cooper's. His legs were long, tucked all the way under the coffee table.

"Hi," Sylvia said.

"Hey. How was your nap?" He put down his tablet and pencil.

"I feel a lot better," she said. "Thank you."

He unfolded himself from the couch and motioned for her to follow him up the stairs to the nursery. In the crib, wrapped in a blanket and sleeping, was her baby daughter.

"What did you do?" Sylvia whispered.

He pointed at the baby, speaking in a normal voice. "I wrapped her tight, like a burrito or a wonton, depending on your preference."

"A burrito?"

"Never fails. I learned this technique from the baby whisperer."

"The baby whisperer?" she said, prepared to laugh. Surely that wasn't a real person?

He looked at her, smiling. "He's a pediatrician who wrote a book about how to soothe babies and get them to sleep the first three months of their lives. He claims all humans need another three months in the womb."

"Really?" She still was not sure if laughter was the appropriate response.

"Best advice you'll ever get."

"Maybe I should get the book," she said.

"Already ordered you one. Arrives tomorrow."

"Really?" She looked at him. "Suddenly you seem like my guardian angel or something."

"At your service," he said, grinning.

She realized, suddenly, that they were talking at regular levels. What if they woke the baby? She asked him, keeping her voice low, "Shouldn't we go in the other room? We don't want to wake her up."

He shook his head, still speaking at a conversational volume. "No, they need to get used to loud noises. My mother used every appliance known to man while we slept. That way they'll sleep through anything."

Sylvia felt the lump forming in the back of her throat, so common these last days. "I don't know what I'm doing." The tears came again. What was wrong with her? She didn't fight them, allowing her fear and self-pity to run freely. "I love her so much but I'm afraid I can't do this alone."

He stared at her for a moment and then came towards her, folding her into a hug. "You're going to be fine. You can do this. And you're not alone. You have Cleo. And me."

She stayed stiff, next to his chest. He smelled like fresh soap and shaving cream. She ached to put her arms around his neck and press closer, to feel his hands on her skin.

"Come downstairs," he said, pulling back. "I had food delivered."

Once in the kitchen, he guided her over to the granite counter, almost like they were at Cooper's and he was serving her as he usually did. Only this time, after he'd set two places for them, complete with silverware and napkins, he joined her. Her heart softened; he'd remembered she was a vegetarian and had ordered mac and cheese and a Greek salad. He gave her the salad first, while the pasta warmed in the microwave. The way he moved around her kitchen made her think of Malcolm. It was strange that he wasn't here, that the life she'd imagined had disappeared in a moment. And now here was Nick, just moving about her kitchen like he'd always been here. But soon he would leave, go back to his own life, and she would feel as she always did after spending time with him – more alone than ever. She felt the tears start again.

"Oh no you don't," Nick said, sounding like he was speaking to a child. "No more crying until you finish your dinner."

She was too tired to fight. And he was right - she needed to eat. She stabbed a cucumber and piece of feta cheese with her fork. As she began to eat, she realized how hungry she was. "I can't remember when I ate last," she admitted after finishing her entire portion of salad.

"That's what I suspected," he said, plopping several tablespoons of macaroni on her plate.

Almost the minute she ate the late bite of mac and cheese, they heard Madison cry through the baby monitor.

She looked at Nick, feeling helpless and embarrassingly needy. "Do you want to stay for a while?"

"Sure," he said. "I have tomorrow off and nothing to do but look for a new apartment. Go on up. I'll make the bottle."

"Two scoops per four ounces," she said. "And heat it up but not in the microwave." He'd already turned on the warm faucet as she said the last part.

"I know," he said.

"Oh, yeah, right," she said, smiling. "Sorry."

She thanked him and went upstairs. By the time she arrived, Madison was in a full scream, her face red and blotchy. Sylvia's hands shook as she put the furious bundle on the changing table and unzipped the cotton sleeper. The baby's legs were flailing and she cried in little bleats that sounded like a goat. Sylvia took the diaper off and cleaned her with one of the wipes. Then she reached for a diaper from the pail but before she could scoot it under Madison's puckered bottom, the baby had urinated all over the changing table pillow. Out of the corner of her eye, she saw Nick.

"That's just a rookie mistake," he said, his voice teasing but gentle. "You have to put the new diaper under the old one and then slip the old one off."

She eyed him, suddenly feeling like she might like to throttle him or at least give him a good punch in the stomach.

"Giving me the stink eye. That's cold," he said, laughing. He stepped next to her and pulled a burping towel from the pile, slipped it under the baby's bottom and had the diaper fastened before she had time to protest. But she didn't feel like crying this time. Perhaps it was the food and the four hours sleep, but she suddenly felt better. She picked Madison up and sat in the rocking chair. Nick handed her the bottle and sat on the floor opposite her while the baby ate.

"Why are you looking for a new place to live?" she asked.

"My landlord decided to sell my place. Which is too bad since I've been there for years and the rent was cheap."

"You can stay here, you know. I have a guesthouse out back. Fully furnished. You can use it as long as you like." She kept her voice casual – just a friend offering to help a friend.

He cocked his head. "What's the rent?"

"That depends," she said.

"On what?"

"If you're willing to help me with the baby."

"Yeah?" he said.

"Free rent in exchange for helping me? How does that sound?"

"Done."

Her heart soared, like a thousand lights were turned on in the dark. They grinned at one another for a moment before they heard the doorbell ringing.

"I bet that's Cleo," she said.

"I'll let her in," said Nick.

"Great," said Sylvia, turning her gaze to the baby and fussing with the collar of her onesie so he wouldn't see she was sorry that Cleo was here. What kind of friend did that make her? But she so seldom had Nick to herself. And now she'd have to watch him watch Cleo with that glint of love in his eyes. It hurt. That was the truth. And now that Malcolm was gone, she couldn't hide behind the consuming energy it took to try and be happy. She was simply alone with her secret.

"Tell her to come up, would you?" she asked, her voice almost catching at the back of her throat.

"Sure," he said as he walked towards the door.

A few minutes later Cleo stood in the nursery doorway. "I came to check on you but it looks like Nick beat me to it."

"He's been here all afternoon. He let me take a nap."

"I wish you'd called me. Naps are best friend territory," said Cleo, hugging her.

"Nick knew just what to do. He taught me how to make a burrito with a blanket and everything."

"A burrito?" asked Cleo, gazing at Madison. "She's gotten bigger since the other day, I swear."

"She eats every two hours," said Sylvia. "No wonder."

Madison was done with her bottle. Sylvia put her on her shoulder to burp her, patting gently on the middle of her back. "You want to hold her?"

"Could I?"

Sylvia stood and put Madison into her friend's outstretched arms. Cleo sat in the rocking chair, gazing at the baby's face. Madison was awake, her blank infant eyes fixed on Cleo. Cleo leaned over, kissing the baby's head. "She smells so good. There's nothing like newborn baby smell."

Sylvia stood over them. "Do you see the dimple in her chin?"

Cleo flinched, something crossing her face that Sylvia couldn't read. "Yes. The dimple. I hadn't really noticed it before."

"It makes her unique," said Sylvia.

"Yes. Yes it does," said Cleo.

Madison drifted back to sleep. Sylvia took her from Cleo and put her in the crib, drawing in a deep breath as she did so. She must act as if it was nothing to her that Nick had agreed to stay in the guesthouse. "Nick's going to stay in the cottage for a bit. Just until he finds a place. He's agreed to help me with Madison."

"He told me," said Cleo.

"What do you think?"

"I think it's great. He's amazing."

"You don't think it's weird?"

"Absolutely not." Cleo looked at her with a blank expression. "Why would it be weird?"

"I don't know. I guess because he's a man."

"Well, lots of people have male nannies," said Cleo.

But not everyone's in love with their nanny, thought Sylvia. *Just me.*

Chapter Fourteen

PETER RECEIVED A CALL from Cleo Tanner in the early morning several days after he'd initially met with her at Cooper's. "Could you meet me at the coffee shop on California and Boone?" Her voice sounded shaky. "I have something I need to tell you."

She was already there when he arrived, staring out the window and twitching her foot under the table. She wore a bulky blue sweater and jeans tucked into black boots. The boots and jeans were somewhat attractive, but the sweater looked like something an aging kindergarten teacher might wear.

The coffee shop was filled with grungy youth, arty types dressed in black, with tattoos and piercings on and in every possible body part. It was Saturday and Peter was dressed casually in khakis and a polo shirt but still felt out of place amongst the shrugging disdainers of the establishment. Glancing around the room, he wondered how sanitary the place was. The tables and chairs were dingy. There was dirt in the corners and along the baseboards, and the orange walls were splashed with drinks consumed long ago. The girl behind the counter with pink hair, a mermaid tattoo on her forearm, and a ring through her lip glared at him, as if his presence was personally offensive to her. He ordered green tea before joining Cleo at the table.

Here was a different Cleo Tanner than the remote and logical woman he'd met the night before. She appeared visibly shaken. Her hands trembled slightly as she lifted a coffee to her mouth. Once he sat down, she wasted no time with pleasantries, launching immediately into the purpose of the meeting. "I need to see the photo of the missing girl again."

He knew to speak softly, to keep her from a rising panic he read on her face. "Sure." He took it from his pocket and handed it to her. Her eyes fluttered. She put her fingers over her mouth. "I'm not imagining it."

"What is it?" he asked, sure to keep his voice even.

"Sylvia's baby's chin. There's a distinct dimple. Just like this girl." The last was said with barely a whisper, as if the words were stuck in her throat.

It took a moment for him to understand what she meant. "The timing makes sense," he said.

Cleo's face flushed. She gripped the sides of the table in both hands, as if holding onto a life preserver. "What did they do to this poor girl to get her baby?"

"Are you all right? Can I get you some water?"

"I think I'm going to be sick." She put both hands over her mouth. He sprang from the table and went to the counter, asking the girl with the pink hair for water. She pointed at a small table with a pitcher of water and plastic glasses coated with condensation. He poured a glass, keeping his eyes on Cleo. She had her face buried in her hands now and her back rose and fell in shallow breaths.

He set the water in front of her. "Here, drink this. Try to breathe."

"What will happen to the baby? Will they take it from Sylvia?"

"I don't know. It all depends on whether the adoption is legal or not."

She cursed, several expletives in a row. Peter almost laughed, given the schoolteacher sweater and all. Then she leaned forward across the table, closer to him than he would've expected and looked him directly in the eyes. "Scott Moore, or his people, killed this girl for the baby that Sylvia now thinks of as her child. Do you understand that?"

"We don't know she's dead. They could've bought her off. She might have run away with the money. She could've been spooked her mother would find out. Teenagers do strange things."

"But you don't think any of those things are really what happened, do you?" She tugged on the legs of her jeans, like they were stuck to wet skin.

He caught a whiff of her scent: caramel and magnolias. "My gut tells me no," he said.

"I'm terrified for Sylvia. I'd been thinking and pacing for an hour before I called you. And I've decided something." She paused, leaning forward again, almost dramatically. "I want to go undercover."

"Undercover?" he looked at her closely. What exactly did she mean?

"Yes, undercover. I used to be a really good actress." She waved her hand in the air again. "It's been a long time but I think I still have it in me."

He started to speak but she raised her hand. "Listen, I've got it figured out. I have absolutely no idea why, but Scott Moore is very interested in me. I know I could get him to think I was interested back." She paused, putting both hands up in the air like a Broadway dancer doing the can-can. "Then, I could infiltrate."

Despite his efforts to hold back, he laughed. She turned red, a deep flush that started at her neck and moved all the way up her face. "Why is that funny?" She crossed her arms over her chest.

He cleared his throat and willed himself to stop laughing. "Well, although I'm sure you're a fine actress, it would be too dangerous to put you into that kind of situation."

She shook her head. "You're wrong. I can do this. I'll make him think he can trust me. I'll get in his house, in his head. Collect evidence."

Peter, quite simply, was at a loss for words. This peculiar woman was clearly crazier than he'd first thought.

"You could put a wire on me. Like in the movies," she added.

"I don't know," he said. But that wasn't entirely true. As he thought about it, he realized it wasn't a terrible idea. She might be able to gain Moore's trust. There was no way he would ever think this particular woman, this sweet Montessori teacher, would ever have the courage to go undercover. "We'd have to make sure you were safe at all times," he said.

She gazed at him, her head cocked to the left. "You think it's a good idea. I can see it on your face." She pulled on the collar of her sweater. "You might not be able to imagine a man would be interested in me, but I could take it up a notch. Start dressing better and all that. You know, sex it up a bit. Like the women you like."

He stared at her, shaking his head. "How do you know what I like?"

"I can imagine," she said, pulling on her ponytail, looking at the table. "Anyway, I used to be a vibrant woman. When I was young."

He eyed her skeptically. "Maybe drop the grandma sweaters."

She looked down at her sweater, pulled it into her hands in clumps. "I know. But I like this sweater. It keeps me warm. And hides my stomach."

He paused, gazing at her midsection. "Curves. Nothing wrong with that."

Her eyes widened and then she looked at the table. "I guess."

"Regardless, this Moore already likes you. Sweaters and all."

"That's true," she said, her forehead wrinkling. "Although, I was wearing a tight dress the night I met him."

The sound of a mournful female singer suddenly filled the coffee shop. The pink-haired girl at the counter let out a whoop and yelled, "Yeah, stereo's working again."

"I have a theory about why he's so interested in me," Cleo continued. "He likes it that I live so simply. That I don't date. I think he's intrigued by my nun-like existence."

"Madonna-Whore thing?"

"Right," she said. "Anyway, what do you think? Can I do it?"

He shook his head, truly uncertain. "Let me run it by my boss and my partner. That's the best I can promise for now."

"Fine," she said. "Call me the minute you decide."

That night, Peter went to the gym after work. It was dark by the time he returned home. Jack was sitting in the dark watching Charlie Rose interviewing an economist about the recession. Reduced to a silhouette in the television's glow, he had one long leg crossed over the other with a pillow on his lap, just as their mother did while watching television. Even in the dim light, Peter understood that Jack continued to suffer.

Jack turned off the television when he heard Peter's keys drop onto the table next to the door.

"How's Misty?" Peter asked.

"Agitated. I sent her to bed."

"She miss her mom?"

"Yeah. But she knows it's best to stay here. Safer," said Jack.

"Five days is a long time to be away from your mom when you're that age. I guess." Peter smiled. "Actually, I have no idea. It's not like I know anything about teenagers."

Jack returned his smile. "Yeah, I don't either and I see hundreds of them every day."

Standing before his brother, Peter's stomach tightened. He shoved his hands into his pants pockets. "I guess I'll head to bed too," he said, moving towards the hallway.

"Peter."

"Yeah?" he said, turning back.

"I'm sorry."

"For what?"

"Everything. All of it," said Jack.

"Sure. I know."

Chapter Fifteen

SYLVIA CROSSED THE YARD to the guesthouse, the baby monitor in her hand, thankful that Madison was down for a late afternoon nap. The weather was warmer than recent days but still cloudy. The leaves on the apple trees in the yard were the light green of early June. Beyond the grass, the lake appeared gray, reflective of the clouds that still hung low overhead. She hesitated at the door, wondering if it was appropriate to come unannounced, but Nick, wearing shorts and a T-shirt, opened it before she had the chance to knock. Behind him, boxes were stacked in haphazard piles, with a path into the small kitchen.

"Hey," he said, grinning. "How are you?"

"Starving. You?"

"I can always eat." He ran a hand through his hair, making it stick up. "Sorry about the mess. It'll take me a couple of days to get unpacked."

"Take your time. It won't bother me," she said.

His eyes moved to the monitor in her hand and then up to the window of the nursery. "You need me?"

"No, she's asleep," she said.

He leaned in the doorway. "You should rest too." It was his voice, she thought, that made him even more appealing than his good looks, so soft and reassuring, so relaxed. She felt the familiar longing, trying not to stare at his bare legs, an image of tackling him down to the floor and straddling him flashing across her mind. She shook her head, as if that would dispel the thoughts.

"Minnie left lunch," she said. "Come eat with me?"

He stepped towards her. "Never one to turn down food."

❧

In the kitchen, she scooped cold pasta salad onto two plates and cut several pieces from a fresh loaf of French bread. Behind her, Nick turned on the teakettle and measured tea into the strainer. "You seem more at home in my kitchen than I do," she said, setting the plates on the small kitchen table. "I never cook. I guess I wasn't a very good wife."

"You sound like my mother," he said, a look of irritation crossing his face.

"How so?" She took two cloth napkins from the drawer next to the dishwasher and grabbed two forks and knives from the silverware drawer.

"She thinks if she stopped making my dad's every meal and waiting on him hand and foot, he'd leave her." He brought the butter dish to the table. "Which is probably true." He placed a cup of tea next to her plate. "Anyway, I thought you kicked Malcolm out."

"Is that what Cleo told you?"

"Yeah." He sat back down, took another bite of his pasta, his eyes on his plate.

Sylvia put down her napkin "That's just like Cleo. Loyal beyond rationality."

He nodded, a look of sadness crossing his face. "Makes her a great friend." He peered at her for a split second before stirring a spoonful of sugar into his tea.

Her heart twisted, knowing how much he loved Cleo. Think of something else, she told herself. *You must never let him know your feelings.* His eyes were so transparent. *Someone with nothing to hide yet strangely quiet about his own life.* "How come you never talk about your father?"

He buttered a piece of bread, glancing out the window. "Nothing to say, really. Can't stand the guy."

She couldn't think what to say. What did he mean? Not able to tolerate your own father? How was this possible?

He stirred his pasta salad around the plate with his fork, watching her. "I've shocked you."

"A little, yes."

"I used to wish she'd leave him but then she always got pregnant again. Treats my mother like shit."

"How so?"

He sighed. "Basically he's a bully. Withholds love from anyone who won't do exactly what he wants. She spends all her time trying to figure out what he needs and yet never seems to please him."

"Is that what he did to you too?" she said, softly.

"Yeah, except I went the other way. I rebelled. Fought back. So now we don't really speak much. I see them, of course, but my dad and I do a good job of ignoring one another until he gets in a couple cracks about my glass hobby and how I've wasted my life working at the bar instead of going to college and getting a real job."

She felt indignant and protective. "He clearly doesn't understand anything about you. And your work is so good."

He shrugged. "Ah, well, he's never really looked at any of it, really. I don't care that much."

There were leaves floating near the surface of her tea. Was it true that there was insight about your life in the shapes and positions of the leaves? She looked up to see Nick watching her. She flushed under his gaze. "What is it?"

"I wonder why you didn't see Malcolm was cheating?"

She pushed aside her plate, folding and unfolding her napkin in her lap. "I was in denial. I suspected something last December. But we were in the middle of in-vitro and my mind couldn't go there." She took a sip of her lukewarm tea. "We had a terrible argument before his company holiday party. I was feeling out of sorts, bloated and sensitive and we fought. I don't even remember what it was about. But he stormed out and went alone to the party. I tried to let it go but something didn't feel right. Always before he'd made such a big deal about me attending functions with him and this time he seemed almost eager for me to stay behind. So I drove alone to the party and when I arrived, his secretary told me he'd left already. She acted strangely, nervous and cagey. I went home and waited for him, alone in the bed, watching that stupid clock tick away. He didn't come home until after three a.m. The next morning I didn't have the courage to ask him about it." She paused, pushing aside her tea, feeling sick to her stomach, an image of Malcolm's face the morning he left like a movie in her mind. *She notices I'm in the room.*

"And I never did find the courage to ask him for the truth," she said. "Because I already knew it. He had someone else. But it was my fault. I shouldn't have neglected him. He was right. All I cared about was having a baby. It consumed me. But there was an elephant in the room, Nick, the whole of our marriage."

"What was it?" he asked, his gaze fixed upon her face.

"That I never loved him as much as I should have. He knew it. I knew it. But once I committed to him I wanted it to work. I refused to give in to my feeling that it wasn't right between us, that I wasn't happy or fulfilled by him. I truly thought if we had a baby it would make us closer, like a real family, and then I'd be happy. I sound like such an idiot when I say it out loud."

"No, not that. Never that." Nick looked into his teacup, stirring round and round with a spoon. She sat forward in her chair, putting her arms on the table. There were no tea leaves in his cup whatsoever. "What happened to your tea leaves?"

"I don't know." He smiled. "You got them all. I wonder what that means?" He hesitated for a moment and then reached across the table with his long arm, brushing her forearm with the tips of her fingers like a brush stroke on a painting. "I'm sorry for everything you went through. I wish I could take it all away. But listen, everyone deserves to be happy. Even you. Especially you. You want to take care of everyone else, but at some point you have to take care of yourself."

A tingle went through her entire body. Her thighs tensed. She drained the last of her tea, swallowing hard, wanting suddenly to crawl onto his lap. This desire was like an illness she couldn't shed. It was always there, just below the surface. "I don't know. I feel like I've made so many mistakes."

"Everyone feels that way," he said.

"Do they?"

"Yes." He took her hand, holding it between his own for a moment before letting it drop back to the table. "I can't imagine letting you go once I had you."

She couldn't breathe for a moment. Did he mean that or was it just a general statement to a friend? And then, a confession. "I don't blame him, actually." Her eyes moved to the doorway. There were several raindrops on the concrete patio. "I had major doubts before the wedding but I felt trapped by then. All those guests coming from out of town. All the money my parents had already spent. On our honeymoon, I remember looking around at all the couples in the hotel pool, arms wrapped around one another, and so obviously in love. I felt nothing but a hole in the pit of my stomach." *And wished it was you with me*, she thought.

"Why didn't you leave then?"

"Because I never do anything I'm not supposed to do. Good girl syndrome." She pushed her plate aside. "My parents are like some kind of love story in a movie. They've been married all this time and then here I was wondering if I'd made a mistake before I even walked down the aisle. But Malcolm just seemed so perfect for me."

"Perfect for you or everyone else?"

"That's it. That's just exactly it. I shouldn't have married him. I know that now. But at the time I didn't see any other choice." She felt the tears again at the back of her eyelids. "You know, if he hadn't left, I don't think I would've ever done it."

There was a tick at the corner of his eye, just once, and then his eyes looked pained. Was she imagining it?

"Does that make me sound bad?" she said, fearing the answer.

"Of course not. Anyway, you don't need to know the answer to whether or not you would have left eventually. He made the decision and now you're free."

"I've never told anyone how uncertain I was about Malcolm. Not even Cleo. Not even myself." She finished the last of her tea. "And you know the only part that bothers me?" She paused, deciding if she should confess this out loud. But his brown eyes were so steady, so kind, that in spite of any doubts, she told the truth. "That he'll probably have a baby with this new, unflawed woman." Nick did not flinch. She noticed this, took note of it like she used to during research for papers, and tucked it inside a box in her mind. *He listens without judgment, like he gets me.*

"You're not flawed, just because you couldn't get pregnant," he said.

"That's not how it feels when you're in it. You look around at all the women who are pregnant out of nowhere, by accident or carelessness or trying for a month or two and you ask yourself, 'how could a natural part of womanhood, the thing God designed us to do, be denied me?' The only answer you come up with is that it's something wrong with you. A flaw in your body."

"There is absolutely nothing wrong with you." He paused, raising his eyebrows. "Or your body."

A shiver went through her. Again, her thighs tensed. Was he flirting with her? She couldn't allow herself to hope for this. She would change the subject. Get him to talk about himself. "Tell me what's happening with your glasswork?"

His faced clouded. "Not much to tell. Still trying to make a decent living so I can quit working at the bar. I have doubts it'll ever happen."

"Is that you talking or your father?"

"You've got me there," he said. "Long legacy of pessimism."

"I think you need a plan," she said. "A business approach."

He laughed. "I'm no good at that kind of thing."

"I know someone who is. He's an expert at making money." She paused, and her eyes wandered to the photo above the light switch, of her mother and father walking on the beach arm in arm.

"We've been over this."

"I know, but my dad would love to help. He's really good at business and wishes he had an artistic talent. Instead, he invests in art and helps fund galleries and scholarships. He has his hand in every art community in the Puget Sound area."

"Sylvia, please. Don't." His eyes were serious now.

She put up her hands. "Fine. Just know the offer is always there."

"Thank you." He paused, moving his teacup several inches back and forth, back and forth. "You must miss your parents. I know how close you are to them. It must be excruciating not to have them here to meet Madison."

"They'll be back in a month and I just can't interrupt their vacation. My mom waited so long to have him to herself without the interruptions of his work. We'll be here when they get back. And they won't have missed much. Right?"

"Absolutely. And I think it's sweet of you to put them first." He patted the counter. "And, lucky you. I'm here."

The monitor crackled and then Madison's loud cry filled the room. "That's the hungry cry." She sighed. "I should go get her."

"I'll fix the bottle," he said, beginning to clear their dishes from the table.

"I'm glad you're here," she said, and spontaneously threw her arms around his neck to give him a quick hug. His arms went around her waist and he held her tight for a moment. "I'm the thankful one," he said. "Helping with Madison is the least I can do." His voice was raspy and soothing next to her ear. She could feel the strength in his arms and torso. He was just the right height for her, she thought, and then quickly dismissed the thought before pulling away and heading to the nursery.

Chapter Sixteen

THE NEWS CAME TO PETER in the early hours of Wednesday morning. They'd discovered a body, pulled in by a fishing net all the way up by Astoria. By the time Peter's father called to tell them, they'd identified the body from dental records. An autopsy was scheduled for later that afternoon.

Jack told Misty, sitting next to her on the couch, embracing her as she collapsed in a heaving clump in his arms. Peter and Jack locked eyes then, in the same way they used to as children, helpless and useless when their parents fought. After the sobs ceased, she pulled her tear-stained face from Jack's shoulder and spoke with a mixture of grief and anger and resolve he'd heard the loved ones of victims use so often during his career. "You'll find who did this, right? Please say you will."

Peter nodded, silent, asking for help from a God he doubted.

Later that morning, Peter and Brent left for Legley Bay. Misty had wanted to see her mother, but they all agreed it was better that she stay in Seattle, under Jack's protection. There was no way to link any of this with either Jack or Peter at this point, and they wanted to keep it that way.

Upon arrival in Legley Bay, they went straight to the police station. Tim Ball was there, looking tired, drinking a cup of weak coffee from the pot on the counter. "Hell of a thing," he said, right away.

"You have anything we should know about?" asked Peter.

"Not much. Initial coroner report thinks death by strangulation with rope. The kind you'd find in any housewife's junk drawer, so almost impossible to trace." Tim paused. "And she'd recently given birth."

"Does Jo know about the pregnancy?" asked Peter.

"My deputy's on the way over now. What else do you know?"

Peter filled him in on what he suspected had happened to Alicia Johnson's baby. With a body, they agreed, the next step was to open an official investigation. Peter told him about Cleo Tanner and the undercover work she'd suggested and that he believed it was the only way to link the case to Scott Moore. They talked of the midwife, where she was, who she was, and that she'd virtually disappeared. There was no one fitting her description who worked at the agency; the only witnesses to her existence at all were the girls, the Montessori headmistress, and Myrna. Surprisingly, Tim agreed that the wire and Cleo might be the only way to link it all together.

Peter and Brent stopped at Aggie's next and had a couple of bowls of bean soup. She and his mother wanted to know details but there wasn't much to tell other than what they'd told them about the case the last time they were in town. After lunch they went out to Jo Johnson's house, a visit Peter dreaded. She answered the door after a few minutes, wearing her bathrobe and holding a tattered tissue to her nose. She stood aside so that they might enter. The trailer was small with low ceilings and the few furnishings only a sagging couch and an armchair with thinning upholstery.

"I'm not surprised," she said. "I've known. But I guess there was still a little hope left in me."

"We're so sorry for your loss, Ms. Johnson," said Brent.

She nodded, wiping at the corners of her eyes. "What now?"

"We continue our investigation until we figure out exactly who did this," said Peter.

"Will you keep Misty?" she asked Peter. "I'll want her to come to the funeral, but it will take me a couple of days to sort through the details."

He nodded. "Jack can stay with her at my place. Safer that way."

"Thank you." She paused and reached for a pack of cigarettes, opening and closing the lid several times. "Do you think we'll ever find my grandchild?"

Peter looked to the floor, thinking of Cleo Tanner and her friend. "I do," he said. "If so, what do you want, Jo?"

"I want what is rightfully mine."

"It might not be that simple," he said.

"They coerced my baby to have a baby and then killed her for it. The baby belongs to us. It's our flesh and blood."

Later that afternoon, back in Seattle, Peter dropped Brent at the precinct and then called Cleo Tanner, arranging to meet her at Alki Beach. He found her standing by a lamppost, looking out at the water, dressed in yoga pants and a T-shirt, her hair in a ponytail. "They found Alicia Johnson's body," he said. "Washed up on the beach."

She put her hand on the lamppost, as if for support, peering at his face. "And were you right? Had she been pregnant?"

"Yes," he said, speaking softly. "And Alicia's mother wants the baby."

"Oh, Peter," she said. "This can't be happening." The sun peeked through full, gray clouds and fell upon her face, contorted with worry.

He guided her to a bench, where they sat. The sunlight glittered on the water. A ferryboat a mile or so out motored across the Puget Sound, the water a V behind it. Several small children played on the shore, digging with sand shovels and buckets.

"Sylvia is that baby's mother now," she said. "There's no going back for her."

"Cleo, I'm sorry," he said, looking into her eyes. "But we have to find out what happened. Justice for a dead girl has to come first."

She looked at him with her head cocked to the side, her eyes both pained and quizzical. "How do you do this work?"

"Cops beget cops and all that," he said, sighing, watching the light like diamonds on the water before glancing over at her. "Get Moore to take you out tomorrow."

She clapped her hands together, a look on her face somewhere between determination and triumph. "Yes, okay. Fine. What made you change your mind?"

"Can't see how else to nail the bastard. Be at my place at five. I'll get you wired."

"I'll be there."

Chapter Seventeen

THE KNOCK ON CLEO'S DOOR woke her from a deep sleep. Glancing at the clock, she saw it was just after 2:30 in the morning. She sat up, heart pounding. Who could it be? Mrs. Lombardi? Was something wrong? She sprang from bed, grabbing her bathrobe for cover.

But it was Nick standing in her doorway, looking disheveled and tired. "Nick, what is it?" Was it Sylvia or the baby?

"Cleo, I can't take it anymore." He slumped against the doorframe. "I can't go home, knowing she's asleep twenty feet from my bed."

"Oh God, Nick. Come in here." She put her arms out and he practically fell into them. "Have you been drinking?"

He spoke against her neck, sounding on the verge of tears. "No, I've just come from work. But I can't go home. I can't go home and not go into her house, into her bedroom and tell her I love her. I've had it with pretending. I can't stand another minute. I made a mistake moving in there. You have no idea what it's like to be with her every day and not be able to hold her, or be close to her like I want to."

She brought him over to the couch. He sank onto it like his legs were giving way. "Nick, listen to me. You must tell her the truth. This is ridiculous. Four years you've loved her and never once said anything. You need to give her the chance to decide if there's something between you. It's not out of the realm of possibility, you know. You're a wonderful guy. I know she loves you as a friend. And she's free now. There's no reason to hide it any longer."

"But I'm not good enough for her. You know that."

Cleo stomped her foot in frustration. "I most certainly do not know that. There is no man in the world I'd rather have her with than you. There's no better man alive, as a matter of fact."

"But now she has Madison and she needs a man who can provide a good life for both of them."

"I'm sorry but what part of filthy rich don't you understand? She doesn't need anyone's money. She needs someone to love her properly."

"I do love her," he said, burying his face in his hands. Through his fingers he muttered. "Everything about her. Just every part of her. So much."

Cleo knelt next to him. "I'm begging you. Go home. Get some sleep. In the morning, tell her the truth."

Chapter Eighteen

CLEO DIALED SCOTT MOORE'S NUMBER three times before she had the courage to let it go through. He answered on the second ring. After the normal exchanges, she launched in with the purpose of her call. "I would love to take you to dinner, in order to thank you for everything you've done for Sylvia," she began.

He quickly agreed, insisting, however, that he pay. "I'd love to take you someplace nice," he said. His voice was low and smooth.

Using a department store gift card Sylvia had given her for her birthday, she shopped that afternoon for a new dress, settling on a peach silk flattering to her curves and complimenting her fair complexion. She also purchased a pair of high-heeled black sandals, sure to make her feet ache within the first five minutes.

It was almost six when Cleo arrived at Peter's apartment. He lived on the other side of West Seattle from her apartment, in a building several blocks up from the ferry dock.

Jack opened the door and led her into the living room. Misty was reading a book on the couch but looked up when she came in. "You look nice," she said to Cleo, shyly. Peter came from the kitchen, wearing shorts and a polo shirt that stretched across his slim stomach.

"Cleo Tanner." His eyes skirted the length of her.

"Like my costume?"

"Much better than the granny sweater," he said, softly.

She smiled. "Stop calling it that."

He shrugged and smiled but his eyes were serious. "C'mon, I have the wire in my office."

His office was small but tidy, with a bookshelf that lined an entire wall, filled with hardback fiction, mostly suspense and cop novels, but with a few classics too: Dickens, Hardy, Hawthorne, Crane, Hemingway. All the male writers, Cleo thought. The desk was black and held only a Mac laptop, an empty blue vase, and two photos. One photo was of Peter in a suit and tie with his arm around Jack, who wore a graduation gown and cap. The other was of a pretty blond woman sitting between a young Peter and Jack with the ocean and a large, jutting rock behind them. "How old are you in this photo?" she asked.

Peter picked up the picture, gazing at it. "Ten. This was the day after my parents' divorce was final. That's Haystack Rock in the background."

"Never been there," she said.

"That's impossible."

"Nope," she said.

"Cleo Tanner, you need to get out more." He put the photo back on the desk and indicated the soft armchair next to the desk. "Please sit." He sat in the chair at the desk. Cleo averted her eyes from his legs but not before she noticed the ropey muscles of his thighs.

"Let's go over how we're going to do this. I need you to be safe, no matter what. Got it?" said Peter.

"Yes. What do I do?"

He pulled a small microphone attached to a cord from his desk. "This is the wire I want you to wear. And I need to tape it onto your skin." He looked uncomfortable, his eyes shifting to the wire in his hands. "It has to go under your blouse."

"Oh," she said, flushing. Was it unusually hot in the office? "Where?"

"Right along your bra line would be best. Best place to hide it."

She laughed, a dry sound that caught in her throat. "Yep. No one's been there for awhile." She motioned towards the wire. "Go ahead. Back in my theater days, we used to strip down practically naked in front of one another back stage." Again with the rambling, she thought. Just be quiet, she told herself, unbuttoning the top part of her dress and shrugging her arms from the sleeves, holding the dress up at her waist. "Go ahead."

He wrapped the wire under her bra line, fingers brushing her skin. She held her breath, hoping he wouldn't notice that her stomach wasn't perfectly flat. But why should she care? This was just business. What was wrong with her? But he seemed not to notice her body at all, securing two-sided tape to her skin with an efficient couple of swipes. "That shouldn't move," he said. "This is the same stuff the starlets use for the red carpet to make sure nothing falls out."

"Perfect," she said, feeling breathless. She could smell his cologne. The curls at the nape of his neck were damp. "My acting career. Resurrected."

"We'll drop you off a block before the restaurant. Then we'll park across the street. I can be at your side in a matter of minutes if anything gets weird." He spoke with an intensity she understood made him good at his job.

She nodded. "What else?"

"Try to get him to talk about work. See if you can get him to tell you how he finds the birth mothers. We just need enough on tape to get a search warrant."

"Any tips?"

"Just act normal."

She thought of the long night ahead of her, of having to sit across from a monster at dinner and pretend to be interested in him, and she felt the fear creeping inside her. But she couldn't let Peter see her fear or he wouldn't let her do it. "I'm a classically trained actress, you know. I have technique to back me up if I get scared. That's what we do on stage."

Peter rolled his chair closer to her. She noticed for the first time that his green eyes had flecks of gold near the pupil. "Listen, you don't have to do this if you don't want to," he said. "I'll find some other way to nail Moore."

She found herself staring at his mouth, noticing how attractive his bottom lip was. A man shouldn't have bee-stung lips. Those should be saved for women.

"Cleo, did you hear me?"

She blinked, moving her eyes away from his mouth. "Yes, I heard you. I can do this. I'm just a little nervous."

Peter glanced at his watch. "It's getting late."

"We should go," she said. "I suspect he's a stickler on time."

✼

Cleo and Scott Moore sat in a quiet booth towards the back of the restaurant. The bar and tables were dark wood with crisp tablecloths and waiters dressed in black with traditional white aprons. Along the wall opposite the bar were photos of Seattle in various decades: the waterfront in 1891, the Smith Tower in 1946, the crowds at the World's Fair in 1969. There was a low rumble of the diners and soft music played overhead. She wanted, like an itch you're not supposed to scratch, to put her hand inside her blouse and assure herself that the wire was held in place. But she kept her hands at her sides, on the smooth wood surface of the bench. The waiter came and asked for their drink orders and described the specials. Cleo wanted to gasp at the prices but told herself that the role she played tonight, beautiful and sophisticated woman out on the town, wouldn't be surprised by these prices, would not calculate them in relation to her utility bill, for example. Drinks arrived, a gin martini for Moore, a glass of white wine for Cleo. They ordered dinner, Caesar salads and tenderloins for both of them. Cleo, from an instinct, knew he would approve of her asking if he'd order for her. After the waiter left, Cleo couldn't think of what to say. Scott reached across the table and touched her hand lightly. "I was glad you called."

She tried to act nonchalant but earnest. "Thanks," she said, feeling stupid.

She saw a slight twitch on the side of his face but his voice was even. "I hope you'll make it a habit."

"I hope so too," she answered, taking a grateful sip of her wine. Get him to talk about his work, she instructed herself. "Did you go to law school with the intent of opening an adoption agency?"

He stared at her. Something flickered behind his eyes, but he answered steadily, with a smile. "I did. From the time I was eighteen I knew what I wanted to do with my life."

"Did you have any idea it would be so lucrative?"

"Lucrative?"

"Isn't it?" She felt herself sweating under the light summer dress.

He leaned closer to her, cocking his head to one side. Was he suspicious or was he just listening well? His eyes didn't move or blink as he reached for his drink, running his finger around the rim. "I don't do it for the money. I do it for the children." He sipped his drink. "It's my job to unite unwanted babies with their rightful mothers. And it just so happens that there's a high demand for white babies."

White babies? Did his agency only adopt out Caucasian babies?

Before she could ask more about this, the first course arrived and the conversation stopped as the waiter ground pepper on their salads and filled water glasses. Scott ordered another drink but Cleo declined. Must keep my head clear, she thought.

"Where are you from?" she asked.

"Mostly Longview," he said. "In Washington."

"On the way to the coast?"

"That's right. I was born in Legley Bay. Ever heard of it?"

"Somewhere over on the coast?" she asked, moving her eyes to the meal in front of her. She cut her steak, casually. *Legley Bay? What were the odds of that?*

"My mother was in and out of jail when I was a kid. Drugs mostly. Petty crimes. When we weren't in Legley Bay, I lived with my mother's sister, Mary, in Longview. My mother died when I was fifteen and I lived with my aunt until I turned eighteen."

"I'm so sorry," she said.

"It's just another sad story," he said. "I didn't let it define me. Left for college on a scholarship and never looked back." He gestured towards the room with a wave of his hand. "Made it my mission to live this kind of life."

"What about your father?"

"No father."

"Are you close to your aunt?" she asked.

"Not really. We're polite and all that. Send a card at Christmas. She had four daughters of her own." He said the last as if that explained everything.

"I'm sorry," she said again and felt a slice of doubt. Was this man truly a criminal?

He shrugged. "I'm over it now. I make sure babies never end up with mothers like mine. Helps me sleep at night."

"Is your aunt still in Longview?"

"Yes. She's a widow now. Husband died in a trucking accident."

"That's terrible."

He shrugged. "Uncle Milt was hardly ever around anyway. Long-distance truckers are gone for weeks at a time. The women in my family had a talent for picking men who didn't want to be around, I guess."

"Did your father leave?"

He smoothed his hand over the tablecloth, as if to wipe away crumbs. "Let's not talk about my father. There's absolutely nothing to tell anyway."

Nothing else of significance came out at dinner. Feeling instinctively that she didn't want to tip him off by being too curious about his work, instead they talked of the theater and music.

After dinner, she allowed Scott to drive her home, disappointed that she hadn't gotten more out of him about the agency.

"Thank you for a wonderful evening," she said, reaching for the car door handle.

He touched her shoulder. "Wait there. I'll get your door."

Her fingers played nervously with the fabric of her dress as she watched him cross in front of the car. She shifted her gaze briefly to the van across the street where she knew Peter and Brent waited, listening. Scott opened the car door and she stepped out, careful not to slip in the awful sandals that were now pinching her pinky toes painfully. She looked to the sky. The night was chilly but clear and several stars sparkled, low on the horizon. A breeze blew the skirt of her dress and she shivered. "Are you cold?" he asked.

"I'll be fine once I get inside. I should've thought to bring a sweater."

He shrugged out of his coat and draped it around her shoulders. It smelled of expensive cologne she couldn't place - not unpleasant but potent. They walked towards the front entrance of her apartment building.

"Thank you for a lovely evening," she said, searching for her keys.

"Can I call you?" He pulled the coat from her shoulders with both hands, arms brushing her own.

She gave him her most dazzling smile. "Please do."

He leaned closer and kissed her on the cheek. "Talk soon." She stifled a shudder.

He turned and walked several steps to his car.

"Scott," she called out to him.

He stopped and looked back at her. "Yes?"

"I lost my mother too," she said. "When I was only fourteen."

He stepped back towards her. "I'm sorry."

"Cancer. I understand how hard it is."

"The motherless club," he said, smiling slightly.

"I just wanted to say, I understand."

"It's not quite the same. Your parents didn't reject you." He laughed, but it was a bitter sound from deep within his chest. She felt cold down her spine. "Anyway, I'll let you get inside. Goodnight, Cleo."

After saying goodnight, she slipped inside the lobby, watching him lope to his car and speed away. Only then did she let herself breathe, leaning against the row of mailboxes. Across the street, the van door opened and Peter began making his way towards her.

❧

She was shaking by the time he opened the door to the lobby. "You okay?" he asked, punching the elevator button.

She opened her mouth to talk but nothing came out.

"I told Brent to go on home. I can take a bus home." He paused, wrinkling his brows. "You're not okay." The elevator arrived and he stepped inside, holding the door for her. "Come on. I'll get you settled."

She followed him blindly into the elevator, trying to calm her mind, the adrenaline flowing. She shivered and continued to shake. "I'm sorry," she said, as the elevator began its slow crawl to the third floor. "I thought I was fine and then when it was over I kind of lost it."

He put his hand on her shoulder as the elevator arrived at her floor. "Totally normal. You were extremely brave. I'm impressed."

She took in a shaky breath, leading him down the hall to her apartment and unlocking her door. "I need a drink," she said, motioning towards the kitchen. "You care for one?"

He shrugged, running a hand through his hair. "Why not? I guess we're done for the evening." He motioned for her to come closer. "Let's take the wire off you first."

She felt her breath catch, thinking of his hands on her skin earlier. "I'll take it off in the bathroom."

"Careful of the tape when you pull it," he said. "Don't want to tear your pretty skin."

"I will," she said, flushing.

In the bathroom, she stared at herself for a moment. Her cheeks were pink and her eyes seemed shinier than normal. *Pretty skin?* Did he think she was pretty? She peeled the tape from her skin and took off the wire, then headed back into the sitting room.

After she handed him the wire, she went into the kitchen, reaching into the cabinet above the refrigerator for her one bottle of scotch. She poured him a generous amount and grabbed a beer for herself.

"My one indulgence," she said, walking back into the sitting area. "Good beer." She held the glass of scotch out to him. "I don't know if this is any good or not. Macallan?"

"Ah, very good." He took a sip. "Let me guess. A gift from a school parent?"

"How'd you know?"

"I'm a cop. I pay attention to the details."

"Like actors. Same thing. Kind of." She indicated for him to sit in the easy chair while she sank onto the couch, shoving off her shoes and rubbing her feet together.

He glanced at the turntable with her rows of vinyl records on the shelf below. "You still have records?"

She smiled, feeling sheepish. "It started out with my mother's collection – she loved music. She left it to me when she died, and it's just continued to grow. I have an iPod too, but this is what I prefer. They're making a comeback, you know."

"I know," he said, kneeling down and flipping through the first several: Eric Clapton, John Hiatt, Bonnie Raitt, James Taylor. "You've got some good stuff here."

"Eclectic. Depends on my mood. Pick something."

He chose Clapton's *Backless* album. "A little something from 1978?"

"Nice choice," she said, standing and flipping open the plastic cover of the stereo. "Besides Clapton's genius, I love the background singer's voice." She took it from its jacket, holding it by the edges, and put it on the stereo. She placed the needle onto the first track. It crackled with static for a few seconds before the first note filled the room.

"Forgot what the old vinyls sounded like. It's in perfect condition."

She laughed. "My mother was particular about her records. I was eight before she'd let me take one out of the jacket. Nine before I could place the needle on and that was after an hour of instruction, I swear." She closed the cover of the turntable and turned towards him. "I thought I might choke on my steak when he said he was born in Legley Bay."

Peter nodded. "I know. I about dropped my equipment. That is nowhere in any of his background checks. Just says Longview, Washington on place of birth and childhood residence."

"Have you heard of his mother?" she asked. "Her last name would be Moore as well, wouldn't it?"

"Doesn't sound familiar. I'll ask my mother and Aggie when I go down for the funeral tomorrow."

Cleo shivered. "They're doing it tomorrow?"

"Jo wanted to get it done."

"Could I go with you?"

"Why?" He took a sip of his drink, his eyes on her over the glass.

She blushed under his scrutiny. "I don't know. Just seems like I might notice something at the funeral that might be helpful. Don't they say that murderers often go to their victim's funerals?"

He chuckled. "You've watched too much television."

"Please," she said. "I'll stay out of your way. I promise."

"I'm staying overnight with my mother and Aggie. You'd have to stay too."

She felt an alarm bell go off, near her temple, but she ignored it. "No problem."

"And my grandmother's a terrible cook."

"Good. We'll have something in common."

Chapter Nineteen

SYLVIA WAS IN THE KITCHEN making a boiled egg when she heard a rap on the French doors. Looking over, she smiled. It was Nick. She motioned for him to come inside.

"Morning," he said. His hair was wet. He smelled like fresh aftershave. "Where's Maddie?"

"We're calling her Maddie now?"

He grinned but there was something almost sad in his eyes this morning. "Maybe just me?" he said.

"How are you?" she asked.

He rubbed his chin, glancing at the floor. "Good. Little tired. Haven't been sleeping well."

"That makes two of us." She smiled, resisting the urge to reach for him.

"When was the last time you went out of the house?" asked Nick.

Sylvia pulled on her ponytail, glancing out to the yard. "When I picked her up." She chuckled. "So, eight days."

"I'm not working at the bar today. I'm on my way to the glass studio this morning. What do you say about coming down and letting me take you girls to lunch?"

Her heart soared. Time with him during the day? What could be better? "I would love it."

"We can take a walk on the waterfront and then get something to eat. Time for you to try out that new stroller."

"Great."

"And I have something I want to tell you," he said.

She looked at him. "That sounds intriguing."

He shook his head. "Nothing big."

But he didn't meet her eyes. He was lying, she thought. Her heart, so happy a moment ago, sank. He was probably going to tell her he was moving out. She turned away, hoping he wouldn't see the hurt in her eyes. "Sure. We'll come around noon then?"

"Perfect," he said.

The glass studio was down by the waterfront in a refurbished warehouse-type building with large glass windows along the front so that people might watch the glass blowers work. A little before noon, Sylvia, her hands gripped tightly on the handle of the stroller, watched Nick. He was talking to another artist, his head bent, listening intently. Several other artists were working together on a piece, possibly a vase, in the shade of a Van Gogh sky. One of them held onto the end of a four-foot-long hollow pipe, moving it in a fluid movement back and forth on a long table while blowing into the hole. The other artist held the round piece of molten glass between wet pieces of newspaper, shaping and smoothing it. She knew from watching Nick several times before that the piece of glass was over 2000 degrees Fahrenheit. After they were done shaping it, the piece would go into a special chamber where it would slowly cool.

Nick looked up just then and waved. He said something to the man he'd been chatting with and then disappeared behind the furnace, emerging a moment later holding a package with a pink bow and coming out the front door.

"Hey," he said, smiling. "You made it." His cheeks were flushed. It was hot in the studio. He always said he never even felt the heat but anytime she'd gone inside she'd been overwhelmed by how warm it was.

"I was a wreck driving over here," she said. "I kept looking in my rearview mirror, sure someone was going to hit me."

He laughed. "You're cute."

She flushed with pleasure. How was it that something so innocuous as being called cute could make her feel this good? "I'm a mess."

He put the package in the bottom of the stroller. "Something I made for you."

What had he done? "Don't I get to open it now?"

"Absolutely not. You have to wait for lunch. Let's set out. I'm hungry. Move aside, beautiful. I want a turn pushing this precious bundle."

Beautiful. There it was, again. The glow that came from her stomach and flowed out to her limbs. "Are you ever not hungry?"

He shook his head. "Not so far."

The day was warm, although overcast, and after a few blocks, Sylvia took off her light jacket and stuffed it in the bottom of the stroller with her gift. She stole glances at Nick. He seemed better this afternoon. Maybe he wasn't going to tell her bad news after all.

Madison continued to sleep as they made their way down the sidewalk, maneuvering through tourists and business people out for lunch. After five or so blocks, Nick pointed to a bistro on the corner of First and Madison. "See there?" he asked, pointing at the Madison sign. "Perfect spot for us. This can be our place."

Our place? Might they have a place? She looked over at him. He looked like a kid suddenly. "You're fun. You know that?"

"I've heard that before," he said with his grin that made her heart thump.

She reached out towards him, putting her hand on his shoulder for a moment. "Seriously, I always feel lighter when I'm with you."

He moved slightly and took her hand in his. "Sylvia, thank you for letting me be part of your life at all. That I make you feel lighter makes me happier than you know." Then he dropped her hand and pointed inside. "Come on, I made a reservation and everything."

He detached the baby's car seat from the stroller and then opened the door for her. The restaurant was small and empty, with tables covered in crisp white tablecloths. It had a distinctly romantic feel to it, she thought. This almost felt like a date. Was it a date? Never mind that, she chastised herself. Just be in the moment.

The server, a young woman in a crisp white apron that matched the tablecloths, stored the stroller in the front by the door and then escorted them to a table by the window. They ordered sandwiches: French dip for him, mozzarella and tomato for her; both came out quickly on crusty rolls that melted in their mouths. The baby continued to sleep. Several other patrons came in but they were seated on the other side of the restaurant so that it continued to feel like their own private room.

"When do I get to open my present?" she asked after gobbling down half her sandwich.

"How about now?" He fetched it from the stroller and handed it to her. "Something I made for Maddie's room. Just so you know before you open it – it's a lampshade. I didn't think you'd know what it was if I didn't tell you."

She untied the ribbon and opened the box. Nestled in tissue paper was a glass lampshade in a delicate shade of pink with splotches of yellow all around the perimeter that looked amazingly like ducks. "How did you do that?" she asked.

"Very carefully," he said. "Yellow glass chips. It took me two tries to get it right."

She traced the ducks with her fingertips. "Nick, this is true artistry."

"Thanks. I'm proud of it, actually."

"I've never heard you say that about any of your work before," she said, staring at him.

"Maybe it's because it was for you two – made with love." He shrugged and coughed, looking uncomfortable suddenly. "The lamp is back at the house. I'll bring it up for you when we get home."

"Thank you. Truly. I couldn't love it more." She paused, looking down at the piece of art in her hands. "I think you could sell these at baby boutiques."

He surprised her when he said. "You might be onto something there. Let's talk about it later. Over wine maybe?"

"Deal." She took a deep breath, afraid to ask but knowing she had to. "What did you want to tell me?"

His eyes darted to the window. "You know what? Never mind. It's nothing important."

"So you're not moving out?"

"What? No."

"I'm so relieved. I thought you were going to tell me we were too much trouble."

He shook his head, picking up the last part of his sandwich. "There is no way either of you would ever be trouble to me." He pointed at her plate. "Now finish your lunch. We should get home and let you have a nap."

I love you, she thought. *I love you. A thousand times, I love you.*

Chapter Twenty

PETER'S MOTHER CALLED just as he and Cleo were heading east to Olympia, asking if he'd like to meet for lunch. "Ben's here and would love to meet you," she said.

Ben. The fiancé. "I don't know," he said. "I have someone with me."

"Who?"

"Cleo Tanner. She's the woman helping me on the case."

His mother sighed on the other end of the phone. "Oh, I got excited for a moment."

"Mom, don't start."

"Bring her to lunch. I promise not to embarrass you," said Louise.

He felt Cleo watching him and glanced over at her. "You want to meet my mother?" he mouthed, smiling.

She surprised him by nodding her head in a manner that could only be described as eager. He could see this Cleo Tanner was, above all else, a person curious in nature.

After he hung up, he turned to her. "Thanks," he said. "It will help me. Having you there for lunch, that is."

She shifted in the seat, shrugging out of her sweater. She looked pretty, her hands folded in her lap, her eyes the same light green as her sweater. "Why will it help you?" she asked.

He shook his head. "I don't know. My mother's been alone for over twenty years. What if this guy's a jerk? Or a womanizer?"

"What happened between your parents?"

"My father was a serial cheater." He slowed the car as they came upon a large truck carrying logs.

She didn't say anything. When he looked over at her, she was peering at him like he was a specimen in a jar.

"It's unnerving the way you look at a person," he said.

Her eyes went wide. "Sorry." She turned and looked out the passenger side window.

He turned on the stereo. Waylon Jennings was still in the CD changer.

"Oh, turn it up. I love this album," she said.

He smiled and turned the knob.

His mother was already at Myrnas when they arrived, sitting with a white-haired man with broad shoulders in the corner booth. Almost every table was taken and the counter seats were filled. His mother smiled wide when she saw him. He felt the sudden illogical urge to hold Cleo's hand, which bewildered him even as he thwarted the impulse.

Both his mother and Ben Schulman stood as introductions were made. Ben was a large man and muscular for his age, with a wide, friendly face and light blue eyes. His hand was soft when Peter shook it. Surgeon hands, he thought. No calluses, probably always protecting them from the environment, sports, and all things physical.

Peter hated him right away.

Ben gestured for them to sit. His mother indicated with her eyes towards Cleo.

"This is Cleo Tanner. She's a teacher too, Mom. Montessori."

"How wonderful," said Louise. "I would've loved to learn more about her methods. How did you decide on that instead of traditional public school?"

"I started working as an assistant after college and decided after a year or two I would get certified," said Cleo.

Louise's eyes sparkled. "That's similar to me. I started as an aid at the elementary school and then my mother talked me into getting my teaching certificate. After my divorce. Do you remember that year I went to school in Portland, Peter?"

"Sure, Mom."

"I felt tremendous guilt over it," Louise said to Cleo, in that way that women did with one another, like they were members of a secret club, the windows of which men could only hope to gaze into, observing yet not participating. "I had to stay three nights a week in Portland, leaving the boys with Aggie."

"It was fine, Mom," said Peter. "We were all proud of you."

His mother's eyes went soft. "Really, Peter? I've never heard you say that before."

"And Aggie took good care of us, despite almost killing us several times with her cooking."

Louise laughed, resting her head on Ben's shoulder for a moment. "Oh, Ben's already been introduced to Aggie's bean soup."

Ben patted his stomach. "It's been good for me. I've lost ten pounds since we started dating."

How often did he eat at Aggie's? What was it with this guy, anyway?

Louise looked up at Ben and then over to Peter, her eyes shining. "He's exaggerating – he was already in great shape when I met him. He can bench press the same as men half his age."

Peter and Cleo exchanged a quick glance. Then Myrna arrived with plastic menus and glasses of water.

Peter tried to observe Ben without being too obvious. Ben and his mother sat with no space between them. Every so often, he touched her arm or moved her glass so it was easier for her to reach. Cleo didn't say much, but as the lunch progressed Louise drew her out, asking questions about her work and her father. Peter could tell she liked Cleo and detected a small spark of hope behind her eyes. He wanted to set her straight, to remind her that the men in his family were either not good at love or, in Jack's case, unlucky in it.

Talk turned eventually to how she and Ben met. Apparently his mother had left some of the detail out of her story. She did indeed meet Ben online, not on a dating site as he'd assumed, however, but as part of an online support group for people with family members who had attempted suicide. Their group met in Portland, his mother explained, and she began attending regularly, once a week, after her son's attempt. What else had happened in his mother's life that he didn't know about?

He felt Cleo stiffen, and when he glanced at her, she was gazing at him curiously.

"No, not Peter. Jack," said Louise, her eyes glassy with unshed tears. Ben put his arm around her, smiling gently in Peter's direction. "They teach us at support group to allow ourselves to feel the emotion, whatever it is, when we're feeling it. Allows us to heal faster, supposedly," he said, with another kind but rather sad smile.

"I'm sorry, Louise, I didn't know about Jack," said Cleo. "I've met him, just recently, and he seems, well, fine." She stopped, looking at Peter. "Does that sound stupid?" She turned back to his mother and Ben. "I've never known anyone who's attempted suicide and I'm afraid I don't know how to talk about it."

Louise smiled in her direction. "It's all right, Cleo. It's good to hear that he seems normal to you. I find myself watching him all the time, looking for signs, so afraid it might happen again."

"This watching is very common," Ben said to Cleo. Then he looked straight at Peter. "There are a few siblings in our group - similar situations to yours and Jack's, actually. You might consider looking into one in your neighborhood."

"I'm not the support group kind of guy," he said, stabbing a potato in his chowder with his fork. Why was this man he'd just met giving him suggestions about his life?

"It was my daughter," Ben said to Cleo, as if she'd asked. "Forty years old and tried to kill herself. Fastest-growing group of suicide attempts, women in their forties."

"I never knew that," said Cleo. "I wonder why?"

Louise spoke softly. "It's the hardness of life that hits you then, if things haven't gone according to plan."

Cleo stared down at her salad, picking at it with the tip of her fork.

Through bites of chowder, Peter observed Ben. He seemed harmless enough. In fact, he was quite likable with his brawny looks and clear eyes. But he wouldn't allow himself to like him. He needed to trust him first. Make sure he wasn't a bastard. His mother was so good - soft, trusting. Who knew what she might do in moments of vulnerability? Really, what kind of self-respecting man went to a support group?

Ben was still talking. His daughter, Allison, had one son from a relationship in her twenties who was now living with Ben.

"Lou's been a great help with him. She has this way of getting him to talk."

Peter's stomach turned. Only close family and Brent called her Lou. Everyone else called her Louise. Even his father had called her Louise.

"It only works with young men who aren't my sons," she said, mostly to Cleo.

"How long have you called her Lou?" Peter asked Ben, spinning a knife in a circle next to his soup bowl.

"Peter," said his mother, with a hint of a warning in her voice.

"It suits her," Ben said, smiling. "Lou, simple, salt of the earth, so comfortable to say. Just like her."

Peter put his spoon down. Comfortable? That sounded like a stuffed animal.

Cleo shifted in the seat next to him. "Is Allison better now?" she asked, leaning forward.

"Yes. Much," said Ben. He paused, looking over at Louise. "But like Lou, I watch Allison all the time. Always afraid for that phone call." He scratched at the side of his face. "I found her, Peter, just as you did Jack. There are so many nights I can't sleep, the image of that flashing through my mind like a movie."

Peter looked away from Ben, from his eyes that were a reflection of his own pain. "Yeah, me too." He wanted to weep. Really, just put his head on the table and cry. For Jack and his mother and this Ben and his daughter who were suddenly in their lives. He stirred his chowder with his spoon, trying to will away the lump in his throat.

"Peter," said his mother.

He looked up, swallowing.

"Are you all right?" asked Louise. Her eyes were damp.

His heart beat hard in his chest. His eyes stung. He stuck his fingers into them, pushing on his eyeballs until they hurt.

"I'm sorry," he mumbled. "But we should get going."

Ben reached his long arm across the table and patted Peter on the shoulder. "Best not to push all this inside."

Peter slid out of the booth, looking at Cleo. "We don't want to be late to the funeral."

Cleo scooted towards him, her face tense. "Thank you for the meal," she said. "It was nice to meet you. And congratulations on your engagement."

Louise smiled. "Maybe you'll come to the wedding? With Peter?"

Cleo's eyes darted to his. "Oh, well, we're just working together on this case, so probably not."

His mother continued to smile. "We'll see you at the house, later, though?"

"Yeah, Mom. We'll see you later," said Peter.

Chapter Twenty-One

IN THE CAR, Cleo didn't say anything until they were out of Myrnas' parking lot. "I thought the funeral wasn't until three," she said.

He shrugged. "So I lied." He headed south on the main street of town. The sky had cleared while they were in the restaurant. "Want to take a walk on the beach?"

"Sure."

Situated above the beach, the state-owned tourist stop included a parking lot and picnic tables, all deserted. They walked through the parking lot and down a steep trail, littered with pebbles and driftwood, to the section of sandy beach known as Seagull's Landing. The Landing, as the locals called it, was a half-mile stretch of beach, its soft, fine sand in the shape of a mussel shell. It was interrupted by massive jutting rocks, covered with mussels and moss, on either end of the sand's curvature. During low tide one could scoot around, between waves, to another section of coast, but Peter never had, fearing he wouldn't get back around and would be stuck. There were tales, Legley Bay lore, Aggie called it, of children who were trapped on the other side of the rock as the tide came in and were swept out to sea.

Now, the tide was out and the small span of beach was laden with pebbles and shells. They walked to the edge of the water, waves almost reaching their feet. Peter breathed deeply, of the salt air and scent of seaweed and fish. No matter how long he was away, it always smelled of home to him.

They walked in silence down the short stretch of beach. Shiny gray pebbles were scattered amongst the soft, damp sand.

"Peter." Cleo tugged on the sleeve of his jacket.

His eyes slid to her. Her cheeks were flushed pink from the sea air. "What is it?" he asked, softly.

"When did you start thinking you had to save the world?"

They'd reached the craggy bank where the stretch of beach ended. He stopped for a moment, grazing his fingers over the skinny leaves of a fern, and turned north, gazing at the lighthouse in the distance. "I don't think that."

"You hold so tightly onto your feelings but eventually they'll come out," she said.

He glanced back at her. "I think that's funny coming from you."

She shook her hair and it moved in a wave down her back. There were tendrils around the sides of her face. Were they as soft as they looked? "Maybe," she said.

At the end of the curve of beach they turned to walk back. "Since the first time I heard my mother crying in the night," he said, suddenly, surprising himself for allowing it out of his mouth. "Waiting for him to come home. Night after night."

"Oh, Peter, I'm sorry. Did your mother know he was cheating?"

"I'm not sure in the beginning but there was a final incident that caused her to leave."

"What was it?"

"I've never talked about it." He paused, searching the waves for something to hold onto, some reason to keep the story locked inside, but found that this woman, this Cleo Tanner, made him want to talk, to tell her every intimate detail of all that had shaped him. And the one night in particular, the night that changed everything came into his mind, unencumbered still, despite twenty-five years between now and then.

"Here," he said, pointing to a rock near the water. "I might need to sit to tell you this."

❦

It was the early side of midnight. Oregon rain fell in slants outside his bedroom window and Peter was curled on his side in the narrow bed, clutching the blankets around him like a shield, the sounds of his mother's waiting and watching from the front room a roar in his young ears. There were real noises, the rain on the roof and the wind ruffling the needles of the fir tree directly outside his window. But he heard only his mother's silent screaming as she sat in her rocking chair near the window, stitching needlepoint, one in a series of well-known homilies surrounded by flowers: *There's No Place Like Home; Home Is Where the Heart Is; Welcome Friends*. She rocked and pushed that needle and thread through tiny holes, crying without sound into tissues he would find stuffed in the bathroom trash basket by morning, like so many days before.

The grandfather clock in the living room struck one. He heard his mother shuffle down the hall towards her bedroom. Her silent cries still found him, keeping him from sleep, as if they seeped down the hall and into his chest where he held everything good and bad. The thought came to him then - he was ten years old, for a week now. Almost grown, he told himself. And for this reason he must go to her, must rescue her from her sadness. He must take his father's place. He rose from bed and in chilled bare feet padded down the hallway towards his parents' bedroom.

He paused in his brother Jack's doorway, watching him with the familiar feeling that a clasp was poised inside his chest, loosening and tightening, depending on the day, always informing: Jack must be protected. It was Peter's job.

He went past the family photos arranged in clumps of threes and fives, as all objects should be, according to Louise. He stopped for a split second, as he often did, to stare at the photo of his father in his University of Oregon football photo. Tim Ball held a football under his arm, kneeling on one knee, looking into the camera like a blaze of unscathed light, with his lips curled over straight white teeth, his square jaw matching his wide shoulders. The fastest, smartest running back in college ball that year, Louise told Peter once, while cleaning the top of the picture frame with a feather duster. Until his career came to a dreadful, crushing end when his knee twisted under the weight of a USC linebacker. But this was never spoken of. It was one of the things Peter wasn't allowed to ask about, ever.

At his parents' room, he peeked through the open crack in the doorway. His mother lay lengthways on the bed, her arms outside of the covers, blue veins evident under translucent skin. Under the covers he saw her hipbones, jutting like two mountain peaks. She was too thin, pushing her food around with the tip of her fork at dinner every night for months now, her eyes darting to the door every time the wind moved the tree over the kitchen awning.

Peter watched her, silent, hand gripping the doorframe. He held his breath. Louise's lips were soft and full, and along with her sympathetic blue eyes made her appear vulnerable and childlike. She reminded Peter of a painting of the Virgin Mary hanging in his Sunday school classroom. Tonight, her right upper lip held a fever blister the size and shape of a raspberry, the sight of which pained him.

On the wall across from the bed there was an antique clock, circa 1953, a wedding present from Aggie, displayed on the pine bureau. Louise's eyes made small movements, following the red second hand. Tick, tick, tick. Peter counted, one-thousand one, one-thousand two, one-thousand three before he said, "Mom?"

She jumped. Then she quickly put on her mother mask: indulgent concern mixed with her soothing middle-of-the-night voice. "Oh Peter. Why are you awake? It's one in the morning."

"I heard you crying." He said it without expression and made his face blank, like his father did.

"I wasn't crying," she said.

"I heard you."

She sighed and tried to sound exasperated, as if to say: *I wasn't crying but I'm too tired to fight with you.* "I'm waiting up for your dad. He's working a case." Then she looked at him for a long moment, in that way she did when she was trying to decide something. "Come in," she said, scooting to his father's side of the bed, pulling back the crocheted afghan in gold and brown squares that smelled faintly of wood burning stove, and patting the spot she'd made warm with her body. He climbed in, facing away from her, counting the number of yellow flowers in the wallpaper so that he didn't have to feel anything but her arms around him.

"Go to sleep now, Peter," she said. "It'll all be fine in the morning."

Morning. He stopped counting the yellow flowers. His body went tight. Yes, Peter understood the morning. That was the time when they'd all pretend nothing was terribly broken inside their house. Peter and Jack would leave for school with their homework tucked neatly inside their backpacks, leaving behind a fury of some kind, like the footage of hot lava streams killing everything in their path when Mount St. Helens blew.

"He's not really on a case, is he?" Peter said softly, almost wondering if he'd spoken the words out loud or not. He felt her chest go up and down and heard her draw in a shaky breath. "I suppose not, Peter," she said, tightening her arms around him. Her skin smelled like vanilla and the Jergens lotion she rubbed into her hands after she washed the dishes.

"Where then?" he said.

"I don't know." A few seconds ticked by on the clock. "I never know."

He fell asleep with her arms around him. In the early morning, before light, he awakened in his own bed to the sound of a telephone ringing but he fell back to sleep. Later, he opened his eyes to daylight showing between the crack in his curtains and the smell of pancakes coming from the kitchen. He felt weary and rubbed sleep from his eyes while staring at a spot on the ceiling where his mother's brush had made a visible stroke in the paint. Then he took in a deep breath, bracing for what was to come, knowing that the walls of the house were seething, expanding to the point of explosion, with all that remained from the wet night.

After a silent breakfast, his father reading the newspaper and sipping coffee, his mother slamming cupboard doors, his brother eating his pancake in a circle like the hands of a clock, Peter grabbed his backpack from the hall table and reached for his raincoat in the orderly hall closet. There was an unfamiliar scent coming from his father's jacket, a mixture of musk and oranges. He leaned close to the black and tan woven tweed that Louise said made Tim look like a professor - and sniffed, long and hard. Yes, oranges and musk. Jack came around the corner then, his blue eyes innocent behind his glasses. "Are you ready, Peter?" he asked. He couldn't yet say his "r's" so it sounded like, "Ah you weady, Petah?"

Peter handed him his jacket, the standard yellow plastic slicker, and commanded him, somewhat gruffly, "Put on your hood. The bus is about to come."

"Okay, Peter."

Peter opened the door and Jack tumbled outside. But in his angst Peter realized he'd forgotten his coat and went back to fetch it. There, as he slipped his arms inside the sleeves, he heard his mother's voice, shrill and loud. "She called here, Tim. She called you in your home. Where your boys sleep. You think Peter doesn't know what's going on?" A pause and then, "Of all the sluts you've been with, none of them have called your home. I know you meet her at the disgusting bar at the Dew Drop Inn. Everyone in town knows. But I'm done caring."

Tim's response was low and calm, too quiet for Peter to hear, but he knew he was pretending to be as innocent as Jack's eyes. Not wanting to hear more, Peter hurried out the door and down the steps.

It was raining, something between a drizzle and the slanting rain from the night before. His mother always said Northwesterners have many words for rain and this was the variety called "large drops." Jack waited at the gate, water dripping off the edge of his hood. Peter opened the wet gate. It squeaked. He made a mental note to use his WD-40 on it later. Water trickled into the space between his wrist and sleeve and ran down his forearm. He heard the whoosh and grind of the bus as it left the previous stop, heading for them. At that moment, he glanced up, pushing back his hood. There was a young woman sitting in a car across the narrow street, also waiting and watching and searching. Her ordinariness captured Peter at once: brown hair cut to her shoulders, bangs over thin eyebrows, and a bland, wide face, neither pretty nor ugly but somewhere in between. She averted her eyes the instant after they captured his, but not before he saw the hunger there, the yearning for the man inside having coffee with his wife.

Two days later, they moved in with Aggie. That first night, he watched his brother's face as he slept under the Scotty dog quilt in their new room at Aggie's. He was still a baby, Peter thought. He didn't know their family was in the act of implosion. He needed protection. He needed Peter to save him. Then, he was hot and threw off the covers. An overwhelming guilt came to him. He was a careless, reckless, and lazy boy. Only his father saw him accurately. It was because of him that he had to leave the house and spend time at a bar with strange women. He couldn't bear to be in the same house with Peter. Perhaps if he vowed to be better, to study harder and use different methods to protect Jack, well then, maybe their father would come home and stay home. Maybe the woman who smelled of musk and citrus would leave them alone.

He would go to him. Now. If their mother was correct, he was at the lounge. Peter would tell him he was sorry. He would admit that he was a wicked boy and that if he would only stay home at night Peter would stop fighting so much at school and study his spelling words with more intent.

He dressed quickly and stood in the doorway of the bedroom, listening. He wasn't worried he would be detained by Aggie, for she slept like the dead, although never mistaken for such, as her loud snore was heard from every vantage point in the rickety house. Louise, however, was a light sleeper from her years of waiting. He must be careful, stealthy like Spiderman. He crept down the hallway, the floorboards creaking so that they sounded as loud as Aggie's snores. At his mother's room, he stopped and peeped through the crack in the doorway. She was asleep, a half glass of wine on the bedside table, curled in a semicircle on the narrow twin bed with a lacy pink comforter clutched between her small hands.

Peter tiptoed past her room, down the stairs—avoiding the eighth and third step from the bottom, knowing they were the ones with the loudest creaks—and into the foyer. At the front door he paused, listening for any sounds indicating someone might have heard, but detected only Aggie's coarse snores. Then, holding his breath, he twisted the doorknob, turning the lock counter-clockwise so he could get back in.

Aggie's house had a dozen steps from the porch to the flat ground of the sidewalk. He ran down the slippery steps, holding onto the handrail and glancing back at the door several times, nervous he might be followed. When he reached the sidewalk, he ran down the hill two blocks and then left onto the main street of town. The night was encased in a thick fog. Locals called it "pea soup," which never made any sense to Peter because fog was white and pea soup was green. Regardless, it was the variety of damp cold that penetrates despite a heavy coat and is only alleviated through the drinking of a hot beverage. Tonight was no exception, and he shivered as he scampered along, mindful to jump behind a tree or bush the few times he saw the headlights of a car. For the most part he ran in sprints between lampposts, their filtered light his only guides.

His heart pounded in anticipation when at last he saw the dumpy motel's neon-green Vacancy sign with the "y" burned out. He stayed behind a shrub near the front windows, waiting for an opportunity to sneak into the bar unnoticed.

The restaurant part of the Dew Drop Inn was empty except for the nightshift waitress. She was of narrow build and had a bouffant hairstyle that reminded Peter of photos of his mother as a teenager. He thought she was young until she straightened from her task and he saw that her face was etched with deep creases. He waited until she disappeared into the kitchen before slipping in through the glass doors and turning left, sprinting past the cigarette machine and restrooms. Then he was inside, unnoticed by either the bartender or any of the patrons, who sat hunched over the pitiful bar, hands around drinks or smoking cigarettes. The place was dark, with a few low lights hanging from the ceiling and a few more displayed behind the bartender's counter. It smelled of booze and fresh cigarette smoke. The smoke was thick, dancing in swirls before lingering like a cloud-cover near the ceiling. There was a jukebox in the corner, playing Ronnie Milsap's, *There's No Gettin' Over Me.*

He searched through the clouds of cigarette smoke that hung suspended midair. There was a table in the corner; a candle in a red glass container shed dappled light. And there he was. His father.

He was sitting next to the woman who smelled of oranges and musk. There was a bottle of Rainer beer in front of him, the label half-peeled. The woman held a can of Tab between her fingers. And she was crying but his father's face was stony, immovable, very much like it had been towards his mother earlier that day.

Just then his father looked up and his eyes went wide for a split second before his face seemed to sag in on itself. Peter was several feet from the table now, and he imagined he emerged from the smoke like a mirage. The woman stopped crying and watched him with a look that reminded Peter of someone watching a horror film.

"What in the name of God are you doing here?" his father asked, too surprised, Peter assumed, to sound stern or angry.

"I came to get you," Peter said, holding his face in an emotionless expression. His hand hovered near his mouth. He was afraid he might be sick.

"Your mother send you?" Tim asked, his eyebrows knit. Was there hope there in his voice?

"No. I decided by myself." And then, suddenly and despite his efforts to the contrary, he began to cry. Blubber really, and in a way that was so unexpected and so abnormal, he was unable to remember that he'd come to tell him he was sorry for everything he'd done. Seeing his father like this, with the woman, in this place, suddenly he'd lost his nerve, his bravado, and the tenacious desire to rectify all his wrongs and bring him triumphantly home. Instead, snot running from his nose unhindered, without a coherent pulling forth and ordering of words, the most simple of phrases came out in a scream between sobs. "I hate you." Peter said it many times, lunging at him and pounding his fists against his chest. Tim allowed Peter to pummel him for several seconds before picking him up in his large hands and throwing him over his left shoulder. Peter immediately felt his body go limp - exhausted from his midnight jaunt and outburst, in addition to knowing instinctively it was futile to fight his father's enormous strength. Tim carried him to his truck without a word, reaching into his coat jacket for his keys and opening the passenger side of his truck before tossing Peter into the seat. Peter bounced slightly before scooting to the farthest point he could get from the driver's side. He watched his father in the side mirror as he crossed behind the truck, where he paused, gazing at the sky before dropping his face into his hands. Peter saw a shudder go through him. It was a small and rapid gesture, one that Peter asked himself if he'd really witnessed or not.

Finally, he joined Peter in the truck. After slamming the door, he hunched forward as if kneeling before a fire, with his right hand holding the keys between the steering wheel and the ignition. Peter thought he might speak, but he seemed to think better of it and put the keys in the ignition. With the start of the engine, the local radio station, "All country all the time, 96.4 FM," blared from the speakers. Tim shut it off with a jab of his forefinger on the knob. Neither bothered to fasten seatbelts as he pulled out of the bar's parking lot. Peter continued to sob, silently now, and in a way that felt as if he might never be able to stop. Nor did he even want to, so deep was his despair, combined with an almost fatalistic belief that nothing would ever be right again. The truth was known now. There was no going back.

Peter thought, for some reason, that his father would take him to their house. But instead he drove to Aggie's, stopping on the street next to the steps. He wiped his eyes. The house was dark. No one had discovered his misguided journey.

He put his fingers on the door handle at the same time as his father reached for his arm. "Son," he said.

Peter didn't look at him. He couldn't. His fingers went tighter on the handle.

"Get some sleep," he said, his voice gruff.

He nodded, sliding from the car and running up the steps of Aggie's house. He slipped on some moss half way up and began to cry again. As he did, he turned towards the street. His father's truck was still there - headlights shining in the fog so that he could see it was really only mist, containing moisture, not something solid. He couldn't see his father's face and yet knew he continued to watch him. Peter thought of the playground hand gesture used by some of the older boys, meant to portray all disdain and rebellion in the mere raising of one's middle finger. But he didn't do it, thinking of his grandmother and mother. He was better than that. He was better than the undeserving man sitting in the truck. He ran the rest of the way without looking back. As he neared the top, Peter heard the truck pull away.

He opened the door carefully, preparing to tiptoe up to his bed, then closed it without making a sound and turned the lock. And there, sitting on the bottom of the stairs, was his mother. He gasped.

"Mom," he said.

"Peter." She stood and came towards him. He searched her face for signs of tears. There were none. Instead, there was a calm quality to her features, placid, resolute. He began to cry again as she put her arms around him and pulled him to her. "Did you find what you were looking for?" she asked.

"No," he whispered. "Pea soup out there," he said, sniffing.

❧

After he'd finished, there were tears in Cleo's eyes. She wiped under them with her fingers and sniffed. The tide was growing higher, coming close to the rock where they both perched. "It's almost time for the funeral," he said. "We should go."

They both stood. And then, something surprising. She reached out and took his hand. "I see that little boy as if he were here right now," she said, softly.

His breath caught in his chest. Without knowing what he was doing, he drew her to him and held her against his chest. Her arms went around his neck and her frame was sturdy and strong with a curve at her hips. He smelled her unique scent: caramel and magnolias. The skin of her arms against his neck was soft. What was this – the clasp inside his chest loosening, just slightly? He took in a deep breath, way into his lungs and felt the urge to bury his face into her hair.

How he wanted to kiss her. That was it. He wanted to kiss her. But he couldn't allow himself to do it. For so many reasons, the least of which was that she was working undercover for him. Let her go, he told himself. He stepped away, immediately feeling the chill come over him without her warm body next to him. *Cleo Tanner, what are you doing to me?*

"I'm sorry," he said. "That was inappropriate."

"It was just a hug," she said, shrugging, but her cheeks were flaming pink. "No big deal."

And as they turned, trudging their way up the hill, he saw the pulse at her neck beating fast.

Chapter Twenty-Two

ALICIA'S FUNERAL WAS GRAVESIDE, with only a pastor, Misty, and Jo in attendance. Peter and Cleo stood to the side, near a tall fir. He scanned the cemetery but saw no one. As the service neared an end, Cleo whispered to him, "Shouldn't we go? It feels intrusive."

"Yeah. They wanted it private. But I told them we'd be here, just checking to see if anything or anyone showed up."

As they drove out of the cemetery Peter's cell phone rang. It was Aggie. "You almost here?"

"We'll be there in five minutes," he said, chuckling and glancing over at Cleo as he hung up the phone. "My grandmother. Asking when we'll arrive."

"Great," she said. "Can't wait to meet the famous Aggie."

The evening light was soft when they pulled into Aggie's driveway. He watched Cleo as she surveyed the house and yard. What did she see? "The house has seen better days," he said.

"I love it," she said, climbing out of the car. And he could see that she did.

They walked up the steps and she turned to look at the view from the front porch. "Peter," she said, opening her arms, like she wanted to take the experience into her body. "It's breathtaking."

He turned to look. The sun peeked through a layer of clouds high on the horizon, sending slants of orange light shooting across the water. He turned back to Cleo. The beams of light played against her face so that her eyes were startlingly bright. *Beautiful.*

Aggie came out onto the porch. What was Aggie's first impression? Did she notice how pretty she was? Did she see the intelligent glint in her eyes? "Aggie, this is Cleo," he said.

❧

Aggie dished them all up bowls of bean soup while Peter rummaged in the pantry for Tabasco sauce. Everything tasted better with Tabasco, he thought. Even Aggie's bland soup. He grabbed the salt, too. Cleo might like salt better than hot sauce. Would she? He was curious now. He wanted to know everything about her. He paused, putting his hand on a pantry shelf and bowing his head. That was a sobering thought. *I want to know everything about you. Cleo Tanner, what have you done to me?*

"Peter doesn't care much for my cooking," said Aggie from the table.

"That's not true," said Peter, turning towards them and throwing his hands up in the air. "I just think adding a few new recipes to your repertoire might be nice."

Aggie shrugged. "No need for that nonsense. People think too much about food in our culture. Anyhow, this is kidney bean soup. Sometimes I make pinto, and, in the summer, Cleo, pea soup. There are a huge variety of beans to choose from at the Shop and Cart, just all lined up one after the other. Matter of fact, last week I splurged and bought one of those mixed beans in a plastic bag instead of the beans out of the bins. Your mother and Ben quite enjoyed it. That Ben's a good eater. Has to be to keep his brain sharp for his work. You know he's a surgeon, Cleo?"

"I did." Cleo pursed her lips and blew onto her spoon before taking a bite. "It's delicious, Aggie."

What a liar, he thought, almost laughing. He passed over the Tabasco sauce without a word. Without meeting his eyes, Cleo unscrewed the top and then shook it vigorously over her bowl. He hid a smile behind his hand.

"I don't know what Peter's problem is with my soup, Cleo," said Aggie. "Surely it's better than the tofu and sprouts he's always eating."

"Aggie, I haven't eaten sprouts in twenty years. Anyway, that was Mom's kick for awhile in the late eighties." He looked over at Cleo. "Aggie's always picking on me for healthy eating when in actuality, nothing is healthier than beans. So, if you think about it, Aggie, I got it from you."

Aggie nodded, looking serious. "Good point. And I'll take that as a compliment." She thumped her hand on the table. "You know what this dinner needs? Some wine. I have a couple bottles stashed away." She looked at Cleo. "Lou doesn't really approve of drinking, so I have to sneak it."

Peter glanced at Cleo. She looked so comfortable here in Aggie's old kitchen. A surge of something warm spread through his chest, loosening the clamp further. And they were staying over; he'd get another twelve hours with her.

As Aggie got up from the table, Peter and Cleo exchanged a glance. "This is fun," Cleo whispered.

"I'm glad you think so," said Peter. And now the tightness of the clamp loosened the rest of the way.

Aggie rambled off to bed around eighty-thirty, announcing she was anxious to get back to the latest spy novel she was reading. While Cleo used the bathroom, Peter poured them both generous glasses of Glenlivet and set them on the coffee table. He'd turn her into a scotch drinker yet.

The sitting room was small and rectangular, designed during the Victorian age when rooms were smaller. It was lit with just two lamps that threw shadows onto the walls, the old green easy chair with the stuffing coming out of it, and a sagging couch, all of which had inhabited the room all his life. As was often the case, there was a chill to the room. He knelt at the fireplace and used some kindling to make a teepee around wadded-up newspaper and lit it, letting it get a good start before putting two dry pieces of fir on top. He was lost in thought, thinking through all he knew of the case thus far, and when he rose from the hearth, he was surprised to see Cleo standing behind the couch, watching him. She immediately moved her gaze, examining her hands. *What did she think of?*

"Everything all right?" he asked.

"Sure," she said.

"I poured you a scotch," he said, fetching it from the built-in alcove. "We have no beer."

Her eyes widened. "Oh, thank you." She took a bird-like sip and then coughed. "Strong."

"Take another," he said, smiling. "It'll grow on you."

He sat in the easy chair; Cleo curled up on one end of the couch, folding her legs under her. He saw her shiver and offered her the blanket from the back of his chair, getting up and wrapping it around her shoulders.

What was it about her sitting there that seemed both familiar and exciting all at once? She was gazing at the fire, which crackled and came alive, giving the room a warm glow when only moments ago it had seemed dark and cold. After a second or two, he realized he'd been staring at her and aimed his eyes at the drink in his hands.

"Will your mother come home tonight?" she asked.

"Yeah, I guess Ben took her to dinner up in Cannon Beach. Takes them forty-five minutes to get home from there. I hope he doesn't drink and drive," he added, his chest tightening again. He shook his head. "I can't get the image of them out of my mind."

She chuckled. "She's a grown-up, Peter. I think she'll be fine."

He set his drink on the coffee table, rubbing his hands together to warm them. "Maybe. But really, how much do I know about this guy?"

"I get the feeling we saw pretty much everything at lunch. He seemed pretty open." She hesitated, taking another sip of her drink. "What is it exactly that's bothering you about him?"

He turned towards the fire, searching his own mind for the answer to her question, and then, there it was suddenly: the truth. "I guess it makes me feel alone."

She raised her eyebrows, watching him. "That's a big thing to say."

"I guess it is." He cocked his head, considering her. Should he ask her the question? Would it make her angry? His curiosity was too much to resist. "Why don't you date?"

She took another sip of scotch. "It's hard to explain."

"Would you ever be open to it? I mean, if the right person came along?"

Her eyes were flat. She shrugged and shifted on the couch so that one leg dangled over the side. "There won't be. Right people only come along once. If you're lucky."

"So you had someone? Once?"

A twinge of pain crossed her face. "Yes," she whispered. "He was my person."

"Will you tell me about it?" He wanted to know, desperately, what made her eyes sad and resigned.

"I don't really talk about it. Sylvia knows because she was there. And Nick knows the whole story because we've been friends for so long."

"Why don't you talk about it?"

She met his eyes for a second or two before glancing back at the fire. "I just don't. I figure people wouldn't understand."

"I might. If you tried me," said Peter. "I'd like to."

Her chest rose and fell as she took in a deep breath and then let it out slowly. "It was when I was at USC. I was twenty years old and in love with a boy who made me feel like I was in a movie."

"Go on," he said. "Please."

Chapter Twenty-Three

CLEO TOLD HIM THE STORY, flat and without expression, letting the words come out of her mouth unfiltered. His eyes never left her, so that it felt almost like a confession to a professional, perhaps a therapist or a pastor.

The day began with the sound of shrieking sirens. They pulled her from an early morning Sunday slumber, sheets twisted about her naked legs, the smell of Simon's cologne and sweat on her skin. She stretched, feeling a slight muscle ache from sleeping double in a twin bed. For a minute or two, she replayed the night before, remembering every sigh and moan, recalling each pleasure with a shudder before sitting up and rubbing her eyes. On the corner of Simon's desk, next to a pile of books about screenwriting and his newly completed manuscript, was a note. *Gone for donuts,* it said, in his angular handwriting. He always left a note, even though it was unnecessary. Cleo knew his habits by then, as if they were her own. Every Sunday he bought donuts for his freshmen, taking his duty as Resident Advisor for a dormitory floor seriously. "Gets them in here if they need to talk," he told her the first Sunday she slept in his room.

His room was tidy, decorated like it was a movie set. Besides the plaid bedspread and matching lamp, there were movie posters hung in a row of three on the wall over the bed: *Casablanca*, *To Kill a Mockingbird*, and *Citizen Kane*. On his desk, next to his textbooks on writing and screenwriting, were two photos: one of Cleo at the beach, the other of his family back in Pennsylvania.

The sirens continued as she fell back onto the bed, wrapping her arms around his pillow, thinking perhaps she might sneak a peek at his closely guarded new manuscript. It was a full-length screenplay about a girl and her ill mother, based on Cleo's own stories of her mother's struggle with cancer. "You've changed me, Cleo," he teased her one afternoon as they walked in the bright sunlight across campus. "Have me writing a drama about women. What's happened to me?"

She'd met Simon in the autumn of her freshman year when she auditioned for his graduate school student film. He had dark brown hair worn slightly longer than the fashion and black-rimmed glasses that made him look artistic and interesting but did not disguise the soft brown of his eyes. Working on the film together, she saw that he was quietly self-confident in the way he framed his scenes for the student running the camera and insightful in his direction to the actors. It felt to Cleo as if his eyes were constantly upon her and it gave her both a sense of excitement and embarrassment. She couldn't tell, in her virginal naiveté, if he was enamored with her acting or if he wanted her. She understood, later, that it was both.

On the last day of filming, he asked her to eat dinner with him in one of the student common areas. It was a Saturday night and they stayed up all night talking about his movie, about her acting aspirations, and then of their families, of things more intimate than she'd ever spoken of to anyone but Sylvia. They consumed four cups each of weak coffee; she used sweetener, he took his black. Sometimes he took off his glasses and rubbed his eyes, making him appear vulnerable. She longed to touch the sides of his face with her fingertips. By the end of that night, as the sun came up over the smoggy orange haze of the Los Angeles sky, they were in love.

They walked across campus in the dew of the early morning, and he stopped her under a Eucalyptus tree and pulled her to him, kissing her so thoroughly that she felt her knees weaken like she'd read about in books. She would have easily stayed there all day, under the spicy scent of that tree and kissed him again and again because in that moment she felt the pieces of her life fall gently into place. She'd chosen and been chosen. There was nothing more to wish for than this. The rest of it, the ambitions, their dreams, were merely set dressing on an already-built stage.

There were times during those heady first weeks of love that she felt ordinary next to his expansiveness, but after a time she began to see herself as he saw her and she understood that love made you feel as magnificent as the other person saw you. She imagined sometimes, while his hands moved up and down her skin, that he was creating her at a potter's wheel, fashioning her into the person she always wanted to be. Only once had fear crept under the outer layer of her caressed skin. "There are so many others you could have," she said, almost not daring to look at him. He shook his head with resolute firmness. "Not for me. There's only you. You're my person."

A filmmaker who has found his muse, he said to her in the middle of one night when she awakened to the Santa Ana winds rattling the windows as he typed away in the dark room, the glow of the computer screen bouncing off his glasses.

Now the siren on the street pulled her away from thoughts because it made one last sharp ping before going silent. Suddenly, a hollow feeling settled in her middle section. She darted from the bed to the window and drew back the curtain, holding the polyester material against her bare skin, peering down from where she stood on the eleventh floor. Near the east campus entrance, a battered motorcycle was on its side. Ten or so feet from the hunk of metal a man was crumpled on the hard pavement. There was a pink bakery box, too, on its side. And, scattered all about were donuts, spilling jelly and chocolate filling from their greasy middles. It was Simon.

No. Not Simon. His name was a wail inside her.

Chapter Twenty-Four

CLEO CRIED AT THE END of her story, which surprised Peter. She swiped at her cheeks with the back of her hand until he handed her a tissue from the box Aggie kept on the coffee table. "He died on impact, they told me later. He didn't suffer. That's given me some comfort over the years," she said, her voice shaky. She blew her nose. "I guess this is why I don't talk about it. After all this time it still hurts."

"Cleo, I'm so sorry," Peter said, keeping his voice soft, wanting to take her in his arms and wipe away her tears.

"I know what you're thinking."

"I doubt it."

As if she didn't hear him, she continued, "You think I should move on, that ten years is too long to mourn someone."

He hesitated before answering, thinking how odd it was that he could talk so honestly to this woman he'd know such a short time. "I understand I have no ground to stand on here, given how I've let my past keep me from living, but I do have to wonder. Isn't it time to let go? Don't you want to love again?"

She put her hand up as if he were coming towards her. "I can't." Her eyes flashed and her words came fast and loud. "Anyway, like you said, who are you to give advice? I suppose you have a different girl every week, none of whom you're close to or have anything even resembling intimacy. All in an attempt to prove what exactly?" She covered her mouth with her hand. "I'm sorry. I shouldn't have said that."

"No, it's fine." He rubbed his eyes, hard, so that he saw flashes of lights behind his closed lids. How did she know all that? "I'm not trying to prove anything. I just don't want to hurt anyone. Like my dad did." The bitterness in his throat surprised him. He drank the rest of his scotch and turned towards the fire, wanting suddenly to punch something. "I don't lack for a certain type of company. This is true. But I never lie to them. They always know where I stand." He went to the fire, warming his hands, feeling the heat on his face, before turning back to her, speaking softly. "I grew up hating my father for his absence and for his betrayals. After my mother left him, he basically dropped out of our lives. But this is a small town so we knew everything he did anyway. He was with woman after woman. Married four times, all of whom he cheated on, I'm sure. But no time for Jack or me. Always an excuse about why he couldn't come by and get us." His voice caught in the back of his throat. "Shit, Cleo, I feared, more than anything, that I would become him. I still do."

"But why?"

"Because from the age of thirteen, I found girls irresistible. The way they smelled, the unbelievable softness of their skin, how they laughed over things boys couldn't possibly understand. As an adult, I love their clothes strewn about before a night out, the way a bathroom smells after they shower, the rise and fall of their voices when they tell a story, each of them utterly unique. Not one of you share the same scent or laugh or voice." He paused, choosing his words carefully. "Yes, it's true, I've been with a lot of women - short and tall, voluptuous and thin, every shade of hair and skin color. And they were all sweet and beautiful with forgiving and yielding hearts, pardoning men's indiscretions and carelessness and even cruelty and yet filled with self-hatred and criticism about their appearance, their intelligence, and everything in between. Over and over I've seen my women friends fall for men who don't deserve their love, just as my mother did." He moved from the fire to stand next to the couch, looking down at her. "I vowed to myself a long time ago I would never be one of those men. I would never hurt something as precious as a woman's heart."

She watched him with big eyes, her face tender. "Aren't you ever lonely?"

He put another log on the fire. The room brightened as it sputtered and caught flame. "I'm the same as you, Cleo Tanner – walking around

half-dead. Only way to do it without succumbing to my own weaknesses."
He went to the scotch bottle, feeling buzzed, and poured another small
portion. "But what about you? No sex for ten years. How is that
even possible?"

She played with the seam of her skirt. "You can shut it off. That
part of you that wants someone's touch."

"I don't buy it."

"Maybe only a woman can do it. But the longer you go without
sex, the more it seems that it's no longer real, no longer part of life
that matters." She untangled her legs, pushing her toes into the rug.

"I think the statute of limitations has run out on you," he said,
attempting a joke.

She tilted her chin up, as if defying an elder. "I don't think of it
that way. I feel like he's waiting for me. He and my mother."

Was it this dead love that was his competition? What was he even
thinking about this for? Neither of them were available, probably
equally so - Cleo waiting for her dead lover. And him? What was he
doing all these years, with all the different women? Trying not to be
his father and yet knowing he was anyway.

"Let me ask you this, Cleo Tanner," he said. "If you were the one
who died, would you want him to wait for you, or would you want
him to move on with his life, to find someone to love?"

She took another small sip of her drink and then ran a finger
around the rim of the glass. "This might be hard to believe, but I've
never thought of it that way before."

"That's very hard to believe."

Neither spoke for a moment. Her eyes flickered and shone in the
firelight. "Peter," she said, finally.

The scotch was making him feel warm and reckless. He wanted
to play with her, wanted to take her into his arms and make her
forget her dead lover. "Yes, Cleo Tanner?"

"I don't think you're one bit like your father."

"No? Well, you're wrong."

"I'd say more like Aggie."

"Bossy, opinionated, stubborn?"

"Tenacious. Quizzical. Curious," she said, smiling. "And sensitive
and caring like your mother."

"Nothing would make me prouder than to be half the person either of them are. Trust me on this."

"The fact that you fear you will become your father is ridiculous, given the way you love and respect women. You have to let go of this."

Just then he heard his mother's key in the front door. A moment later she came into the sitting room. Her hair was disheveled and her lipstick smeared. His stomach twisted. Surely they hadn't been fooling around in the car?

Louise came to stand at the side of the couch. "Peter, why didn't you tell me you were staying over? We could've all had dinner together."

He shrugged, glancing at Cleo. "We just wanted a quiet night here with Aggie." He took another sip of his drink, eyeing the hallway. "Where's Ben?"

"Parking the car," she said. "We had the most wonderful dinner."

His mother's eyes were actually shining. How was this happening? Louise turned towards Cleo. "It's so nice to see you again."

"Oh, thank you," said Cleo, standing up, holding onto the arm of the sofa. "I seem to be a bit tipsy. It's Peter's fault. He gave me scotch."

"Peter," said Louise, disapproving. "It's not polite to get a young lady drunk."

He was about to protest when they heard the front door open and close once again. There were heavy footsteps in the hall before Ben appeared in the living room doorway. He greeted them all, sticking his hand out for Peter to shake. As he matched the older man's strong grip, Peter tried to look at him but couldn't stop staring at his mother's skirt. It was wrinkled, like someone had pressed against it.

"Peter," Louise was saying. "Did you hear me?"

"What? No, I'm sorry."

"I just said we're beat and going up to bed."

"Here?" asked Peter.

Louise nodded, firmly. "Yes. Ben stays over." She turned to Cleo. "I hope to see you in the morning before you go."

Ben stays over. Stays. More than once. On a regular basis.

"That would be nice," said Cleo, blushing and smiling. She was so pretty, Peter thought, despite his sudden foul mood.

After his mother and Ben left the room, he flopped onto the couch, propping his feet on the coffee table. "I can't believe they're sleeping together without being married. This is not the same mother who raised me. I mean, what does the church think?"

Cleo laughed. "I'm surprised about your double standard," she teased. Then she yawned.

He sat up. "C'mon, Cleo Tanner. Let's get you to bed. You can sleep in my old room upstairs. I'll take the couch."

"No, I can't take your room."

"Wait until you see it before promising anything. Aggie still has the twin beds from when Jack and I were kids. They're as uncomfortable as this couch."

"I doubt that," she said.

"Oh, I can prove it to you. Follow me."

He held out his hand and she took it. *Her hand feels like warm silk,* he thought. He led her up the stairs, the familiar creaks all still there and some new ones too. When they reached his old room, the first in the hallway, he reached in and turned on the light. The twin beds were made up with the same old mismatched patchwork quilts.

"Which was yours?" she asked.

"The one closest to the window."

"Of course it was."

"Why do you say that?"

"You had to protect Jack." She sat on his old bed, her feet dangling off the side. "What happened with him, Peter, that made him so desperate?"

He took a step towards the window, drawing the shade. Could he talk about it? It came again, the image of Jack on the floor, the blood covering the tiles, and the clasp in his chest tightened. "I've never talked about it to anyone."

"You don't have to," she said. "I shouldn't have asked."

"No, you told me about Simon. It's only fair." He closed the door and sat on Jack's bed. "Jack's wife was shot and killed outside a movie theater while he was in the restroom. She bled out in his arms while they waited for an ambulance. He couldn't forgive himself for letting her walk outside the theater by herself. I had flown out on a redeye to D.C. when we got the news about Miriam. That morning, at his apartment, I found him bleeding all over the bathroom floor, with his wrists cut. Jack wouldn't see me at the hospital. My mother had to fly out and take care of him. For eighteen months I didn't hear from him. And then, last week, he shows up at my doorstep and asks me to help find Misty's sister."

Cleo watched him as he talked, never taking her eyes from him. "So this is why you're so hell bent to help with this case?"

"That's right. It's my chance to try and repair our relationship." He shivered and pulled a knitted blanket from the end of the bed, wrapping it around his shoulders. "I don't make it a habit to talk about myself this much."

"But it feels good, doesn't it?"

"It does," he whispered, his voice hoarse now.

"It felt good to me too. And I'm sorry. For all of it." She reached her hand across the space between the beds as if to touch him but pulled back. She lay on the bed, turning on her side with her head resting on the pillow and her hands under her cheek. "Are you tired?" she asked.

"Very. But I can never sleep."

"Really? All the time?"

"Pretty much," he said.

"Just stay here," she said, yawning, tucking her hand under the covers. "Downstairs is so far away. And I'm afraid of the dark."

"You sure?"

She murmured something in the affirmative as she closed her eyes. He stretched out on his bed, watching as her face relaxed into sleep. Was she really afraid of the dark? *I'll protect you from the dark night*, he thought. *For as long as you'll let me.*

He rested his head on the pillow that smelled of his childhood and continued to watch her, memorizing every detail of her face: the slight bump on her nose, the freckle near her right ear, the arch of her eyebrows, the way her eyelashes curled. And he knew then. *I'm in love with her.* For the first time in his life, he couldn't turn his thoughts elsewhere. *Cleo Tanner, what have you done to me?*

It was Cleo Tanner he'd been looking for all these years, looking without knowing he was empty of anything until he saw her face, heard her voice, felt the softness of her skin. She believed him to be good, of strong moral code and compassion like his mother and Aggie. And when she gazed at him, he saw himself as she did: a loyal and loving man that would hold a woman's heart in his hands like the precious gift it was. But now what was he supposed to do? She loved a dead boy. How did one compete against someone who hadn't walked the earth for ten years? It was impossible, he supposed. And yet, he wanted her. There was no way around it.

When he finally drifted off to sleep, her face was the last image in his mind. He didn't wake until the morning.

Chapter Twenty-Five

IT WAS JUST AFTER SIX A.M. when Peter slipped into his running clothes. The house was quiet, with everyone, including Cleo, still sleeping.

He started at the base of Aggie's steps, ran the mile down the main street of town, and then turned right, past the library and Myrnas, to The Landing. The sky held clouds, the kind that looked like gray cotton balls. The early morning sun peeked between them and the horizon, shooting yellow beams of light onto the beach as his feet pounded against the moist sand. As he ran, the sand, wetter in some spots than others, splashed onto the backs of his calves. He thought about his father, of all the memories he'd shared with Cleo. He moved his eyes from the sand at his feet towards the sea and beyond to the horizon, his eyes half-lidded, and thought, as he so often did, of the smallness of one individual compared to the enormity of the ocean. He pushed a little farther down the beach, running faster, as if there were someone behind him. His breath came faster now, but he continued at the same speed, more of a sprint than his usual steady pace, four times down and back, touching the rocks on either end as if it they were relay partners in a race. All the time, foot after foot upon the sand, he thought of his father, of the type of man who missed his own life, who let it trickle away into the air, as if it were never real in the first place. And, he realized, this was how he was like his father. He'd let his life trickle away, living life on the sidelines.

At the end of his run, he caught his breath and stretched his hamstrings against a decaying post at the base of the trail. The light was brighter now and there were large patches of blue sky. He wiped his face with his T-shirt before walking back to the edge of the ocean. The tide was growing higher with each passing moment. It swept over pebbles, covered only minutes before. He reached for one, gliding his finger over its smooth surface before tossing it into the water. Watching the waves come in and out in giant, unpredictable surges, he remembered the empty spaces that held his father, all the baseball games missed and family dinners and school conferences. And he was consumed with rage and grief as big as the body of water before him, and he leaned over, putting his hands on his thighs, taking in gulps of air, hating Tim Ball, sobs coming suddenly and in abundance, as if his tears might fill the ocean.

Finally, disgusted by his tears for a man whose only consistency was absence, Peter wiped his face with his fleece jacket and made his way through the sand to the trail and up the bank, careful now not to trip in the muted light, touching the foliage as he moved into the reality of the world above The Landing, where he knew his life would not continue as it had for so long. His love for Cleo Tanner was as big and bold and wide as the ocean itself.

The drive from Legley Bay to Seattle took them six hours and they arrived at Cleo's apartment close to the dinner hour. As he grabbed her bag from the back of his car, he watched as she stretched her arms above her head. He didn't want to leave her. What excuse could he make to go upstairs with her?

"You want to grab some dinner?" he asked as they walked into her lobby.

She smiled, tugging at her hair. "We could order take-out." She punched the elevator button. "You could come up?"

"Great." He tried not to sound too eager.

They took the elevator to the second floor and she let him inside.

"Your place is nice," he said. "I meant to tell you that before."

She shrugged and waved off the compliment. "I've been here eight years. Isn't that crazy? Everyone tells me to buy, which drives me insane. Guess I've never been comfortable with the commitment. Seemed too grown-up, maybe."

Or, just a life on hold, he thought.

"You want something to drink?"

Despite the fact that he rarely drank two nights in a row, he found himself saying yes.

"Red wine, beer, or your bottle of scotch?"

"Scotch," he said, following her into the kitchen, noting the curve of her backside as she leaned into the refrigerator, which was empty but for several cartons of yogurt, a bag of grapes, and a six-pack of beer.

"You could starve on the contents of that fridge," he said.

She laughed. "I cook for my dad at his house. He likes the same things every week. That's about as much cooking as I can stand. During the school year I have lunch at school with the kids. I'm always trying to lose weight but I have no discipline."

He leaned against the counter, sipping his drink. She opened a bottle of beer. "Cheers," she said, gesturing towards him with the glass.

"Cheers. You don't need to lose any weight, by the way."

She looked at him for a moment, as if trying to discern if he were sincere. "That's kind of you."

"Just the truth."

She blushed and pulled on her ponytail. Neither of them spoke for a moment.

"You want me to run to the Thriftway?" he asked. "Pick up something from their deli. You like tofu?"

She grimaced. "God no."

"Chicken?"

"Much better," she said, smiling.

⚜

When he returned, she'd put another album on the stereo: Emmylou Harris, *Blue Kentucky Girl*. The small dining table was set with silverware and napkins. "I hope you don't mind," she said, pointing at the table. "I never have visitors, so I don't even have a tablecloth."

She'd changed into shorts and a tank top. Her bare legs were muscular. What would they feel like under his hands? The window facing the street was propped open and the evening's air hinted of lilacs and also of the Puget Sound, salty and fishy.

Cleo held up a pair of socks. "I hate to be in the kitchen without socks," she said, slipping them onto her feet.

"Really? I hate wearing socks inside." In the kitchen, he took a roast chicken and a side of lentil and mint salad out of the paper bag. "I also got us a bottle of wine," he said. "Something halfway decent."

She glanced at it, lighting up. "More than halfway decent."

After they ate, they took their glasses of wine into the living room. She sat on the floor, leaning against the couch. He sat by the easy chair and did the same, legs spread out in front of him. "Something nice about sitting on the floor, isn't there?" he asked.

She smiled, hooking her hair behind her ear. "I suppose there is."

"Wine's good," he said. "Little chocolate on the finish."

He told her about his trip to Napa several years before, leaving out the part about the woman he'd travelled with, and as he talked, the wine appeared to give her cheeks a pink flush.

"I'd love to go to Napa sometime." She stretched her legs out towards the middle of the room.

In spite of himself, he reached out and touched her foot with his. "Your sock has a hole in it," he said.

Her foot jerked away, as if she'd been burned. Then she rose to her feet and went to the stereo, taking the needle off the record mid-song. "How about a little James Taylor instead?" She tugged at her ponytail holder so that her hair came loose about her shoulders. "Are you warm? Does it seem warm in here?"

"Feels fine to me." He tried to smile but it didn't work. He was unable suddenly to do anything but want her.

She put the other album onto the turntable and turned, catching him staring at her.

"What is it?" she said.

He shrugged, his fingertips playing with the carpet. "Nothing. You want more wine?"

She nodded, plopping onto the ground and closing her eyes, resting her neck on the seat of the couch. "Why not? No school tomorrow. Summer's the best time to be a teacher."

From the kitchen, he poured the rest of the bottle into their glasses and rejoined her in the living room. She was staring at the ceiling, a look on her face he couldn't read.

"I have something I want to share with you," she said, as he took his seat on the floor. She got up, going to the hall closet and pulling out a hatbox. Then, she pulled out a DVD and put it into her player. She took the needle off the stereo and switched on the television. "This is the student film Simon made."

It begins with a close-up of two sets of hands. The young hands ladle soup into a bowl grasped by a set of gnarled, arthritic hands. Then, a close-up of a young woman's face, her eyes filled with horror. It is Cleo, twenty years old, ten years ago now, her face rounded, unlined, her hair soft about her shoulders. The camera shifts and we see the old woman's toothless grin, and we hear a crusty voice: "Give us a little more now, won't you?"

Cleo flinches and steps back, splashing soup onto her white tank top.

The camera shifts to the floor. The old woman wears a ratty pair of boots, a shredded dress skimming her fleshly knees. Cleo wears a pair of flip-flops. Her toes are painted pink and she wears a toe ring on her middle toe. On the floor near the girl are shopping bags, with soft tissue paper between clothes. Cleo's hands take the bags. Then, a long shot of Cleo running down the steps of the building, a pink skirt billowing around her long legs.

The closing shot is of Cleo sitting in a convertible, eating an apple, her face tilted towards the sun.

"Cleo, it's really good. And so are you."

"I'm so young."

"Yes. You're even more beautiful now," he said. "But my God you were so talented. Do you miss it?"

176   TESS THOMPSON

"A lot, actually, but I said goodbye to it a long time ago."

"I'm sorry," he said. Their glasses were empty. "I'm a little drunk."

She laughed. "Are you? After a couple drinks?"

"Three," he said. "I don't think I can drive." He knew, conceivably, that he could walk home. But he wanted to stay. That was all. He wanted to be wherever Cleo Tanner was and he'd find any excuse to do so.

"You're kind of a lightweight."

"You're a bad influence. I hardly ever drink," he said.

She grinned, her voice teasing. "You'll have to stay over until you sober up. I'll make up the couch for you."

He looked at her, long and hard. "I don't know if that's a good idea."

"Don't be ridiculous. It's fine." But there was a flicker of fear behind her eyes. "I have extra sheets but they're flannel."

"It's fine," he said.

She stood and disappeared into her bedroom, coming out a few moments later with a stack of blue plaid flannel sheets and a white blanket. Unfolding the sheet, she leaned over the couch, her T-shirt opening slightly, revealing a lacy pink bra over round breasts. He averted his eyes and helped her to tuck the sheet between the sofa cushions.

"This couch isn't bad to sleep on," she said, stuffing a pillow into one of the cases. Her voice was strange, back in her throat as if she might choke. "Well, I've never actually slept on it. Or had anyone else sleep on it."

"It'll be fine."

"Took me three years to pay it off. One of those places that will let you pick your own fabric. I have an extra toothbrush. Brand new. I'll put it out for you."

"Thanks."

She straightened. "Well then, I'll just let you alone. And there are extra towels under the sink if you want to shower in the morning." She put her hand on the frame of the door, and he noticed that it was shaking. "Anyway, we have a big day tomorrow. What with Scott and all."

"Right," he said, stuffing his hands in his pants pockets.

"Okay, well, goodnight."

After she was gone, he used the bathroom. The new toothbrush was still in its package. But there was no toothpaste. Should he bother her for it? Would she fall apart if he knocked on her bedroom door? He stepped out of the bathroom. And there she was, no more than two feet from the door. "I have toothpaste," she said, holding it out to him.

"Great."

"I'm sorry," she said.

"For what?"

"Forgetting the toothpaste."

"Don't worry about it."

Then she was gone, her bedroom door shutting firmly behind her.

After he brushed his teeth, he lay on the couch, his mind still foggy from the wine. He imagined what she was doing in her bedroom. The idea of her undressing caused him to flop and toss for at least an hour before he fell into a restless sleep.

Chapter Twenty-Six

SYLVIA SAT UP IN BED with a start and looked at the clock. It was four in the morning. Madison hadn't cried since ten the night before. Why hadn't she cried? Sylvia threw off the covers, running towards the nursery, her body covered in perspiration. But she was there, pink and plump, sleeping peacefully, her chest rising and falling. Sylvia put her head on the railing of the crib and felt the sort of love she'd never thought possible. It was there in every nerve ending, and in her flesh, her bones, her organs. Nothing would ever matter to her as much as this child.

But she was alone in this love, she thought, and sank into the rocking chair, watching her daughter sleep. The thoughts came in a spiral, twisting until she felt the breaking point come. Could she do this on her own? Would she be a good enough mother? If only Nick loved her. The three of them could be a family. But it was impossible, just as it had always been. He loved Cleo.

No one would love this child as she did; there was no father to share and brag with about milestones, like first steps or soccer games or proms or weddings. She was alone in this and she was afraid - more afraid than she'd ever been in her life. She put her face in her hands, crying silent tears, ever mindful not to wake her sleeping baby but allowing herself to mourn the end of her marriage and the futility of her feelings for Nick.

She dried her eyes and moved to the window, peering out into the dark yard, then looked up to see Nick standing in the nursery doorway. Her hands went to her nightshirt. Was it even buttoned? And her hair? When was the last time she brushed it?

He smiled and said, "Hey." He looked haggard. His clothes were rumpled and his hair looked like he'd been tearing at it with his hands. "Are you just getting home?" she asked him, motioning for him to follow her into the hallway.

"Yes. It's Saturday. Late night. Did I scare you?"

"No, just startled me." She searched his face. His eyes were bloodshot. "You must be exhausted. I don't know how you work these hours."

"You get used to it." He shrugged and put his hands in his pockets. He looked at the floor and then up at her. "I saw the light on in your bedroom and wanted to make sure you were okay."

"Oh, well, that was sweet of you. She's been asleep since ten. I thought she was dead." She smiled. "No, I really did."

He chuckled. "I know you did. I know you. But I'm surprised at her. That's really great for a baby this age. She's a sweetheart. Like her mother."

She leaned against the wall. "That was a really nice thing to say."

"I only point out the obvious."

They stood like that for a moment, gazing at one another. "Have you been crying?" he asked, his brows wrinkling.

"No," she said, her eyes darting to the floor.

"Liar," he said softly. He stepped closer. "It's all right to feel bad, y'know. Or scared."

"I am scared. Terrified, actually."

"You're not alone. You know that, right?" He paused and reached out his hand, lightly touching her bare arm. "You have Cleo. And me."

Her heart felt soft suddenly, like he'd just wrapped a warm blanket around her. "Thank you."

"Most especially me."

She couldn't think. Why was he so close to her? What was in his eyes?

"Sylvia, would you ever consider me?"

"Consider?" What did he mean?

He flushed. She'd never seen him fumble. "Consider seeing me. I know it's probably too soon and everything."

"What are you saying?"

"I'm in love with you, Sylvia. I have been forever."

"With me?"

He scooted backwards down the hallway, with his hands out in front of him as if he were shielding himself from harm. "But I know you could never love me. I just had to tell you. Finally. Or I thought I might die."

Thoughts were scrambled in her mind. He loved her? But what about Cleo? "Nick," she said, so faintly it was almost a whisper. "Stop."

He did so, gazing at her. "I shouldn't have said anything."

"What about Cleo?"

"What about her?" he said, his forehead wrinkling.

"Aren't you in love with her?"

He smiled, shaking his head. "No. She's like a sister. As a matter of fact, she knows I've been in love with you for years."

"She never said a word."

"I made her promise," said Nick.

"But why haven't you ever told me?"

"Because I'm not good enough for you. And then you married that idiot. But lately, being here with you, I can't take it. I don't think I can live here any longer." His eyes were red. "And I love Madison already. It's going to kill me to leave you two but I can't do this. It hurts too much."

She put out her hands. "Nick. I've been in love with you since the first time I ever met you. All this time I thought you loved Cleo. I've never told a soul. Not even Cleo."

His face changed as she spoke, from grief to confusion to something that couldn't be mistaken for anything other than joy. "You love me?"

"So much it hurts. I loved you when I married Malcolm. All these years I've been trying to set it aside. You have no idea how I've tried. But it's no use."

Suddenly he was standing beside her. He brushed a finger on the side of her face and then picked up her left hand. "See that there," he said, pointing to the line that curved from the middle part of her hand to the edge of her wrist. "It's your life line. You're going to have a long life. You're already here," he said, indicating the first third of the line. "I've already missed so much." He dropped her hand and tilted her face towards him. "Is it really true? You feel the same way?"

"Yes. A thousand times, yes."

He leaned closer, as if to kiss her.

"Wait," she said, putting one hand on his chest and the other over her mouth. "I have to brush my teeth. And I smell like baby vomit."

"You smell awesome. Like always." He pinned her against the wall with his thighs and kissed her neck, once, lightly. She shivered and felt her body push into him, despite her intention to keep her wits. He put his hands on either side of her hips and pressed gently. "Fine. I'll wait. But hurry."

She took his hand and led him into her bedroom. "Just give me a minute to clean up. I can't remember when I showered last."

He smiled, sitting on the edge of the bed. "I've waited this long, I can wait another five minutes."

Just then they heard the baby crying. He put up his hand. "I'll feed her and change her. You take a shower."

"Thank you," she said, feeling like she'd just won the lottery. She escaped into the bathroom. Once there, she examined herself in the mirror. She really was a mess: dark circles under her eyes, uncombed hair, pajamas stained with formula.

She showered, shampooing her hair and shaving her legs. Afterwards she rubbed lotion all over her body and dabbed a little perfume on the back of her neck and combed through her long brown hair. She looked at herself in the mirror. Things were not as firm as they should be. She'd taken too much time off from yoga, what with all the in-vitro tries. It couldn't be helped. Using her electric toothbrush, she scrubbed her teeth and then swished a generous amount of Listerine around her mouth. There was a short, silk robe hanging on the back of the bathroom door. When had she worn it last? She couldn't remember. She slipped into it. The soft material against her bare skin made her shiver.

When she opened the door of her bathroom, he was there, perched on the edge of the bed, still fully clothed. His eyes lingered on her face before moving down the length of her body. "You look amazing in that robe," he said. "Truly."

He stood, coming towards her, holding her gaze in his. She leaned against the wall, letting herself melt into his chocolate eyes, until he reached for her and pulled her into his arms.

"It's you," she said, wrapping her arms around his neck. He smelled so good. She closed her eyes, waiting to feel his mouth on hers.

Then he kissed her, gently at first and then harder, pushing her against the wall. "You're unbelievable," he said, kissing her neck and pulling gently on the lobe of her ear with his mouth, which made her shudder. Then he was back at her mouth, kissing her hard again until their breath was ragged.

She buried her fingers in his hair, pressing against his body as his hands seemed to move all over her at once. He caressed the sides of her thighs and her backside, and then he reached under her robe to graze her breasts with his thumbs. She quivered and moaned softly against his mouth.

"Are we moving too fast?" He pulled back.

"No," she whispered, fumbling with the top button of his shirt. "Not fast enough."

He continued to kiss her as he unfastened the remaining buttons. Her hands moved over his chest, his stomach. He was solid and muscular. She tugged off his shirt and tossed it on the floor, taking in his bare torso. It was better than she'd imagined all the years she'd watched him. He groaned when she unbuttoned his jeans and tugged them below his hips with her hands. He pulled away for a brief, cold moment to slide his legs out of the pants and take his socks off, tossing them to the floor. Then he stood and pressed against her. "Please tell me now if you don't want this because I don't know if I can stop after much longer," he muttered, pushing her harder into the wall.

"Don't stop," she whispered, her hands in his hair. "Please don't stop."

He untied her robe and it fell around her ankles. He grabbed the backs of her legs and hoisted her up around his waist, continuing to kiss her as they crossed the room, then tossed her onto the bed as if she weighed nothing. Next, he moved his mouth down her neck, her breasts, her stomach. He pushed her legs open and splayed his hands over her inner thighs, using his thumbs to stroke her until she arched up with her hips, wanting more than anything to feel him inside her.

"Do you want me to use anything?"

"No, it doesn't matter." I can't get pregnant, she thought. "Please, I can't stand it another second." She moaned as she put her hands on either side of his face, pulling him up to her and wrapping her legs around his hips. "Please, now." And he entered her, thrusting hard and fast until they climaxed together.

A few minutes later, sweaty and spent, he pulled her into his arms and kissed her soft, lingering at her mouth. "Give me a few minutes and let's try that again. Slow this time."

She nodded, smiling and running her hands down his chest. "If you insist."

Chapter Twenty-Seven

WHEN CLEO WOKE THE MORNING AFTER Peter slept on her couch, it was after eight. How had she slept so late? Was Peter still here? She opened her bedroom door a crack, looking towards the couch. No Peter, just the sheets and blankets folded into neat squares on one end of the couch. She went into the kitchen and started her coffee brewing in the single cup coffee maker Sylvia had gotten her for her last birthday. She watched as the coffee dripped slowly into the cup. Drip, drip, drip, into the lone cup. One cup of coffee at a time was all she needed. There was no one here to share it with.

She thought of Peter. How nice it had been to share a meal and music with someone. *Not just anyone. Peter. Just Peter.*

She glanced at the clock. In less than seven hours she would get to see him in preparation for her pretend date with Scott. The day seemed long, stretching out in front of her like empty space.

She remembered, then, that she hadn't checked on Mrs. Lombardi over in 3C for two days.

After a shower and her cup of coffee she went across the hallway and knocked on Mrs. Lombardi's door. There were footsteps and then Mrs. Lombardi stood in the doorway, smiling, with her hands on her hips. "Cleo. Get in here and tell me all about these young men that keep showing up here."

"I'll tell you all about it if you let me come in and make your breakfast."

"I just happen to have some fresh eggs." Mrs. Lombardi stepped aside so Cleo could pass.

Over scrambled eggs and toast, Cleo told her the whole story. When she was done, Mrs. Lombardi's wrinkled face was pinched with concern. "I'm so worried about Sylvia," said Mrs. Lombardi. "And this poor little girl they murdered. It's just too awful."

"I know. It's sickening. So you can see why I had to do something."

Mrs. Lombardi rose to her feet, tucking a strand of hair behind Cleo's ear. "You're a brave girl. Just be careful."

She felt herself soften under the older woman's touch. This is what it would be like if her mother were still alive. She could ask her for advice. She could talk to her about things. An image of Peter's mother came to her then. There was something wonderful about Louise, maternal and nurturing but also interesting and vibrant. The mother anyone would want.

Mrs. Lombardi carried their plates to the sink. "Now, I have to run out and get Stewie's medicine."

"Medicine?"

"Well, while you've been busy working undercover, I found Stewie a cat psychologist."

"A what?"

"A psychologist. She came here to the house and looked Stewie straight in the eyes." Mrs. Lombardi held up her hands, dramatic like a dance move in a musical. "And she diagnosed him right away. Schizophrenic."

Cleo felt her mouth drop open. "Is there such a thing in a cat?"

"Apparently. I know. It was a surprise to me too. But, I mean, it makes perfect sense, given all his different moods."

"A cat shrink?" Cleo shook her head.

"Psychologist."

Cleo made a mental note – *do not leave Mrs. Lombardi alone for two days in a row.* "How did you find this person?"

Mrs. Lombardi looked at her with an expression of pure innocence. "She was at bingo the other night, passing out fliers to all the ladies who love our cats. She refers to herself as 'The Cat Soother'."

"*The*?" said Cleo.

"Well, there aren't that many of them in the world," said Mrs. Lombardi, sounding defensive. "Anyway, I just have to run down to her office and pick up some pills."

"How much is that going to cost you?"

Mrs. Lombardi busied herself at the sink. "Never mind that."

"How much?"

"Hundred and fifty," Mrs. Lombardi mumbled.

"Well, how are you going to eat for the rest of the month?"

"I'm not that hungry. Not compared to taking care of Stewie."

How she wanted to say – *that awful cat needs to be euthanized instead of using up your small social security checks.* But she held her tongue, her love for Mrs. Lombardi outweighing her sense of righteousness. Mrs. Lombardi loved Stewie. Obviously, there was nothing rational about love. She would just have to bring leftovers from her dad's dinners, make a trip to Costco and buy one of those enormous trays of breakfast pastries to get her through the month. Mrs. Lombardi, not tempted by most foods, did love sweets.

"You want me to water your plants on the balcony while you're gone?" said Cleo.

"That would be lovely." Mrs. Lombardi smiled widely. "You're so thoughtful."

Cleo carried a full watering can out to Mrs. Lombardi's balcony. The sky was overcast but it was warmer today, perhaps in the middle sixties, which in June was expected. Mrs. Lombardi's plants of various sizes were lined up on the far left of the rectangular balcony. Cleo sprinkled water on the spider plant in the one hanging basket first and then leaned down to spray the snake plant and Peace Lily next. The watering can was empty already, so she turned to go inside.

And there was Stewie, blocking the door. "Shoo, Stewie." Waving her hands, she moved towards him. He rose on his hind legs and hissed, batting his front paws like a boxer.

Cleo took a step back. "C'mon, Stewie. I need to get inside."

He curled himself into a ball. He yawned, as if to say, *I'm bored with this already.* Should she just wait for him to fall asleep and then make her move to get inside? But his eyes were open, glittering in the light, never moving from her face. This was ridiculous. She couldn't allow herself to be scared by a common household cat.

But this was no ordinary cat. This cat had mental problems. It didn't take a cat shrink to discern that truth.

She took two steps towards him, holding the empty watering can in front of her like a shield. Again, he rose on his hind legs and this time he growled and then hissed. Did his eyes just shoot out bolts of light? She backed up, all the way to the edge of the balcony. Now, she realized, she really needed to use the bathroom. How long until Mrs. Lombardi came home?

Stewie paced back and forth, back and forth, never taking his eyes from her. She watched him, making eye contact. What was it there in his green eyes? Intimidation tactic? Sure. Or was it something else?

"What do you want, Stewie? Some of my chicken cacciatore? I'll bring you some next time I make it. I won't even discourage Mrs. L from giving it to you. I promise."

He stopped pacing. He hissed, baring his teeth.

She had her cell phone in her pocket. She carried it everywhere these days in case Sylvia needed her. But whom would she call for help? Mrs. Lombardi did not have a cell phone, only barely knew how to call out on her landline. Cleo knew she couldn't call Sylvia; she would not find this amusing in the midst of taking care of a newborn. Her dad was at work and almost never answered his cell phone. Still, maybe he would this time. She dialed his number, keeping her eyes on Stewie while it rang. After five or so rings, it went to voicemail. Now what?

Peter. She could call Peter. Could she call Peter over something so silly? Of course she couldn't. He was working on solving a murder. He didn't have time for this nonsense. This was embarrassing anyway, trapped on a balcony by a crazy cat.

She moved towards Stewie once again. There was no way she was letting this mutant creature get the better of her. This time he lunged at her. She screamed and dropped the watering can. Stewie went back to his place in front of the entryway.

She dialed Peter's number. He picked up after the first ring. "Cleo Tanner, what's up?"

"Hi Peter. I'm…well…I need your help."

"What's going on? Moore?" His voice was louder than the moment before. He cared about her, she thought, warmth spreading from her stomach all the way down to the tips of her toes.

"No, nothing like that," she said. "It's embarrassing. I don't know if I can tell you."

"Hey, you're scaring me. What's going on?"

"I'm trapped on Mrs. Lombardi's balcony."

"Wait? What?"

"You heard me."

"Did you lock yourself out?" he asked, sounding amused now.

"Um. No. It's Stewie. He won't let me inside."

"Stewie? The crazy cat you told me about on our drive to the coast?"

"The very same."

He started to laugh. Loud. The kind of sound you made when your head was thrown back. She'd never heard him laugh like that before.

"Hey, it's not funny," she said. "I really can't get inside and I have to go to the bathroom."

"Okay, I'm sorry. I'll be right over." His voice was shaking as he tried to control his laughter.

"This is serious," she said, smiling in spite of the fact that it annoyed her that he didn't understand the gravity of the situation.

Just then, Stewie rolled onto his back and stretched, meowing in a way that could only be interpreted as contentment before strolling into the kitchen. "Wait. He just got up."

"You're kidding?"

"I'm not."

"Does this mean I don't get to rescue you?"

She laughed. "I guess not. I'm kind of disappointed."

"Me too. I have kitty handcuffs and everything."

"Handcuffs?" She let her voice lilt up, teasing.

"Whoa. Are you flirting with me, Cleo Tanner?"

"Of course not," she said, sobering instantly and speaking in her best prim and proper voice. But she had been. She was flirting with Peter Ball. What was she doing? What was he doing to her?

There was a short silence between them before he said, "Well, I'll see you later at my place. Come around five."

"Got it." She paused, tiptoeing through the apartment entryway, just in case Stewie decided to slip into his evil persona again. "And thanks for being willing to rescue me."

"Anytime," he said, sounding sincere now in a way that made her heart pound. "And I'm glad it was me you called."

"Me too," she said, flushing with heat as she hung up the phone. *I'm glad it was me you called.*

Stewie was on the couch, licking his paws. He raised his head and blinked at her and she heard a voice inside her head, clear as if there was someone in the room. *My work here is done.*

Was Stewie talking to her?

If so, his voice sounded just like Gilbert Gottfried, the comedian she remembered from watching Hollywood Squares with her mother years ago. He had been the voice of the duck on Aflac Insurance commercials. How she knew this, she didn't know. Peter was right. She needed to get out more. Regardless, Stewie, the crazy cat, sounded like a guy imitating a duck. Well, of course he did, she thought, even as she chastised herself for clearly losing her mind in the middle of an ordinary June morning.

Chapter Twenty-Eight

AFTER GETTING CLEO WIRED, Peter stood at the window of his home office, trying to concentrate as they went over tactics on how to get Moore to talk. But she was wearing a red dress, fitted around her waist and slit up the side to reveal her muscular legs, her red toenails poking out from high-heeled sandals. She was flushed and her hair hung in long waves about bare shoulders. It seemed to him she was the most beautiful woman in the world.

He began to pace the room while they talked but she sat calmly in the chair at his desk, her legs crossed so that if he allowed himself to look he could see almost to her mid-thigh. He went to the window and looked at the Olympic mountain range, still encased in snow. "The weather's good," he said. "That bodes well."

"What?"

"Nothing. Just something my father used to say." He pivoted from the window and saw that she watched him, not with the distance she'd possessed when they first met but something that could almost be described as open. Was it possible she was softening towards him? Were a few of her barriers lessening? She'd called him for help earlier. He almost smiled, thinking of her on the balcony, trapped by a cat. Only Cleo Tanner would get herself into that kind of situation.

He adored her. That was the truth.

"What's wrong with you tonight?" she asked. "You seem antsy."

"Honestly, I'm having second thoughts about you doing this. We don't know enough about this guy to know how dangerous he is."

"We're doing this," she said.

"I think we need to tell Misty and Jo and Sylvia the truth. Tomorrow."

"I was thinking the same thing," she said, wringing her hands. "As much as I don't want to."

"I'll help you. Jack went down yesterday and brought Misty back with him from Legley Bay. I do not want her out of our sight as long as the midwife knows what she looks like and knows Misty could identify her."

She stood, straightening her dress and picking up her purse to rummage inside. "I just want to get Moore to admit something tonight." She went to the oval mirror that hung by the door and covered her lips with pink gloss. He watched her reflection until she glanced up, catching him.

"What?" she asked.

"You look great in that dress. That's all." He came to stand behind her, wanting to take her into his arms, to feel what her body was like next to him. He stared at her, taking in every detail of her face: the way her chin came to a point, her high cheekbones, and her hair the color of straw and honey.

Her gaze locked with his in the mirror's refection. "Peter," she said, her voice a whisper. "What is it?"

"You're beautiful."

She closed her eyes. And she twitched, like she might if she were preparing to dive backwards into a pool. Her body was just brushed up against his. "When you look at me that way, I feel like it's true."

"It is," he whispered. His arms, as if they had a mind of their own, went around her waist. He breathed in her scent, magnolias and caramel. How he ached to feel her skin under her clothes. He spoke softly in her ear. "Cleo Tanner, what're you doing to me?"

"I don't know," she said.

He pulled her even closer against him, one hand splayed just below her breasts where the wire was attached. With the other hand, he moved her hair all to one side and watched her in the mirror before leaning down and brushing the spot just below her ear with his lips. He felt her shudder. He turned her so that she faced him. "Would you let me kiss you, Cleo Tanner?"

"I don't know if I can. Or if I should. You only kiss women you don't plan on having in your life for long."

"What if I'm different now?"

"Different?"

"Since I met you," he said.

"What're you saying?"

"That you're special. And that I adore you."

Her eyes widened. "You do?"

"Yes." He paused, tracing her jawline with his fingers. "I'll be gentle," he said, wanting to smile but feeling instead like he couldn't get enough air in his lungs.

Just then the door opened. It was Jack. Seeing them, Jack jerked back, his eyes on the floor. "I'm so sorry. I didn't realize you were still here. I just came to borrow a book for Misty."

Cleo flushed red as Peter stepped away from her. "It's fine. Cleo has to go anyway."

"Right. I do."

"Oh, well, good luck," said Jack, backing out the door, still unable to look in their direction.

Peter took her hands in his. "We'll discuss this kiss sometime later. Right now, the main thing is for you to be careful, stay in public places with him. Don't compromise your safety. And don't hesitate to call for help. Even if it blows your cover."

She put her purse on her shoulder. "I won't."

"I'll be listening every moment. You ready to do this, then?"

"As ready as I'll ever be," she said.

Later, from inside the van, Peter and Brent listened to Cleo and Moore talking through dinner. The conversation was mostly benign: talk of television they both liked, Moore's travels in Europe - none of it incriminating or noteworthy. But towards the end of dinner, Cleo did something surprising.

"Would you like to come back to my place? For a nightcap?"

"Love to," said Moore.

Of course he would, the bastard. But this was not the plan. She was supposed to stay in the restaurant, under the watchful gaze of other patrons, not bring him up to her apartment.

Peter looked over at Brent. "What's she doing? I told her distinctly to stay in public places."

"She's got good instincts. Must see something there that might work," said Brent.

"But that's when people get in trouble. You know that."

Brent looked at him with a strange expression. "Dude, what's going on here? She's perfectly fine."

"Whatever," he muttered under his breath.

Brent drove, with Peter still monitoring Cleo's wire from the back of the van. They followed Moore's car onto the freeway and over the West Seattle Bridge until they came to Cleo's apartment. It was harder to hear what was being said because of the background noise in the car but he made out Cleo telling him how long she'd lived in the same place.

"Renting for that long," said Moore. "You should buy something."

Cleo didn't say anything. Peter had to smile, knowing how much she hated it when people said that to her. They saw Moore turn down Cleo's street and find parking right in front of her apartment building. Brent circled the block, waiting for them to go inside so as not to draw attention. Peter heard a rustle on the microphone as Cleo got out of the car.

Just as Brent came back down the street, parking half a block from Moore's car, Peter saw them walk inside her building.

A few minutes later, he heard Cleo tell Moore to have a seat and she'd fetch them something to drink. After a few minutes she said, "I hope a beer's okay. It's all I have."

Good girl. Don't give him the Macallan, he thought.

"Sure. It's fine. Come sit with me on the couch?" said Moore.

A second or two later, the microphone went to static, like there was something pressing against it. He heard Cleo, say, "No, please don't."

"What's the matter?" asked Moore, like he was trying to tease her but sounding more like he was irritated. "Isn't that why you invited me up?"

"No, actually," said Cleo.

"Guess I read you wrong," said Moore.

"It's fine. I'm just not comfortable after only one date," she said.

Peter rocked back in his chair, fidgeting with his earphones. "I need to go up there," he said.

Brent was leaning forward, listening intently. "No, she's got it handled."

Then they heard Moore say, "I guess I should get going anyway. Tomorrow's an early day."

"Sure," said Cleo.

They heard the door open and shut. A few minutes later Moore came out of the building and got into his car, pulling out quickly and driving away.

Using his cell phone, Peter called Cleo. She picked up on the first ring. "You want me to come up?" he said.

"Yes."

After Brent drove away in the van, Peter ran across the street to her apartment. She opened the door before he knocked, moving aside to let him pass through.

"You okay?" he said.

"Little shaky. He tried to kiss me."

"So I gathered." *Bastard.*

"And he was aggressive about it. Almost leaped on me on the couch." She paced near the window, reaching inside her dress and pulling off the wire.

He went to her and put his hand on her arm to still her. "Cleo. Stop. Look at me."

She turned to him, her hands fluttering at her thighs. "Yes?" she whispered.

He put his hands on the upper part of her arms, looking into her eyes. "You're safe now."

"Yes. Of course. I'm being ridiculous."

"Why did you bring him here?" He hated the accusatory tone to his voice. Keep it business, he told himself. But it was impossible. Cleo Tanner was not business. The thought of that idiot putting his hands on her made his stomach turn.

She averted her gaze. "I don't know. I guess I thought he might tell me something helpful if we were alone." She looked up at him, her forehead wrinkling as if she were worried. "Are you mad?"

He softened. "Of course not. But you scared me. I told you to be careful."

Her arms were still resting by her side. "I know. I'm sorry."

"It's all right," he said. "But I was dying out there. I can't stand the thought of his hands on you." The last part came out of his mouth before he could stop himself.

"I didn't think he'd be so aggressive," she said, her eyes big.

He put his arms around her waist. "You're so damn beautiful he probably couldn't stop himself." He pulled her tighter. She was solid, muscular against him. "Just let me kiss you. Once. That's all I ask," he said.

"Why?" she said, still watching him with those eyes the color of new growth fir.

"Because I can't think of anything but you. All the time. Every minute."

"Peter, really?"

He held his breath for what might come next.

"I'm perfectly fine alone," she said.

"Obviously." He paused, his voice dry. "Living in here like a nun for the last ten years."

"Eight in this apartment. Two in L.A.," she said, under her breath.

He moved his left hand up the center of her dress, slipping his finger below the fabric by her collarbone. "Don't you want to remember what it feels like to be alive?"

He felt her catch her breath. Her arms went around his neck. She spoke softly, near his ear. "It's true that I've been half alive. And now, here you are, out of nowhere. But I'm terrified of having my heart broken. How do I know it won't be cast aside like with all your other women?"

"I have your heart in my hands and I take that very seriously. Despite how I look on paper I know what it is to hold something precious. I'm not going to hurt you."

She removed her arms from his neck, backing up slightly so she was looking into his eyes once again. "I feel awake for the first time in ten years. And suddenly I want more than anything else in the world to be kissed properly by someone who loves me. Just one more time before I die. But I understand it's too much to hope for anyway."

"What is?" he asked, gently.

"That you could love me. That this is anything other than chemistry. This is the way of the world. We love the wrong people. We love the ones that don't love us, or are bad to us, or can't love us properly, or are simply not available. It can never be just right. Simple. A snap. I already had that once. You don't get it twice."

"Who says?"

"I say."

"Well what if you're wrong?" He ran his finger along her bottom lip. It felt just as he thought it would, like cream tastes, silky and filling. "Cleo Tanner, it's time for you to get off the sidelines. Learn to feel again." He paused, looking into her eyes that stared back at him with uncertainty. "Just let me kiss you. Once. Let me show you what I feel."

"Yes. Do it now," she said. "Before I lose my nerve."

He leaned in and kissed her, soft, knowing he held a skittish, frightened creature in his hands and wanting more than anything to treat her with the care and love she deserved. An image of the hush of a first winter's snow, the way it covers every imperfection of a landscape and becomes flawless under muted white ice, floated across his mind for a brief moment, as her mouth responded to his. Then he drew back, watching her face, but her eyes were closed, her lips soft and vulnerable. He leaned in and kissed her again, this time pulling her closer and pressing his mouth harder against her. He felt her body yield, just ever so slightly against him. He kissed her a third time and this time she wrapped her arms around his neck and pressed into him with her entire body. Then he lifted his mouth from hers for a brief moment, catching his breath, and kissed her again, moving his hands under the skirt of her dress and caressing the bare skin of her legs with his thumbs. He felt her breath catch. She whispered into his ear, "Let's go into the bedroom."

Chapter Twenty-Nine

BY THE FOURTH KISS, Cleo could think of nothing but wanting more. She was helpless against his mouth that both pulled and pressed, his tongue that made artful darts against hers. She felt breathless, every nerve-ending springing to life from its long-dormant state. She surprised herself when she suggested the bedroom, knew she was heading towards danger but the force of wanting him was too strong.

He did not hesitate at her suggestion, taking her hand and leading her into the dark bedroom.

Near the bed, she stiffened, unsure suddenly and afraid. He turned on the lamp so the room was dimly lit and their bodies made long shadows. "I want to be able to see you," he said as he came to stand beside her, pulling her into his arms again and kissing her before moving his mouth to the base of her neck and then her collarbone, until she shivered. "You might have to take charge," she said. "I'm out of practice."

"I'm the man for the job." His voice was rough.

"I'm afraid. All of a sudden," she said, pressing into him.

He looked into her eyes. "You can trust me. Say the word and I'll stop."

Unable to speak, she nodded.

"Lift your arms over your head," he said.

She did so and he tugged at her dress. He kissed her again as he slid her zipper down and then pulled the dress over her head. Then his hands were inside the back of her panties, caressing her hips. He pushed her gently so that she was sitting on the side of the bed. First, he unhooked the back of her bra and removed it, gazing at her breasts, hesitating for a split-second before taking in a deep breath.

He slid her panties off, all the way down her legs and then, kneeling on the floor, slowly made his way up, kissing and flicking with his tongue every inch or so until he reached her hips and then guided her onto the middle of the her bed, all the while kissing her. "Don't move," he said, unbuttoning his shirt. She watched, hungry, for what he looked like under his clothes. He did not disappoint. His chest and shoulders were muscular, his stomach lean. He stood and pulled off his pants, tossing them onto the chair next to her bed. Shy, she moved her eyes to the ceiling, not wanting to see him take off the last article of clothing. She heard him take something out of his wallet. A condom, she thought, grateful that he had the sense to think practically.

He joined her on the bed, hovering over her as he trailed his mouth slowly down her neck, her chest, and then to her breasts, stopping to stroke one nipple and then the other with his tongue. She arched her back, heard herself moan softly, and then he put his hands on her thighs, pushing them open and stroking her with his fingers and thumb, until she was writhing under his touch.

"Can I put my mouth there?" he said.

She could only whisper yes, unsure if the word actually came out or not. He moved down her body until his mouth was on her and his tongue darted and sucked until she exploded with a shudder and then another and then the last one so hard against him that her hips arched and she cried out.

He moved up next to her, putting his ear against her left breast, as if to hear how hard her heart pounded, letting her catch her breath for a moment before kissing her again and moving his hands over every inch of her skin, slowly making her excited again. "Hold on," he muttered, reaching for the condom he'd left on the bedside table. She kept her eyes closed, hearing the package rip open and then a moment later he was on top of her. Then he entered her, slowly, carefully, as if he were worried he might hurt her. But she was ready for him, wet and excited and she urged him farther inside by wrapping her legs around him and thrusting upwards, her hands on his shoulders. He thrust shallow and then deep, teasing her almost, until she couldn't stand it any longer and pressed her hands into his backside, urging him inside deeper and harder. He did what she wanted and then she was out of her head, feeling only the pleasure and yearning even as she watched his face in the light. His eyes were closed, his face tense with pleasure, and the proof of his desire made her even more excited, and then the climax came, even bigger this time, and she moaned, beyond sense, beyond thought. As her climax subsided, he whispered her name and made a small sound at the back of his throat, and then thrust once more, hard, and then cried out too, shuddering as he emptied into her.

Afterwards, he buried his face in her neck as their breathing returned to normal. "Cleo Tanner, you're a woman of surprises," he said. "Thank you for trusting me."

Then he rolled to the side and disappeared into the bathroom. While he was away, she slipped between the sheets and stared at the ceiling. How had she let this happen? How had she allowed herself to get so carried away?

He came out of the bathroom and joined her on the bed. She rolled over, resting her head on her arm. What she saw there surprised her. His gaze was tender, searching. "Are you all right?" he said.

She nodded. "Little scared."

"Why?"

"I'm afraid you're going to break my heart."

"Maybe it's the other way around." He pushed back a lock of hair that had fallen into her eyes. "I can't compete against a memory."

She touched his face now, running a finger along his jawline. "I haven't thought of him for days. All I can think of is you."

He smiled. "Really?"

"Really," she said. She ran her fingers through his hair. It was damp and curled around his ear. "Peter, I had no idea it could be this way. I was so young the last time."

He smiled. "Give me the chance and I'll dedicate my life to making up for lost time."

"Is it different between us than with your other women?"

"Cleo Tanner, since the first time I ever met you, I can't think about anyone else. This thing between us is different than anything I've ever experienced. I didn't know I could feel this way."

"Really?"

"Really. Have a little faith. I won't let you down."

"Will you stay with me tonight?" she said.

"I'll stay as long as you like. But I'm a terrible sleeper. Restless. Wake up twenty times a night. Usually can't fall asleep until way past midnight. So if you wake and I'm not in bed, I'm just in the other room. I don't want to keep you up."

"Will you at least stay in bed until I fall asleep?"

"Of course." He shifted onto his back and pulled her into his arms. She closed her eyes, smelling his scent mingled with her own, but her mind was racing still, every nerve ending alive. A few minutes passed and then she felt Peter jerk slightly. She raised her head to look at him. He was asleep. Well, how was that, she thought, smiling. She nestled farther into his chest and let herself drift away.

She woke the next morning to the sound of Peter in the shower. She lay there for a moment, watching the morning sun peeking in between the cracks in the shades. Birds chirped outside her bedroom window. It was an ordinary June day, and yet, everything in her world was different than two weeks before. She loved a man - a great man. How was this possible? And Sylvia was a mother. For now. Cleo's heart raced, her mind tumbling and turning over all the possible outcomes of this situation and none of them seemed positive. And how could she tell her best friend in the world that the sweet baby she thought of as her own might not be hers to keep? But surely they could come up with some kind of compromise with Madison's birth family. Jo Johnson was a good woman. She might see right away that Sylvia was kind and good and that she loved Madison with her whole heart.

She got out of bed and put on a robe, knocking on the bathroom door. "Come on in," he called to her.

He was just getting out of the shower when she opened the door. He grinned at her. "Good morning," he said.

She blushed, unable to look at him. "Morning," she mumbled, reaching for her toothbrush.

"You want to hand me a towel?" he asked, a tease in his voice.

"Sure." She opened the cabinet under the sink and grabbed a clean one, handing it to him without meeting his eyes, and then turned back to the sink, brushing her teeth. In the mirror she saw Peter rubbing his towel through his hair. "I should shower too," she said.

He wrapped the towel around his waist. "Absolutely." He reached for her, taking her chin in one hand and forcing her to look at him. "Do that. And then come find me. It's still early. We've plenty of time before we have to go to Sylvia's."

She felt tears start at the back of her eyes, and she began to tremble. "Okay."

"What is it?" he said, his hands at her hips.

"I was just thinking about Sylvia. I'm so scared for her. I don't know if she'll survive if the baby gets taken from her."

"I know, sweetheart. I know."

"How can I tell her this today?"

"I'm going to be with you. I've got your back if you need me." He peered at her, looking right into her eyes. "What else?"

"I don't know. I'm overwhelmed. Last night. I'm frightened." She stopped, her voice shaking, unable to say exactly what she meant. *You made me feel again. I love you. I'm in way too deep.*

"Cleo, it's all right. I'm still here. And I feel the same way." He leaned down and kissed her so tenderly that she thought the tears might come in earnest. Then he untied her robe and pushed her against the sink. "I'm not going anywhere. You just have to trust me." He kissed her again. "Maybe you could shower later."

Chapter Thirty

SYLVIA HADN'T THOUGHT IT WAS POSSIBLE to have as much sex while continuing to care for a baby. Well, she hadn't thought it was possible to have this much sex, period. In the last two days, they had been all over one another every chance they could. Nick made love to her before he left for work in the late afternoon, and then woke her up when he came home at 2:30 a.m. In the morning, after she fed the baby and put her down for her mid-morning nap, they were at it again.

After he gave her the second orgasm of the morning, he rolled over, plopping onto the pillow and grinning at her. "You were worth waiting for, you know that? I never thought I could be this happy."

She gazed into his eyes. "I didn't either. Everything I've ever wanted just suddenly fell into my life. I'm scared it's going to end."

"Don't say that. Just be grateful. I'm not going anywhere."

"And I'm not going anywhere," she said, smiling.

"And Madison isn't going anywhere." He reached for her, drawing her towards him with his hands on her hips. "So just let me love you. And just be happy." He kissed her, gently at first and then harder, rolling on top of her.

"Yes. Just be happy," she said against his mouth, her heart beating wildly once again.

Chapter Thirty-One

IT WAS MID-MORNING BY THE TIME Peter and Cleo arrived at his apartment; they sat with Misty and Jack in the living room. Peter had called ahead to let Jack know they were on their way and had told his brother the news about Alicia's baby, asking him to help him tell Misty if he stumbled. "Of course, I will," Jack had said.

"How was your trip yesterday?" asked Peter. *Best to start with small talk,* he thought. *Or maybe not?* He shifted, uncomfortable, wishing he didn't have to tell them what he knew.

"Fine. Long. You know," said Jack.

"What is it?" Misty asked, sounding both fearful and impatient. "Did something happen?"

"We have something hard to tell you," said Peter.

She blinked, glancing between Peter and Jack. "Go ahead," she said.

"We think we might know where your sister's baby is. It'll require a DNA test but we're pretty sure we know who adopted her."

"How?" asked Misty.

"Because she has the same dimpled chin as your sister had," said Peter.

"What?" said Misty. "The baby has the same dimple?"

Cleo sat forward, her hands clasped over her knees. "The reason we know, and the whole reason I wanted to help with this case is because…" she trailed off, her eyes darting to Peter.

"We think your sister's baby is with Cleo's best friend," said Peter.

"She wanted a baby more than anything," said Cleo, with tears in her eyes. "She named her Madison and loves her very much."

"Does she know what happened?" Misty asked.

Cleo shook her head. "No. She'll be devastated to know the truth."

"And if it's true that the baby was essentially kidnapped, the adoption would be illegal," said Peter.

"Meaning?" asked Misty.

"That the state would first try to place the baby with a biological relative—your mother."

Misty sat staring into space for a moment, clearly trying to assimilate all this information at once. "My mother wants the baby," Misty said.

Peter's eyes flew to Cleo. She was pale and wringing her hands. "We know," he said. "What do you think about that?"

Misty folded her hands in her lap, as if she might pray. Her eyes flickered to the ceiling and then to Jack. "I feel disloyal saying this, but my mother, well, she's great, but with her job at the bar she just isn't around much and we're constantly broke. Alicia and I took care of one another for a long time. If we take the baby, I'll end up raising her and as much as I loved my sister and would love the baby too, I can't give up my dreams. Right, Mr. Ball? Isn't that right?"

"Misty and I talked about this a lot last night on our way back to Seattle," said Jack. "She doesn't want to take on the responsibility of a baby."

"But if my mother wants her, I don't see that I have much choice," said Misty. "Because my mother will think of it as all she has left."

"I'm sure something could be arranged so that you and your mother could be part of the baby's life," said Jack. "Do you think she'd be willing to think about a legal visitation schedule?"

Misty's eyes were glassy. "Maybe. But she's hurting. She isn't thinking rationally. You know what I mean?"

"Yes, we do," said Cleo. She looked over at Peter, her eyes worried. His heart thumped hard in his chest. He did not want Cleo hurting and worried. He wanted only to solve this mess, but there was nothing to do except tell everyone the truth.

Misty looked over at Jack. "I need to go home and talk to my mother about all this. I want her to hear it from me."

"Pack your stuff," said Jack. "I'll take you."

❋

Peter and Cleo went to Sylvia's next, parking in the curved driveway. Still in the car, he glanced over at her. She sat with her arms crossed, clearly tense. "You ready for this?"

"No. Never in a million years," said Cleo.

"You can do this. I've got your back. The truth will set us free."

Sylvia answered the door with baby Madison in her arms. Her face lit up when she saw Cleo. "Oh, I'm so happy to see you," she said, kissing her cheek. "Where have you been?" She looked at Peter, surprise crossing her features. "Who's this?"

"This is Peter Ball," said Cleo. "He's a detective."

Sylvia's face went from pleased to confused. "A detective?"

"And a friend," said Cleo. "We need to talk to you about something."

"Well, come on in," said Sylvia.

Walking behind Sylvia into the large sitting room, Peter caught a whiff of baby powder and honeysuckle.

They heard a voice from the kitchen. "Sweetie, was there someone at the door?" And then Nick appeared, wiping his hands on a towel. He stopped dead in his tracks when he saw Cleo. "Oh. Crap. Cleo. Hi."

Cleo's mouth flew open as if to say something but nothing came out.

Sylvia smiled, flushing, looking over at Cleo. "There are a few things I need to tell you, too."

"I guess," said Cleo, looking stunned.

"What brings you here?" said Sylvia, glancing at Peter with curiosity.

Cleo looked over at him, her eyes pleading for help. Knowing she needed him to tell Sylvia, he began with, "Cleo's been working undercover for the police."

Now Sylvia looked shocked. "What? Is this true, Cleo?"

"Yes," said Cleo. "I did it for you. For Madison." It came out of her mouth like a confession.

Sylvia went pale. "This is about Madison?"

Nick came to stand next to Sylvia. "Let's all sit down," he said, gesturing towards a sitting area near the large windows that overlooked Lake Washington. He looked over at Peter. "I've seen you at Cooper's. Is that right?"

"Yes. I was following Cleo," said Peter. He then told them as succinctly as possible everything they suspected about Scott Moore and his adoption fraud, ending with the murder of Alicia Johnson. "We're fairly certain Alicia Johnson was Madison's birth mother."

Sylvia's face was white and her fingers trembled as she ran them over the top of Madison's head. "Does the girl's family know about Madison?"

"Yes," Peter said. "They do now. But her mother didn't even know she was pregnant."

"Oh my God," said Sylvia.

"Listen, Sylvia, we know the sister and mother," said Cleo. "It's just the two of them. They're good people. But the grandmother wants the baby."

"Oh, God, no. This can't be happening," said Sylvia, clutching Nick's arm. "What if they take her? I won't survive it," said Sylvia. She started crying, and Cleo moved from her chair to sit on the other side of her as Nick put his arm around Sylvia. She looked small next to his wide shoulders.

"Surely something can be arranged," said Nick. "A compromise of some kind. Madison is your baby. And they are her family. These two things don't have to be separate."

Sylvia looked at Cleo. "Do you think they'd be willing to meet us with the baby? We could drive to Legley Bay tomorrow."

"I know they would," Cleo said.

"Maybe if they meet me in person they'll see that Madison and I belong together," said Sylvia.

"We'll get through this. I promise," said Cleo.

But Peter knew she wasn't convinced.

On the way to the car, Cleo took Peter's hand. "Let's get the son of a bitch."

Chapter Thirty-Two

AFTER CLEO AND PETER LEFT, Sylvia went to her piano. Pulling the cover up, she put her hands on the keys and rested her forehead on the cool black wood. She tried to breathe but the room had no air. *Madison. My baby. My daughter. My life.* How could she let them take her? Could she run for it? Take the baby and head south to Mexico? She had money. She could start a secret life. But no, it was impossible. They would find her within hours. And she couldn't flee with an infant to some third world country.

Nick came in with a cup of tea but she waved it away, feeling nauseous.

"What're you thinking?" he asked.

"I used to think there was nothing that music couldn't heal, no obstacle I couldn't work through as long as I had my piano, my music. But it's not true, as it turns out."

"I'm sorry, Sylvia. I would do anything to fix this for you."

"I can't let them take her," she said.

He knelt next to the bench and took her hand. "Listen to me, when they meet you, they'll see what a good mother you are and how much you love her. They'll see what a wonderful life you can give her."

"I've never been this terrified. They have the legal right to cut us out completely. We have no claim on her."

"But it sounds like this is a decent woman, a woman who wants what's best for her children."

"A woman who just lost her daughter, looking for something to fill the empty space in her heart. Think about it, Nick. There's no way she's not going to want Madison." She sobbed as he took her into his arms.

❋

Nick talked her into taking a sleeping pill that night, telling her he would get up with Madison for feedings. The pill worked well and fast. Sylvia drifted into a dreamless state until dawn, when she awakened with a start, the sick dread immediately coursing through every part of her.

Madison.

She lay, aching and worrying in the dark, Nick breathing steadily beside her. The house creaked and settled. After ten minutes or so, she slipped out of bed and padded down the hallway to the nursery. In the muted light, she stood by the baby's crib and watched her sleep. With every breath the tiny baby took, it felt as if her heart was outside her body, big and bruised and full. To love a child, your own child, left one exposed and terrified, she thought, like no other love.

If only she could talk with her mother. *I wish you were here,* she thought. *I need you.* There was no one like her mother. No one understood her better. No one could dissect a problem better. No one loved her more. It was nine hours ahead in Italy – around two p.m., she figured by counting on her fingers. They would be back at their villa, resting after lunch.

Her mother picked up on the second ring. "Mom, it's me."

"What's the matter?"

It took several minutes to fill her in on Malcolm and Madison and Nick. After she was done, her mother was silent on the other end of the phone. "Mom, are you still there?"

"Yes, just taking it all in."

"I'm sorry to spring it on you. I didn't want you to cut your trip short and I knew you would if I told you everything."

"My poor baby, dealing with all this. Honey, I'm so sorry."

"Mom, I think I'm going to lose her. And I don't know if I can survive it." She let the tears come. It didn't matter anymore if she was strong or not. This was her mother and she understood everything about her.

"Madison is yours in your heart. You're her mother. And mothers, real mothers, always put their children first. What is best for Madison?"

"I want to say me, Mom."

"You can provide for her, yes. You love her, yes. But it's also true that she'll have a great desire to know her biological family at some point. It's their right and hers. They are her family. Go tomorrow with an open and humble heart, honey, and in good faith ask for a compromise of some kind."

"I'll try."

"But be prepared. You may have to let her go."

"Oh, God, mom, I can't."

"Remember the story of splitting the baby in the bible?"

"Of course. But it isn't the same. I'm not her real mother."

"Yes, you are, whether you gave birth to her or not. And because of that, you won't allow her to be split in two. I know you'll do the right thing."

As her mother spoke, Sylvia moved to stand at the window, looking out into the yard. There, in the filtered light of dawn, she saw the guesthouse, sitting empty now that Nick lived inside with her.

"Call me the minute you know something," said her mother.

"I will."

"I love you."

"Mom, I know you do. Like I've never known before. And I love you."

They left Seattle at daybreak, so it was just after one p.m. when Sylvia and Nick arrived with Madison at the address Peter had given them. The trailer was rundown, mildew covering the faux green flooring on the porch and the roof sagging. Sylvia rang the doorbell, her grip tight on the baby seat. Nick shuffled from one foot to the other.

A teenage girl, presumably Misty, opened the door. Behind her was a middle-aged woman with bags under her eyes. "I'm Misty," she said, with a shy smile. "And this is my mom, Jo."

"Nice to meet you both," said Sylvia. "This is my friend, Nick. And this is Madison."

Misty took in an audible breath. "Oh, wow. Mom, look at her."

Jo didn't say anything. Her gaze was fixed on the sleeping bundle. Misty gestured for them to come inside.

"The name's good. I think Madison suits her," said Misty. "I mean she looks like a Madison. Don't you think, Mom? And, wow, she *does* have the same dimple as Alicia."

Sylvia's eyes flickered between them and then back to Madison. "Would you like to hold her, Mrs. Johnson?"

"Oh, everyone calls me Jo," she said. "And yes, I would."

Sylvia unfastened the baby carrier's buckle and picked her up. Madison's mouth opened and then closed, her face scrunching up before relaxing into sleep once again. Sylvia put the baby into Jo's outstretched arms. She seemed to go slightly limp, like she might faint, as she sank into the couch, cooing, with tears streaming down her face. "She smells so good."

"I brought photos," Sylvia said. "I take a photo every day. There's twenty-five so far." Nick handed her the diaper bag with the photos before sitting in the chair by the window opposite the couch. Sylvia found the photo album and set it on the coffee table. "Just to look at whenever you want."

"Twenty-five days of life. Twenty-five days since Alicia died," said Jo.

This poor woman, thought Sylvia. How do you live after losing your child? "I'm so sorry, Jo, for your loss. I can't imagine."

"Thank you," said Jo. She leaned over the baby, kissing the top of her head. "So much hair. Both my girls had all that hair too. At about six months it starts sticking straight up in the air like a horn."

Sylvia sat on the couch, searching for Nick's chocolate eyes to steady her. And he was there, just as he always was now, something to hold onto in the storm. She tried to keep her voice from shaking but it was no use. "I want to say straight out that I understand I'm at your mercy. If you want her, you should have her. As you can imagine, the thought breaks my heart." She paused, fighting the lump forming at the back of her throat. "That said, I talked with my mother last night and she reminded me of the story in the bible of the two women fighting over the baby."

"King Solomon's judgment. Sure," said Jo.

"And it humbled me, thinking of the mother willing to sacrifice her own happiness to save her child. I love Madison as if I'd given birth to her. It's important for Madison to know you and be loved by you. But I know, too, that I will be a great mother to her if you're willing to let the adoption go through and, if so, I would welcome any and all involvement in her life by you both." She took a breath. "I don't know if you'd even consider it, of course."

Jo never took her eyes off the baby's face. She was silent for what felt like minutes but was probably only seconds. "More we talk about it, Misty and me, that is, we just can't figure a way we could take care of her properly and survive. Misty's headed for college in a few years. She's so smart, and I don't want her quitting school to take care of this baby. And I have a full-time job that barely supports us. But the thought of not seeing her is so hard. But what you say about Solomon's judgment is humbling to me too. You can offer her things I never could."

Sylvia felt a surge of hope. She looked over at Nick. He nodded, smiling encouragingly. "I have an idea," she said. "A solution that might be good for all of us."

"What's that?" asked Jo, caressing the top of Madison's head.

Sylvia spoke softly, not wanting to offend, but wanting to make the offer in good faith, hoping it would be well received. "I have a little cottage off my main house. It would be a perfect place for you both to live. And that way you could be part of Madison's life every day."

Misty's eyes flew open wide. "You mean, move to Seattle?"

"Right. There's a really good high school in my neighborhood," said Sylvia. "And, Jo, you could help me with the baby. If you wanted."

"What about my job?" said Jo.

"Mom, you could get a bartender job in Seattle. Right?"

Nick spoke from the other side of the room. "That's my work too, Jo. I could help you out."

"Or, you could just stay home with the baby," said Sylvia. "We could work something out. Grandma pay." She paused, trying to gauge if this hurt Jo's pride or not. "I'll need to go back to work at some point anyway. I took family leave from work but I have to go back soon."

"Grandma pay?" Jo smiled slightly. "I guess that would be a pretty great job."

"We could be a family. A different kind of family," said Sylvia.

"A patchwork type family," said Jo.

"And if you let me adopt her, we could put together legal documents to ensure you have full access to her life. You know, just so you felt secure in that."

Jo was quiet. Sylvia wasn't certain if she was contemplating her offer or thinking of something else. "I blame myself for what happened," Jo said, finally. "If I'd been around more, I might've known what was going on with Alicia. I didn't have any idea and I have to wonder what kind of mother that makes me."

"That's just simply not true," said Sylvia. "Bad people did this. Not you. You're a good mother. Anyone can see that."

"Mom, she's right," said Misty. "This was not your fault or Alicia's."

"I wanted so much for these girls," Jo said. "But I just could never get ahead. And I missed so much because I had to be at work."

"But Mom, you did that for us. And we knew that. We admired you for it. Especially Alicia." Misty turned to Sylvia. "Alicia wanted to go to masseuse school so she could earn money. Mom, so you didn't have to work so hard."

Jo kept her gaze on the baby, rocking her gently in her arms. "She was a good girl."

"Your daughter left a great gift for us." Sylvia paused, trying to think of what to say next. "And I'm so grateful."

Jo looked over at Misty. "Yeah, Alicia did good."

"Yes, Mom, she did," said Misty.

"The other thing is - I don't know if anyone told you my situation?" Sylvia stopped, unsure how to explain about Malcolm leaving and her relationship with Nick. Would it dissuade them from considering her offer if they knew about Nick?

"You mean that your husband left?" asked Misty.

"Right," said Sylvia.

"Cleo told me all about it," said Misty. "And that Nick is your boyfriend."

"She did?" asked Sylvia, surprised.

Misty smiled over at Nick. "She said you're the greatest guy that ever lived."

Nick chuckled. "Might be a slight exaggeration there."

"Not really," said Sylvia.

"Cleo Tanner is our hero," said Misty. "Without her and Peter Ball we wouldn't know what happened to Alicia."

"Yes, and they brought Madison back to us," said Jo. "So if she says you're okay, you're okay with us too." She glanced at Nick and then back to Sylvia. "And I have no room to judge anyone for getting a divorce. I haven't had the best luck with men myself."

"Thank you, Jo, for saying that. It's generous of you," said Sylvia.

Her heart pounded, knowing she had to ask, but afraid at the same time. "Misty, do you have any idea who the biological father might be?"

Misty shook her head. "I really don't. She never mentioned anyone. We had no idea she was even pregnant."

"I'm afraid at some point he might try and come after her," said Sylvia.

"If Alicia didn't think so, I seriously doubt it," said Jo. "From what we know, she probably picked someone unlikely to want much to do with her."

Sylvia took in a deep breath, relieved. Nick let out an audible sigh. He'd been worried about that too, she thought. He'd never said anything.

"So, will you think about my idea?" Sylvia said to Jo.

"There's nothing to think about," said Jo. "It's the perfect solution for all of us."

Sylvia felt like she could breathe for the first time in twenty-four hours. "Thank you, you've just made me very happy," she said, standing and reaching for Nick, who drew her into his arms.

Chapter Thirty-Three

CLEO BEGAN THE EVENING by giving Scott Moore a quick hug and kiss on the cheek, lingering there so that he might smell the fragrance that came from her neck, so that he might anticipate his reward for a night of shared intimacy, a night of shared secrets. He took her to yet another nice dinner, at Canlis, a true Seattle landmark. It was a restaurant reminiscent of an older time that evoked visions of Frank Sinatra and Manhattans.

They sat at the bar before they moved to the dining room. And then, a bit of luck. Scott excused himself to use the men's room. When the bartender approached, she ordered Scott a martini and a white wine for herself. "I'm trying to get this gentleman a little tipsy tonight," she said to the bartender. "I've purchased something without his permission and I'm going to have to beg for forgiveness."

The bartender smiled, raised an eyebrow. "Okay?"

"So could you make his drinks doubles?" She smiled widely and a little flirtatiously.

He grinned. "As long as you promise to drive."

"Done."

Just then she saw Scott coming back from the bathroom. She felt alive tonight, despite her nervousness, or perhaps because of it, but she knew mostly that it was mostly Peter and the flush of her feelings for him. But she put them aside, remembering the advice from her college acting professor, to be in the moment, listening, always listening and responding.

"I ordered for us," she said.

"Wonderful."

The bartender put their drinks in front of them. "Thank you," she said. Then she looked down at the counter, feigning distress, and sighed, as if she were suddenly distracted by a problem.

"You all right?" He took a sip of his martini.

She looked at him through her lashes. "I'm worried about Sylvia."

He cocked his head. "In what way?"

The hostess showed up just then to take them to their table. Another bit of luck, they were given a rounded booth, and as much as she dreaded being this close to him for an extended period of time, she scooted into the middle and patted the seat, asking if he'd sit next to her, which he did. "Have another drink," she said. "I can drive." She said it casually, but while looking into his eyes flirtatiously.

"Why not?" he said. "I feel like celebrating."

This was a big risk – get him drunk so that he imagined he might have a chance to take her to bed, and then move in for the kill. Although she wasn't sure he was safe to be alone with, especially given the other night. But she couldn't worry about that. She must get him to tell her everything tonight.

The waiter brought menus and told them about the specials. Scott ordered another drink and then turned back to her, staring at her intently. "Cleo, I want you to understand something. I'm growing quite serious about you. I need to know if I'm wasting my time or not."

This shocked her. She looked at her bread plate to give herself a minute to adjust to this. But this was good. He obviously trusted her. She looked up, giving him the most open expression she could manage. "I feel the same." She scooted closer to him. "But there is still so much I don't know about you. And I want to know everything."

After they ordered steaks, they talked of his education, of prep schools and law school, of his desire to have a family and his upcoming trips. The waiter brought Scott's new martini and asked, "Was there something wrong with your wine? Can we make you something else?"

"No thank you," she answered, feeling suddenly homesick for Cooper's and Nick. And Sylvia. Especially Sylvia. She was doing this for Sylvia, though, and all the other people this man had hurt. *Stay focused*, she told herself.

After the waiter brought their meal, they ate and meandered through various subjects, a recent movie he'd seen on cable, her work schedule. They both declined dessert and coffee and Scott quickly paid the bill. She put her hand on his. "Time to go?"

He spoke quietly, almost in her ear. "Let's go to my house."

"Can I drive?" she asked. "I'm just dying to try your car."

He smiled and winked at her. "You have no interest in my car. You think I've had too much to drink."

She did her best to look indulgent, demure. "Just hand me the valet ticket, Mister."

Cleo's heart pounded as they drove up to Scott's gated community. The black interior of his BMW sedan smelled of leather and new car. She stopped the car in front of the closed gate. "Can you tell me the code?"

"6818," he said.

She punched it into the pad. Good, this way Peter would know it, she thought.

She parked the car in his rounded driveway and took Scott's offered arm as they walked across the pebble stone walkway. It was a lovely warm night, but Cleo shivered as he escorted her into the house.

"May I take your sweater?" he asked.

"No, I'm fine," she answered, thinking of the wire.

The house was enormous, with cathedral ceilings and cold, modern décor: gray floor tile, black and white furniture, everything in clean, sharp lines. He escorted her into the sitting room.

"I'd love to use the powder room," she said, still holding her purse.

"It's near the front door. Can't miss it. I'll pour us some wine."

"Great," she said.

Once inside the powder room, she sat on the closed toilet seat and texted the gate's code to Peter to make sure he'd heard it, then flushed the toilet, washed her hands, and put on a new layer of lipstick.

He was pouring them both a glass of red wine at a bar between the sitting room and kitchen. After handing her a glass, they sat together on a couch by the window, the lights of Bellevue shining from across

Lake Washington. He appeared more relaxed than she'd ever seen him. From the booze, she thought, feeling a pang of worry. Would Peter and Brent be able to use confessions gained under copious amounts of alcohol? "Here's something I was wondering about, Scott."

"What's that?"

"How come all the babies placed out of your agency are Caucasian?"

"Client demand," he said. "You can judge them if you want, but the truth of it is certain couples want a family that looks like them, where there won't be questions later about why the kids look different from their parents."

"So, if your clientele were Asian-American, let's say, you would've wanted the same for them?"

"Of course. But let's face it, Cleo," he said. "We live in the whitest part of the country." He made a sweeping gesture that Cleo took to mean his neighbors. "These are my clients." *Rich, white people.*

"But how do you do it? How do you only find white birth mothers?"

He looked at her, as if deciding whether or not to share it with her. Perhaps it was his ego that won out, his desire to prove his cleverness, but suddenly he unleashed, talking quickly, with pride in his voice. "It was five years ago that it came to me. There was an article in the *Times* about a pregnancy pact on the east coast. Poor, uneducated girls with no business having babies had made a pact to get pregnant together. And I started thinking – what if we had them get pregnant for a fee and then adopted their babies out to my clients."

"But…" she said, unable to think of what to ask next.

"Before you feel sorry for them – these girls flock to us. All it takes is waving cold hard cash in front of their faces."

"Like five hundred dollars?" Cleo asked, pretending to be on his side, acting as if these girls disgusted her.

He laughed. "Five hundred wouldn't do it. Even for these girls. No, we give them each ten grand. That's enough cash to them, enough that they then sell the idea to their friends."

"And where?" she asked. "Where are these girls?"

"All over the Northwest. All the little towns with nothing to offer to anyone, most especially girls with no future."

All over the Northwest? Not just Legley Bay? How many were there? Cleo felt ill, thinking of all the poor, desperate girls that succumbed to the idea of doing something so drastic for such a small amount of money. Didn't they know how easy it was to let ten thousand dollars slip through your hands? How little money it was in the course of a lifetime? "And you charge $150,000? Doesn't it seem steep? What about couples who want a baby but can't afford one?"

He shrugged. "This is my niche. Other agencies have to take care of those other couples."

"Was Sylvia's baby from one of these girls?"

"I suppose. I don't keep track. I have people who take care of the details." He got up from the couch. "More wine?"

She looked at her glass. It was still full. "No, but you go ahead. I'm a slow drinker."

He poured himself another generous portion and rejoined her on the couch.

"Do the girls ever change their minds?" She studied the contents of her glass.

"Not usually." His eyes were steely, watching her.

"But what if they do? What then?"

"They go on their merry way," he said. "There's always another girl willing to have a baby."

"How do you convince them?"

"Again, I have people for that." There was an edge of impatience in his voice now.

She needed to get him to tell her more. But what could she ask? She looked down at her lap, thinking about Sylvia and Madison. Real fear, real emotion, made the tears start coming. "I had a dream the other night," she said, looking at him, letting her lips tremble. "That the birth mother came back, wanting Sylvia's baby, and Sylvia had to give her up." She was on an improvisational roll at this point, as the made-up story unfolded. "And then Sylvia was riding a motorcycle in and out of traffic in Los Angeles and a truck swerved and..." She didn't go on, a vision of Simon crumpled on the street an image in her mind as clear as if it were yesterday instead of ten years ago.

"Like what happened to your boyfriend."

That startled her. She stopped crying, peering at him. "How did you know about Simon?"

"I had my people look into you." He smiled, throwing up his hands. "I hope you don't mind."

"It's very sweet," she said, putting her fingertips on his forearm, fighting the sense of violation in her chest. "Scott, I'm so afraid for Sylvia. Please tell me we won't have any trouble."

He stared into her eyes. "Cleo, I promise you, nothing is going to happen. Alva took care of that."

"Alva?"

"My right hand person. She takes care of all the details."

"What do you mean, took care of it?"

"The girl's gone."

"What does that mean? Because those people always come back to haunt you. Just look at politicians."

His eyes were slightly glazed. He played with a lock of her hair. "Stop worrying, Cleo. I don't want to alarm you, but the girl's dead."

Cleo's heart was beating so fast she was afraid he might see it move the bodice of her dress. She watched him, looking for signs, trying to think of an angle to get him to tell her more. "How did she die?" she asked, softly, hoping to lull him into telling her. "Was it in childbirth?"

He spoke in a soft purr with a hint of slurring. "No idea. She washed up on shore last week. So, you see, you've nothing to worry about."

"Who is Alva, anyway? Do I need to worry?" *Play the jealousy angle* she told herself. *Get him to talk.*

"Oh, God no. You should see her. I don't think she even likes men."

"Well, what does she do exactly?"

"She handles everything with the girls. She's a midwife. Makes sure they're safe during childbirth. Helps them keep the pregnancies a secret from their families." He stroked her cheek. "Listen, these girls are nothing but white trash. Like my mother. They don't deserve your sympathies. They're getting something out of it."

Had he just called his own mother white trash? She tried not to stare at him.

"When I was a kid, before we moved from Legley Bay, I figured out who my father was. It's a small town and one day I heard my mother talking to a friend. Turns out my father was the town cop. And I walked around with this knowledge that he was my father and yet no one would talk about it. Not my mother. Not my father. He had two sons from another marriage and they were a big deal in town. The older son was a major athlete – a runner who went to state one year – the other one was some kind of mathematical genius. Their photos were in my middle school display case, for different awards and such, and I would look at their faces, burning to know them, to tell them about myself, searching for some kind of recognition that they were my family. So that I wouldn't feel so alone. But no one would tell me the truth. And I just walked around like that all the time, with this knowing that no one would say."

She couldn't comprehend at first what he was saying. Then, it came, like a flood, an understanding that changed everything. He was talking about Peter and Jack. "Scott, I'm sorry. That's terrible. Did you ever meet your father in person?" *Peter. Peter, just hang on and I'll be there. We can talk it all through.*

"No, my mother wouldn't tell me the truth. Pretended like he was dead. Then she drank herself to death." He closed his eyes. "Speaking of which, I've had too much to drink."

"No worries," she said. "I can find my way home on my own."

"I'm sorry. Don't know what got into me tonight. Just take my car. I'll send someone over to get it in the morning."

She rose, taking his hand. "Come on. Show me your bedroom. You can sleep it off," she said. He staggered, leaning into her as they walked down a long hall to his bedroom. In the bedroom, he slumped on the bed and she gently guided him over so that he fell onto a pillow.

The second she heard him snore, she let out a breath that felt like she'd been holding all night. She'd been playing a part, but like a curtain going down on stage she shifted back into her own life and wanted nothing more than to get out of this house and to find Peter, to have his arms about her, knowing he was probably reeling from what they'd just learned. This man was Peter's brother? She filled with a rage then at Peter's father, for all the ways he'd remained absent and yet so present for these men that were once his little boys. She brushed her hands down the front of her legs - as if there was something tangible there, some remnant of Scott on her clothes - as she made her way down the hall and into the living room, grabbing her purse from the coffee table.

It was then she heard the door open. She froze, heart thumping, hoping it was the housekeeper but knowing instinctively that it wasn't.

A stocky woman with purple glasses was in the foyer. *Alva*. From Misty's description, Cleo would know her anywhere. She carried something with her, a box of some kind, like the sort you put files into. Cleo's instinct was to sneak out the back, to run, but it was too late. Alva had spotted her.

"Hello," Cleo managed.

"Hey," she said, coming into the room and setting the box down on the floor, near the coffee table. "Brought some files over for Scott." She peered behind Cleo, to the couch. She had a rough voice, like a person who shouts too much and has damaged their vocal cords.

"He had too much to drink," said Cleo. "I was just about to drive myself home."

Alva was inspecting her, her eyes moving up and down so that Cleo felt almost violated. "That right?"

Cleo held out her hand. "Cleo Tanner. Pleasure to meet you."

Alva shook it briefly and then took a step backwards. "I can drive you home," she said.

Alarm bells went off in Cleo's head. There was no way she was getting into a car with this woman. "No, that's all right. I prefer to drive myself."

"Take Scott's car out for a little spin, is that it?" She crossed her arms over her ample chest, with an accusing look on her face, a look that said: *I know how you people are.*

"Oh, nothing like that. I couldn't care less about cars. I just prefer to drive myself."

"As Scott's number one employee, I think it's best that I drive you instead of letting you take his car. We barely know you."

We barely know you. This woman was possessive of Scott. Perhaps she was in love with him? "You know what?" Cleo said. "I think I'll just call a cab." She headed towards the door, reaching into her bag for her cell phone. "I'll show myself out." Her hand shook as she pressed the button for Peter. When he answered, she felt immediate relief. "Could you send a cab to 1284 Maple Parkway?" she said.

"Get out of there," Peter said into the phone, and she could hear the fear in his voice.

"Yes." She paused for a moment. "It's a gated driveway but I'll come to the gate and wait for you." She hung up and reached for the front door handle.

Alva was following her, so close behind that Cleo imagined she could feel the horrid woman's breath on her neck. "I don't trust you. Just a gut instinct I have." And suddenly Alva leapt in front of her, blocking the doorway with her square body. "I didn't think you were anything to worry about what with your ugly sweaters and boring life but now I'm not so sure."

"How do you know about my ugly sweaters?"

"After I saw your picture in the paper with him I went to your school and got that ridiculous headmistress to give me your number. I followed you the next morning but I could see you were no threat to him and me. We have something special. Always have. I figured he'd lose interest in you in a week. But now, I see I shouldn't have allowed him to see you. I do not permit anything or anyone to harm him. He's all I have."

"I have no intention of harming him," said Cleo.

"Then why all the questions tonight?"

If it was possible, Cleo's heart began to pound harder. Her body went icy with fear. "Questions," her voice was pinched.

"I saw the whole thing," said Alva. "I had a nanny cam installed last year. Nothing happens in this living room without my knowing. And I don't like that you were asking so many questions. Don't like that he told you so much. And when I think about it, the questions were pretty leading and that makes me wonder what you're up to." She reached into her pocket and pulled out a pistol. She pressed it against Cleo's neck. "What are you up to, Cleo Tanner?"

"Nothing," she whispered.

"Tell me what you're doing."

"Nothing, I'm just really into him. And my friend just adopted a baby and I just wanted to understand that it was safe. It happened so fast, that's all. He was just reassuring me."

"And are you reassured?"

"Absolutely," Cleo said, her voice squeaking.

"Well I'm not." Alva shoved Cleo against the wall. She pushed the barrel of the gun into Cleo's chest with one hand and with the other reached under her shirt and found the wire. She yanked it, the tape taking off a piece of Cleo's skin.

"Oh, for fuck's sake," Alva screamed. "You have a wire?"

Chapter Thirty-Four

PETER AND BRENT WERE IN THE VAN at the end of Moore's long driveway, having followed them from the restaurant, listening to everything through Cleo's wire. When they understood that Alva had seen the entire conversation via her webcam, they looked at one another and, without a word, Brent jumped from the back into the driver's seat and began driving full speed ahead down the dark driveway while Peter called for backup.

Simultaneous thoughts went round and round his brain. *Scott Moore is my brother. The woman of musk and oranges. Cleo. I must get to Cleo.*

"Let's move," said Brent. The van lurched to a stop in front of the house. They both pulled their guns out.

"You go around back. See if you can get in. I'll go to the front."

Peter ran up the stairs, stopping at the door. It was the heavy kind, impossible to kick down. As that thought came to him, the door opened and he was face to face with Alva and Cleo. Alva held the gun at Cleo's temple. Cleo was white and shaking.

"Peter," Cleo whispered, her frightened eyes never leaving his.

Alva stepped back several feet; he'd surprised her. This was good. Maybe Brent could figure out a way in through another entrance and come at her from behind. Peter moved closer, trying to back her into the house. "Take it easy now. I'm just here to talk to you."

"Don't get any closer or I shoot her," said Alva.

Peter kept his hand on his gun. "You don't want to do that. There's still a chance to walk away. We called for backup. In a few minutes, they'll be swarming the place. You shoot her and you won't get out of here alive. Let her go and I'll help you."

Alva tightened her grip around Cleo's waist and pressed the gun even harder into her temple. Cleo gasped, wincing. "I told you not to get any closer," said Alva.

Scott Moore appeared then, standing in the doorway, dazed and unsteady. He held a gun in his left hand. "Alva, what're you doing?"

Alva shifted slightly towards Scott. Her gun was now at Cleo's neck. "This bitch was working for the cops. And you told her too much. She had a wire on, you idiot."

"Cleo, is this true?" Scott seemed almost childlike, like a trusted friend on the playground had just betrayed him.

Cleo didn't say anything but her eyes darted to Peter.

Scott came closer, peering at Peter, his expression one of disbelief. "Peter Ball?"

"That's right," said Peter.

"Do you know who I am?" said Moore.

"I do now. I didn't. None of us knew about you," said Peter, keeping his voice low and calm. It had been a long time since he last saw the woman of oranges and musk. But here were her eyes. Her son had the same eyes. He remembered, suddenly, that he'd seen her once in the grocery store, years after his parents' divorce, holding the hand of a little boy with brown hair. He'd averted his gaze and run from the store over to the school where he proceeded to pound his fists into the punching bag in the gymnasium. Then he'd blocked it out. It never occurred to him that she had been pregnant. No wonder she'd been desperate enough to call their house that morning. And there was a little boy. Another little boy with empty spaces left by Tim Ball. *My brother. Scott Moore is my brother.*

"Tim Ball knew. He knew everything and chose to pretend I never happened," said Scott, cocking his gun.

"Scott, just put down the gun," said Peter. "Talk sense into Alva here. We can do this nice and easy. No one has to get hurt."

Moore went on as if he hadn't heard him. "Do you have any idea what that felt like? Walking around town and seeing him, knowing he wouldn't even acknowledge my existence?"

"Listen, the guy's a dick," said Peter, keeping his voice conspiratorial. "Has been all his life and will continue to be. He betrays everyone he ever meets. It's no reason to ruin your life." He tried to sound reassuring, like they were best friends. "We can hire a good attorney, get you out of this somehow."

"You think I would ever trust you?" said Moore, coming closer.

"I don't know," said Peter. "Alva killed a girl over in Legley Bay for her baby. Sylvia Green has the girl's baby. Did you know that?"

Scott turned his gaze to Alva. "Is this true?"

"You really think I'm going to answer that?" Alva pushed the gun harder into Cleo's neck. Cleo yelped, her eyes pleading with Peter to be careful.

Scott took several steps closer. "I never meant for anyone to get hurt. There were always plenty of girls willing. We didn't need to kill anyone. I just wanted to help people like Sylvia. Deserving women. Not sluts like my mother."

Peter, keeping his gaze fixed on Alva, spoke softly. "Scott, your mother was practically a girl when she met my father. Our father. It wasn't fair what he did to her. Or to you. Or to my mother. But we can't let it define our lives."

"Don't trust these people, Scott," said Alva between clenched teeth. "I'm the only one you should trust. I did it all for you."

"Why, Alva? Why did you hurt that girl?" said Scott.

"She threatened to expose the whole thing." Alva's face was almost as purple as her glasses. A vein down the middle of her forehead bulged. "The little bitch changed her mind when she saw that baby. I couldn't let her go. It would've ruined both of us."

"Oh my God," said Scott. "So it's true."

Out of the corner of his eye, Peter saw Brent moving silently behind them, until he was directly behind Moore. Brent rushed Moore, knocking the gun from his grasp and shoving him to the floor, aiming and shooting his gun at Alva. The shot hit her in the leg. She screamed and lurched. Her gun went off. Peter felt a surging pain in his chest and staggered back into the wall before sliding slowly to the floor. He was aware, through his pain, that Brent had Alva on the ground, forcing her arms behind her back and putting handcuffs on her. Then Cleo was above him, saying his name over and over. And then it was black.

Chapter Thirty-Five

CLEO SAT NEXT TO SYLVIA in the emergency room of Seattle's Swedish hospital, watching the second hand tick by on the clock hanging above the nurses' station. Nick was at the window, pacing back and forth with Madison in his arms. Jack sat in the corner, near the coffee machine, staring at the floor, his elbows resting on his knees.

"Sylvia, do you remember the day we sat in the ER waiting for news of Simon?" Cleo asked quietly, so no one else would hear.

"Oh, sweetie, of course I do."

"I wanted to die with him when they came out and told us."

"Cleo, you did die that day."

"That's what Peter said once. And then he woke me up. And now he could be in there dying." She put her face into her hands, feeling the panic rising in her chest. "I don't know if I can go through this again."

Sylvia put her arm around her. "He's going to be okay."

She looked into Sylvia's sympathetic eyes. "You don't know that. No one knows what could happen on any given day."

Nick put the baby in her carriage and sat on the other side of Cleo, taking her hand. "He's getting the best care in the city. And he's tough as nails. You said that yourself."

She felt the tears coming; they spilled out of her eyes and into her hands. "I gave him my heart and now he could die on me. Just like last time. And then where am I? Back to dying myself."

Jack shuffled over to them, hands in his pockets. "Cleo, my brother is the toughest man I've ever met. He's a fighter. Came out fighting, according to our mother. He's not going to let this beat him." He paused. "Especially now."

Hours dragged by, the second hand moving tick by tick around the clock. At midnight, Brent arrived. "I've just come from booking Alva and Moore," he said to Cleo. "Confessions from both. And now the unraveling begins. Literally hundreds of people are affected. It's a mess." Brent rubbed his eyes and sighed. "Sometimes this job feels too hard."

"I can't imagine what he thought, learning about Moore that way," said Cleo, reaching for his arm.

"I know what he was thinking about," said Brent. "You. Only you."

Cleo paced by the windows, a chant inside her head - *Please, God, let him pull through.*

Sylvia sent Nick home with the baby, promising to call him the minute Peter was out of surgery.

At two in the morning, Sylvia and Brent dozed but Cleo and Jack were awake, watching the clock. Finally the surgeon came out, approaching with quick steps, waking Sylvia and Brent. "He made it through the surgery remarkably well," he said. "It helped that he's in such good shape. I removed the bullet from his chest. It missed his heart by only an inch. I've repaired the damaged tissue and sewn him up. I have every confidence he will be fine, after a recovery period."

"Thank God," said Jack, taking Cleo's hand. "See, I told you he was tough."

It missed his heart by only an inch. She felt numb. How was it possible that he'd come so close and yet would be fine?

"When can we see him?" asked Brent.

"Come back mid-morning," said the doctor. "He should be awake by then."

Brent drove her home. The night was clear. Stars twinkled over Puget Sound as they drove across the West Seattle Bridge. When they turned onto her street, Brent looked over at her. "I've never seen him happy before you. I didn't know he had it in him."

"How many times are you guys in situations like we were tonight?"

"What do you mean?"

"I mean almost getting killed." She heard the judgment in her voice.

"Not that often," said Brent gently. "Really. It's not like the movies." He pulled the car in front of her apartment building. "No reason to get spooked. I'll introduce you to my wife. She can tell you it's nothing to worry over. Much as she might wish otherwise, I keep coming home."

She didn't say anything as she got out of the car, holding her breath until she reached the front door, the doctor's voice like a recording in her mind. *It missed his heart by only an inch.*

Once inside, she collapsed onto the couch, exhausted but unable to sleep, the image of Peter bleeding out on the hardwood floor playing over and over in her mind. She thought of Simon then in a way she hadn't for weeks, so absorbed in Peter that she'd almost forgotten him, had let the memory of his face fade. This was her mistake. Because the remembrance of her lost boy had kept her company all these years. He'd been safe; as long as she had him to hold on to she didn't have to go out into the world, did not have to venture into love. She could see it clearly now. She'd let in another man that could die on her, that could leave her in the moment a truck roared around a corner or a bullet shot through the air. And there was his family too, Louise and Aggie and Jack. She loved them already too. And with love came the possibility of loss. She couldn't live this way, with this uncertainty. It was better to be half-dead, awake only in certain parts of her life. It was too much, this loving of a man who might leave.

He was a cop, one of the most dangerous careers a person could have. Night after night he would venture out into danger. Night after night she would wait for him to come home. And one night he might not come. One night she might wait forever.

❧

She woke to her cell phone ringing. It was Jack. Peter was awake, he told her, relief in his voice. He was asking for her. Could she come right away?

After a shower and a change of clothes, she drove to the hospital, shaking, knowing what she must do. She asked at the front desk for his room number and then walked blindly down the hallway until she saw Jack standing over a bed where Peter lay, looking white and wan.

Despite the fact that he was in obvious pain, he grinned when he saw her. "Cleo Tanner."

Out of the corner of her eye, she saw Jack leave the room, shutting the door behind him.

"Hi, Peter." She started to cry.

"Don't cry now," he said, taking her hand. "I'm going to be fine."

She sobbed harder. How could she ever say goodbye to this man? How could she leave this man that made her heart pound and that she loved more than she thought was possible?

She stared at the sheet that Peter's arms rested upon, a painful-looking IV piercing his skin.

"Cleo Tanner, I know I look bad but I'm going to be fine. Soon I'll be out of here and throwing you on the bed."

"No. No," she said, backing up slightly and dropping his hand. "I can't do this. I can't love you and lose you and survive. You almost died."

His face transformed in that instant from adoration to shock to dismay. "Oh, Cleo. Don't do this. I'm not going to die on you."

"You don't know that," she said. "No one wants to die but it happens every day. Every day a cop dies and there's a widow holding nothing but air in her hands. I cannot let that happen to me again."

"So your solution is to walk away now? That makes no sense."

"Maybe not to you," she whispered. "But to me it's just about survival. My own."

"Cleo, things don't have to end between us. Ever. Not when there are feelings like this between two people. I never understood until now what that feels like, how sure I am that I can love you as you should be loved, faithfully, over time."

"I'm sorry, Peter, but I have to go." She turned, unable to look at his face, pushing at the door with both hands.

Louise and Aggie were standing in the hallway.

"Cleo," Louise said, grabbing her in an embrace. "We're so glad you're all right."

"Thank you," she said, still sobbing. She extricated herself from Lou's arms. "But I have to go."

"Why?" asked Aggie, her eyes sharp, scanning.

"Because I can't love a cop. It's just too risky," said Cleo, swiping at her eyes.

"That's a bunch of bull if I ever heard it." Aggie looked at her straight in the face. "Thought you were made of tougher stuff, Cleo Tanner."

"I'm sorry," she mumbled, wiping her eyes with the back of her hand. "But I'm not."

"To love is the biggest act of bravery in this uncertain life," said Aggie. "No doubt about it. Isn't for the faint of heart."

"Cleo," said Louise. "I understand it's frightening but what else is there in this life but to love?"

"Safety," Cleo said. "Just that." And she turned, fleeing down the hall, running until she reached the parking garage, where she slumped against the side of her car, sobbing.

"Cleo."

She looked up, wiping her eyes. It was Jack. He brushed a hand through his hair in exactly the same way Peter did. "Peter would probably want to beat the crap out of me if he knew I'd followed you but I couldn't let you go without saying something. I know it's not my place, but given my own past, I feel compelled. When I lost Miriam, I wanted to die too. Wanted the pain to end and all I could think to do was to take my own life. And what I've learned since is that so many of us choose death over life, even if we don't go to such drastic measures. The rest of you may not slice your wrists. Instead, you just choose to walk around dead, never taking risks, never allowing yourselves to love without caution, without cynicism."

"I know."

"Peter was the same. Since our dad left. But he's chosen you, Cleo. Chosen life." He stuffed his hands into his jeans pockets. "I guess I just want you to think about what a miracle that is, given his past and all the ways he was hurt as a kid. You did that for him. Don't throw it away because you're scared. Finding love is a miracle."

"I know that," she said, bitterness in her throat. "No one knows that better than I."

"I lost someone too, Cleo. I know what it's like. But if I had the chance at love again I would jump at it. Just think about it long and hard. That's all I ask."

Chapter Thirty-Six

THE PAIN MEDICINE HELPED EASE the ache from Peter's surgery but the invisible clasp in his chest was clamped tight. He closed his eyes, trying to think of something besides Cleo Tanner but nothing came. How could you leave me now? he thought. *I need you. How can I go on without you?*

His mother and Aggie were at the hotel, sleeping after having driven most of the night to come see him. The nurses were in and out, checking on him and bringing various meals. It all tasted like sawdust in his mouth. He could take only small sips of ice water. In the late afternoon, Jack came.

"Hey," Jack said. "How you feeling?"

"The same."

Jack stood next to the bed. "Dad's on his way."

"You can't be serious."

"I tried to talk him out of it," said Jack.

"Does he know we know about Scott Moore?"

"I told him."

"I don't know if I can deal with him."

"I'll stay with you. If you want," said Jack, sitting in the visitor's chair.

"I can't stop thinking about Cleo."

"I know." Jack pulled the chair closer to the bed. "I'm sorry."

"She thinks I could die," he said, his voice faltering, the clasp in his chest tightening so the pain was almost unbearable. "Like her other boyfriend."

"Well, the truth is, you could," said Jack. "Anyone who loses someone knows that."

Peter turned his gaze to the ceiling. "I'm the one who knows that. First Dad. Then you. Now Cleo. Everyone I love eventually leaves me. And by choice, not death. It's worse. Miriam didn't want to leave you. She loved you. She chose you. She wanted nothing more than to spend the rest of her life with you. That must be of some comfort to you." He tried to breathe but the pain in his chest was too much. A sob came, choking him. He moved his arm over his eyes.

"Peter, I'm back. And I won't leave again. I'm sorry for how much I hurt you. But the truth is, I was ashamed. I knew you'd never have given in to despair like I did. I couldn't face you. But I love you. I admire you. I always have."

Peter removed his arm, looking into his brother's eyes. "I never got it before, but I do now. I've been fighting all my life. Fighting to protect you and Mom. Fighting Dad by hating him. Fighting so hard to make it in this shitty world by keeping a distance from everything. But now I love her so much and nothing I do will convince her that love is the opposite of fear. But I get it now – what it is to despair. I remember what you said when I found you on the floor that day. I'm sorry you had to be in that kind of pain. I spent my life trying to protect you from it."

Jack's eyes were soft. He took Peter's hand, squeezing it. "Listen to me. You're going to get through this. I'm here for you."

Peter's mouth twitched in a half-smile, even as the clasp in his chest tightened further. "Thank you."

As it turned out, Jack was gone by the time Tim Ball appeared in Peter's hospital room. Peter was in and out of sleep all afternoon. When he woke at three p.m., his father was there, sitting in the visitor's chair, reading a magazine.

"Why did you come?" asked Peter, without even a polite greeting.

Tim Ball stood, coming close to the bed. Peter expected the same bland expression he'd seen on his father's face all his life but he was different. There was a look of defeat about him. The last time Peter had seen that expression was the night in the fog as he stood behind the truck. "I know you don't want me here," Tim said. "I understand why."

Peter remained silent, shifting his eyes to the ceiling.

"I did know about the kid."

Disgusted, Peter turned to look at him. "The *kid*? You mean, your other son?"

"Yes," said Tim Ball.

"So you just chose to bail on him like you did us? I guess that's fair. And expected."

"I'm not proud of it. I'd do things differently now."

"Dad, I could really give a shit at this point. I accepted your absence a long time ago. But, once, we were all little boys and we needed you. And nothing you do now is going to make up for it. The damage is done."

"I understand that, Peter. But I want you to know I'm sorry. And I love you. That's all."

Tim stepped towards the door as if to go, but then, seemingly changing his mind, he came back to stand by the bed. "If you could just think about giving me a chance to be in your life in some way. On your terms. I'm here, if you ever want me."

And then he was gone.

Chapter Thirty-Seven

IT WAS JUST AFTER TEN P.M. and Sylvia stood at her bathroom sink, preparing for bed. Nick was asleep in the bedroom, worn out from several late night shifts at Cooper's. Madison was asleep in her crib, sleeping through the night now fairly consistently. Tomorrow Jo and Misty would arrive. She and Nick had moved his things into the house after spending several days packing up Malcolm's remaining clothes and personal items.

She washed her face and then put her regular mint toothpaste on her mechanical toothbrush. What was this? The mint tasted strange. She felt nausea coming. This was the third time in the last three days she'd been sick. The first was after a sip of coffee the previous morning. Then at dinner she'd poured a glass of wine and just the smell of it had her running to the toilet. Now she knelt at the toilet, barely making it in time to vomit. She sat back on the floor, leaning against the wall.

What was wrong with her? Could she be pregnant? The thought had occurred to her earlier but she'd pushed it aside. Her breasts were tender and she couldn't remember having a period since late June. Was that right? Actually she couldn't be certain. Everything was such a whirlwind the last month with Nick and Madison that she hadn't really been paying attention. And it wasn't like she had to worry about getting pregnant. She was infertile. Or was she?

Kneeling on the floor, her cheek resting on the lid of the toilet, she took deep breaths. It didn't seem possible. Not after all the tries with Malcolm, all the treatments, that after six weeks or so of sex with Nick that she could be pregnant. They hadn't bothered with any birth control, hadn't even talked about it, now that she thought about it. The passion between them was so palpable, so intense that she couldn't even think when he was in the same room with her. Getting up from the floor, she reached into the back of the cabinet under the sink. There were several pregnancy tests, leftover from all those hopeful days of peeing on the stick, praying for two lines.

Ten minutes later, she stared at the stick. Two lines. After all these years, two lines.

Later, she lay in bed, watching the ceiling fan turn round and round. Nick snored softly next to her. She put her hand on her stomach, pressing her fingers lightly between her hipbones, marveling that in inside her was the beginning of a life. A baby, made by her and Nick. She fell asleep to that thought, only to wake in the morning with midsummer light streaming in through the shades. There were sounds coming from below - Nick in the kitchen, probably feeding the baby and making her breakfast. She put her arm over her eyes. What would Nick think? She only filed for divorce a week ago. And her mother and father? And Jo and Misty? What would they think?

But it didn't really matter what anyone thought but Nick. He was the only opinion that counted in this or anything else. He was her person, as Cleo always said. *Nick is my person.* To be loved by him outweighed everything else.

She heard Nick come in, and with him the smell of food. She took deep breaths, trying to control the nausea. When she opened her eyes she saw that he was holding a tray with a roll and some eggs. "Hey, good morning," he said, grinning. "I was getting worried about you. It's late. Madison's down for her morning nap already." He wore sweatpants low on his hips and a T-shirt that stretched across his broad chest.

She put her hand to her mouth, swallowing. "Please, take away the food," she said.

He looked surprised, retreating backwards. "Are you sick?"

She nodded. "Yes," she said, her mouth dry.

"I'll get rid of this. I'll be right back." He disappeared and she rolled over, looking out the window at the sparrows' nest in an attempt to control the nausea.

When Nick came back, he knelt on the side of the bed. "Do you think you have the flu?"

"No. Will you get in here with me?" She patted the space next to her on the bed. "I have something to tell you."

"What is it?" Nick climbed in, putting his head on the pillow next to her, resting his hand on the curve of her hip, as he so often did, his face concerned. His face that was so dear and familiar to her, like he'd always been here.

"I'm nervous to say," she said.

"You know you can tell me anything," he said. "No matter what."

"I'm pregnant."

His eyes opened wide. "What did you say?"

"I'm pregnant. Took the test last night. I figure I could be six or eight weeks. I won't know until I see the doctor. But the baby's yours. I know for sure because Malcolm and I hadn't been intimate since before the last in-vitro round."

He was silent for a moment, taking in a big breath. "How can this be?"

"I don't know," she said. "I didn't think it was possible." She paused, searching his expression in the morning light. "Are you angry?"

"My God, no." He pulled her into his arms, burying his face in her hair. "Of course not. I'm thrilled. But surprised."

"And a little overwhelmed?"

"Well, yes," he said.

"Me too."

He pulled back, looking in her eyes. "Sylvia, I love you. I always have."

"I love you too," she said, feeling scratchy tears coming. "I always have."

"I know I don't have any money but I could still make a good life for you. And Madison. And this baby. We could be a family."

"Nick, we already are."

He smiled. "I suppose that's true. But I want to make it official."

"Madison or us?"

"Both."

"Deal," she said.

Chapter Thirty-Eight

THE ADDRESS SIMON'S MOTHER GAVE HER over the phone brought Cleo to a quiet street of small, brick houses in a small town in western Pennsylvania in the late afternoon. The air felt dense and still, especially given the low-seventies Seattle weather she'd flown out of that morning. Dressed in a light cotton dress, carrying the hatbox with Simon's things, she was hot and damp as she rang the doorbell at his childhood home. A petite woman with dyed black hair and Simon's deep-set brown eyes answered the door. Susan Randall smiled and held out her arms. "Cleo, it's so good to meet you after all these years."

"Thank you for seeing me, Mrs. Randall," said Cleo, leaning into the woman's soft hug.

"Call me Susan, please." She showed Cleo into a small living room that reminded her of her father's house, stuck as it was in another era. There was an orange and brown plaid couch, upright piano, and high school portraits of Simon and his two sisters displayed on either side of a wood-burning fireplace. The house smelled of cooked cabbage and cinnamon. "Here, sit." She pointed to the couch.

"I'm sorry to hear about Mr. Randall," said Cleo, tearing her eyes away from Simon's photo. She sat upright on the couch, questioning why she'd come. Was this the right thing to do?

"Thank you, dear. It's been three years already. I've adjusted. And I have my daughters and their children so I'm never lonely for long." She lowered herself into the rocking chair across from Cleo. "You're exactly as he described."

"Am I?" said Cleo, looking at the hatbox she still held in her hands. "Except I'm ten years older."

Susan Randall folded her hands in her lap, a look of pain crossing her face. "Strange to think he'd be thirty-three years old now."

"I think of that so often. What he would look like. What he might have accomplished by now." She stopped, fighting the lump in her throat. "I came here to tell you how much I loved him. I don't know why I never did that. I should've at least written at the time. But it was so painful and then too much time passed and it felt awkward to contact you after that." She brought the hatbox closer to her chest. "When he died, a part of me never got over it."

Susan's eyes filled. "He loved you too. He talked about you all the time on the phone. Promised me he'd bring you to visit. He told me one time you were the finest actress he ever saw. Famous or not. All these years I've looked for you on television."

Cleo waved her hand dismissively. "Oh, he always exaggerated that. 'A director and his muse.' Gave me chills every time he said it."

"Are you still acting?"

She shook her head. "I couldn't. Not after Simon died."

"Oh, Cleo, well, that's a shame." She leaned forward in her chair. "Matter of fact, that would've made him mad."

Cleo smiled. "I know it would. But after I worked in front of him, in front of his camera, his eyes, I couldn't think of doing it for anyone else, ever. He was my person. From the first time I ever met him." She paused, glancing at his photograph. "I haven't been able to let him go."

Susan looked at her in a way that reminded her of Simon, with her head cocked to one side and eyes that seemed to see everything about her at once. "Is that why you're not married?"

Cleo's hands tightened on the hatbox. "I guess."

"He wouldn't have wanted you to be alone."

"You're not the only person to point that out to me," said Cleo, thinking of Peter. "I brought you some of his things I've kept over the years. They've been precious to me. You have no idea how often I've looked at them but it occurred to me recently how selfish it was that I hadn't shared them with you." She opened the box and showed her the photos and DVD of his short film and then, finally, the manuscript. "He was working on this when he died, fussing over small details. But it's complete, at least in my viewpoint. It's about a girl losing her mother to cancer." She paused. "It's my story but Simon told it, which means that you should have the chance to read it. I was the only one he ever let look at it and then he died before the world had a chance. I don't know what you'll do with it but I know it will give you comfort to read it, to see how truly gifted he was."

"Why now? After all these years?"

"I've met someone."

"Ah, I see." Her eyes sparkled. "Now that's some good news."

"And I know to love him well, I have to let Simon go." She held out the hatbox to Susan. "I will never, ever forget him. Or stop loving him. But, finally, I have to say goodbye."

Susan took the box from her, hugging it against her chest. "Thank you, dear."

Cleo stood, taking in a deep breath. "Would you take me to where he's buried? I want to say goodbye in person."

"Of course."

The cemetery was on a gently rolling hill with rows and rows of tombstones, some dating back hundreds of years. Susan held onto Cleo's arm as they strolled along the paths, stopping when they reached the Randall family plot. There, next to that of his father, was Simon's gravestone.

> *Simon Randall*
> *1980 – 2002*
> *Son. Brother. Friend.*

Susan moved away, leaning against a tall maple. Cleo knelt near Simon's gravestone, feeling the damp grass on her bare legs. She traced her finger in the etching of his name. "I've missed you," she whispered. "So much. But I found someone worthy. Finally. I know you'd approve of him. Rest in peace." She closed her eyes, praying silently. *Watch over him, Lord, and my mother too. Tell them I'm choosing, finally, to live, to love, to be chosen.*

Then she stood and held out her arm to Susan Randall. "You like beer?"

"Oh dear, no. But I like a good scotch. Neat."

"I know just the one," she said, smiling, and, as always now, thought of Peter. "Come on. I want to toast Simon before I have to catch my plane home."

And as they made their way across the cemetery in the hot July afternoon, a breeze came up, like a whisper from her long lost love. *Go. Choose to live, to love, to be chosen.*

Chapter Thirty-Nine

PETER WAS AT HIS PRECINCT DESK when he typed the last word. He saved the document and pushed print, listening for the whir and clank of the printer, sounding, always, as if it might expire at any moment. His hands hovered over his desk's surface, preparing to tidy and organize but it was already neat, orderly, everything in its proper place. Even his mug was on its sand dollar coaster, empty but for a used green tea bag withered at the bottom. There was a muted quality to the precinct this time of night, the flickering of the overhead fluorescent lights more obvious in the hours before twilight. Most of his coworkers were already home enjoying warm suppers and bad television with their families. But he remained, uncertain now of what to do next. Of when to go. And where to go. And to whom.

And like a hundred other times that day, he wondered what she was doing right at this moment? And the awful ache in his chest felt like it might overwhelm him, like it might squeeze every ounce of life from him.

Brent came in from the coffee room, eating a stale donut. Peter didn't have the heart to even tease him about it. His brow wrinkled in worry, he pointed at Peter's injury. "Sure you're okay? You take anything today?"

"Don't need it. Makes me stupid, that stuff."

"You're one tough bastard," Brent said, chuckling. Then, his face turned serious. "You know, I don't say it enough, but I admire you. I hope you know that." He said admire, but Peter knew he meant love. And this show of affection, different from their usual affable ribbing, embarrassed him, as he was still unaccustomed to being vulnerable, to being known by the people in his life, and he felt the heat of the room suddenly.

Brent, hovering near the desk, said. "You go see him yet?"

"No. Tomorrow. At his house."

"I know what he did was wrong," said Brent. "But in some twisted way he actually thought he was doing good. And it's clear Alva murdered Alicia Johnson without his knowledge."

"I know," said Peter. "And the guy never had a chance. You know, given his parents. But it's also true that the lives of everyone involved will never be the same. The whole thing makes me sick."

"I know," said Brent, his eyes pained. "Each one of these cases has to be looked at on an individual basis. I can't imagine getting that phone call."

Peter waved him away then, home to his wife and children. He knew, by the way Brent frequently glanced at his phone that his mind was already there, anticipating the heated grill and marinated steaks his wife would have waiting for him, the potato salad in the refrigerator, the children playing on the sidewalk in front of his house, their eyes scanning the street for their daddy's red truck.

As the papers of his report printed, he walked to the window. The evening sky was flushed pink over a July blue Puget Sound, the jagged Olympic mountains free of snow, trees lining the street flush with green leaves, everything deep into the throes of summer. *Almost a month since I've seen her,* he thought. *Every day as painful as the one before.*

Below, spilling onto the sidewalks and patios of bars and restaurants were people wearing sundresses and shorts and T-shirts, skin glistening with sunscreen. Happy people, he presumed, without this paralyzing knowledge that life is unpredictable and heartbreaking - without this feeling of a clasp inside their chest, without this terrible missing of a person that was now gone to him forever, leaving nothing but an empty space. He turned and with his good arm swept Brent's discarded lunch into the trashcan. He took their cups to the break room. Someone had left an almost empty coffee pot on the warmer and the room smelled of burnt Starbucks French Roast. He flipped the red light to *off* and put the glass pot in the sink, pouring cold water from the tap over the fried coffee. He tossed his used teabag in the trash.

Then he leaned against the sink with this feeling inside like he was dying from this ache that wouldn't go away, this ache that was Cleo. Yes, his chest hurt, even more than his injury, like it did when he was a kid. But it is over now, he told himself. Case closed, his undercover civilian back to her real life. Things must return to normal. She made her choice. And he must continue forward, as if he'd not been transformed by this love.

The document was done now. He gathered it from the printer, holding the pages in his hand. He found a paperclip in his desk, one of the small black ones so coveted – everything orderly and put together. He'd just leave the report in Wilson's office, he thought, so he could read it in the morning. Everything neatly packaged and explained, all the stories of this particular case intact within the pages. But he continued to hold it in his hands, as if he might keep it all close. As if he might keep Cleo with him.

Then, suddenly, he heard footsteps coming down the hall. When he looked up the clasp in his chest pulsated. It was Cleo, just feet away from him – her hair floating loose about her shoulders, wearing that violet dress that clung to the curve of her hips. She hesitated at the doorway, watching him, gathering a bit of the filmy dress material in her hand. He stood, pushing his chair behind him, and came around his desk. "Cleo?"

"Hi."

"What're you doing here?"

"I don't know, really. Checking on you." She looked at the floor, playing with a bracelet at her wrist. "I miss you." She hesitated before looking at him. "So much I can't think."

This was their destiny. The other. He took a few steps towards her. She smiled, just a small curve at the sides of her mouth. But there was still that wariness around her eyes.

"I'm lost without you," he said. "Truly. A mess."

"Oh, Peter, I'm sorry. But seeing you in that hospital bed. And knowing how I love you and how you could die on any given day in this crazy job you have. It made me insane." She put up her hands, as if for protection.

He inched closer to her. He wanted to say to her. *It's too late. We're done. We've jumped into the abyss. We already know what it is to cling to the other. There's no turning back.* But instead he said, "Cleo Tanner, I love you. I'll fight every day to stay alive for you. I'll fight every day to take care of you, to cherish you, to love you."

"Are you certain?" she said.

"I'm alive for the first time in my life. Because of how I love you."

Her eyes filled. "Peter, I can't stop thinking of it all the time. Losing you."

"Yes, I know. But that's what it is to love. Just out there risking a broken heart every day of your life."

She remained in the doorway, hands at her sides. A tear escaped, making a trail down her beautiful cheek, and he moved quickly towards her, until he was right there, wiping it away with his finger.

"Cleo, I'm here now. And I'm unable to walk away. Unable to imagine another day without you." He pulled her to him and her arms slipped around his neck. She was warm and soft and familiar and smelled as only she could, of caramel and magnolias. He put his mouth to her neck, aching now, wanting to crawl inside her. "I was just sitting here, unsure where to go. Lost."

"Come to me," she said. "Come home to me."

"You said once you wanted to be kissed one more time by someone who loves you. May I kiss you properly, Cleo Tanner?"

"Yes, please," she whispered.

They kissed then, long and sweet, in the dimming light of the summer evening, choosing to live, to love.

The End

MORE GREAT READS FROM BOOKTROPE

Grace Unexpected by **Gale Martin** (Contemporary Romance) When her longtime boyfriend dumps her instead of proposing, Grace avows the sexless Shaker ways. She appears to be on the fast track to a marriage proposal... until secrets revealed deliver a death rattle to the Shaker Plan.

Riversong by **Tess Thompson** (Contemporary Romance) Sometimes we must face our deepest fears to find hope again. A redemptive story of forgiveness and friendship.

A State of Jane by **Meredith Schorr** (Contemporary Women's Fiction) Jane is ready to have it all: great friends, partner at her father's law firm and a happily-ever-after love. But her life plan veers off track when every guy she dates flakes out on her. As other aspects of Jane's life begin to spiral out of control, Jane will discover that having it all isn't all that easy.

The Puppeteer by **Tamsen Schultz** (Romantic Suspense) A CIA agent and an ex-SEAL-turned-detective uncover a global web of manipulation that will force them to risk not just their fledgling relationship, but their very lives.

Devil in Disguise by **Heather Huffman** (Romantic Suspense) Reporter Rachel Cooper is America's Sweetheart—but that won't help her when human traffickers kidnap her sister. Can an old flame help her protect the ones she loves?

... and many more!

Sample our books at:
www.booktrope.com

Learn more about our new approach to publishing at:
www.booktropepublishing.com

CPSIA information can be obtained at www.ICGtesting.com
Printed in the USA
BVOW080337250113

311545BV00003B/16/P